Praise for Christopher Priest

'Simultaneously familiar and weird, grippy and slippy, *The Evidence* is a tour de force of intimate alienation'
Daily Mail

'*The Evidence* is an essential missive from Priest's "Dream Archipelago" . . . Years hence we will look back at this loose collection and be amazed' *The Times*

'Priest writes with charm, grace, and a wistful individuality' *Guardian*

'Priest's mesmeric power is formidable' *Independent*

'A novelist of distinction' *Sunday Times*

'Priest is a powerful and underappreciated writer'
Daily Telegraph

Also by Christopher Priest from Gollancz:

The
Evidence

Christopher Priest

This paperback first published in Great Britain in 2021 by Gollancz

First published in Great Britain in 2020 by Gollancz
an imprint of The Orion Publishing Group Ltd
Carmelite House, 50 Victoria Embankment
London EC4Y 0DZ

An Hachette UK Company

1 3 5 7 9 10 8 6 4 2

Copyright © Christopher Priest 2020

A CIP catalogue record for this book is
available from the British Library.

ISBN (Mass Market Paperback) 978 1 473 23138 2

Typeset by Input Data Services Ltd, Somerset

Printed in Great Britain by Clays Ltd, Elcograf S.p.A.

www.gollancz.co.uk

To John Clute

Contents

I

Snow Upon the Rails

What am I doing here? Why did I agree to it? Two whole days of this?

Such thoughts. I was leaning my head disconsolately against the window, feeling the cold from outside as it seeped through the toughened glass, watching as the train passed through an endless frozen landscape of heavy industrial works, derelict buildings and spoilage. At intervals, white and orange flood-lights glared down on concrete emplacements. I felt I did not belong, because no one could belong in such a place. The sky was the darkest grey, like an old cinder, daylight was only grudgingly admitted. The hills were streaked with thin snow, the train went slowly. Sometimes it stopped. Sometimes it went even more slowly.

I dreaded what would happen if the train broke down, or I was told to leave the carriage, or there was an unannounced change of trains at some remote junction. This train and this compartment were my only protection, and a degree of famili-arity. They insulated me from the frozen landscape beyond the glass.

I was on an all-expenses visit to a distant university, where I was scheduled to deliver the keynote speech at an academic conference. It was on a subject in which I was believed to be an expert, but in fact there was a twist to it I knew nothing about. The title of my lecture was the same as the title of the conference itself: *The Role of the Modern Crime Novel in a Crime-Free Society*.

Crime free? That was a new one on me. The paradox interested me, and it was one of the reasons I had accepted the invitation, but only after much indecision. I lived and worked in a place which was most certainly not free of crime. We experienced the usual range of thefts, assaults, drug and alcohol abuse – less often there were cases of fraud, arson and murder. Not everywhere and not all the time, but at a level where it remained necessary to maintain a full police force. Anyway, I had a vested interest in crime: I earned my living indirectly from it. I wrote thrillers, and there were readers everywhere who loved to read a mystery, a noir detective story, a police procedural.

The assumption being proposed in the title made me wonder if the place I was going to was in some way different from everywhere else. Was there really, in this modern world, anywhere without criminals? Had the fear of crime been factored out of people's lives? Did everyone live a peaceable, law-abiding life? Maybe not – the conference would almost certainly be speculative, idealistic, proposing social reforms which would lead eventually to a state in which crime became unknown. That seemed more likely.

However, I had been to academic conferences before: they are built around big ideas, but many of the individual papers produce much dry theorizing about side issues. I had already pleaded a busy schedule: I was not planning to stay for the whole three days.

But still, somewhat against my better judgement, and in spite of similar past experiences, I had accepted the invitation. This one included extras that I found attractive, if not compelling. A flight instead of a long sea voyage, a train journey that promised a first-class private sleeper compartment, meals prepared by a chef of international repute, free drinks and personal attendance by stewards. The president of the society which had invited me, Professor Soradauy Wendow, of the University of Dearth Historical and Literary Society, would meet me in person on arrival. There was going to be a suite at the best hotel in town. Although I was warned that I would be visiting during the winter months, I was assured that every creature comfort would be anticipated and catered for. I would, for instance, be driven everywhere in a university car. And not least there was an honorarium. Not a huge one, but sufficient.

So why did I sit unhappily in my first-class compartment, still close to the beginning of the venture, regretting the fact that I had said yes?

Trips like this one always used up more time than I allowed for, and more than anyone else might expect. As well as the four days of actual travel (two there, two home again) there were the days spent preparing for the trip, writing and rewriting the text of my lecture, worrying about it, worrying about the journey, feeling distracted by having to go away. Work on my latest novel had been hopelessly disrupted and I knew that when I finally returned home, more days would be lost as I tried to pick up the thread from where I had left off. My publisher had also just sent me proofs of my last one, which needed to be checked. I find it impossible to concentrate on work when travelling, so I had left them at home.

There was also the weather. I had been warned of sub-arctic temperatures even during the days, requiring heavily insulated outer wear. I had had to order this specially, and although the agreed expenses refund included a contribution to the cost, it was a contribution only. The padded coat, hood, trousers, were so bulky they required an extra case, which I had had to pay for as hold baggage on both aircraft, making a total of four baggage charges in all.

My first flight had been early. The plane had taken off at about four a.m., but that was a short internal flight only, followed by a long wait. The second plane, to Tristcontenta Hub, had suffered a delayed take-off because of an adverse wind forecast, which meant there was a chance I might miss my connection. In practice I was still able to catch the train with time to spare, but I knew there was only one sleeper train per day and I had no idea what I would have done if I had missed it. Apart from a snack at the airport, and another snack during the flight, I had eaten hardly anything all day.

All of this was stress I could have done without. My first-class compartment was modern, clean and compact, but I felt strangely isolated. Once or twice I had ventured out into the corridor, hoping to see a steward or some of the other passengers, but there was no one about. It was almost as if I were the only one on board.

The invitation to the University of Dearth, in Dearth City, the administrative centre of Dearth Island, had arrived more than eighteen months earlier. The name was not appealing. I knew little about Dearth, and had no ambitions to visit the place – I knew it only by its reputation for long, storm-riven winters and an economy based on heavy engineering and mining.

I had spoken at two or three academic conferences in the past and so would not feel out of my depth, but I had said I would not stay the whole course. The general subject was within my sphere: I had published more than a dozen novels, as well as essays and criticism. I was known in the world of crime writers, had even won a few prizes, but I was no academic. The prospect of prolonged and detailed academic discourse from theoreticians who knew little of the art and craft of writing filled me with dread.

The months slipped by. Suddenly it was a year and a half later and here I was, inching my way south across the island of Dearth, feeling hungry, wondering where the stewards were, staring gloomily at the bleak view outside. There was free wifi on the train, so as soon as the train left the railway station at Tristcontenta Hub I had sent an email to my partner Jo, just to let her know that I was on my way. I knew she was busy, preparing for a business trip of her own, one that sounded much more interesting and lucrative than my descent into the south polar regions.

Jo Delson and I had lived together for many years on an island called Salay Raba, which translated from the island patois as 'fourth island in the Salay Group'. Unlike chilly Dearth, Salay was in the subtropics and consisted of five main islands: Salay Ewwel, Sekonda, Tielet, Raba and Hames: first, second, third, fourth and fifth. They were all of more or less equal size, and because of the latitude, the trade winds and the oceanic currents, they had similarly warm climates. All five islands had developed in different directions. Salay Sekonda, for instance, was a popular holiday resort, attracting visitors not only from the rest of Salay but from all over the world. Salay Raba, where we lived, had emerged as a centre of financial services, and most of the largest banks, insurance companies and pension funds had their HQs in Raba City. Jo and I lived in a tithable house on the edge of the sea, close by the unspoiled forest that covered much of that part of the island. We were by no means well off but on the money I earned from my books, plus Jo's freelance income as a theatrical designer, we were able to get by.

Dearth could hardly be more different from Salay. Setting aside the climate, what I had glimpsed from the train so far was a grim industrial landscape, with huge factories and furnaces, cooling towers, pipelines, broad access roads, advertising signs everywhere, much open-cast mining in the hills, towns built of small houses crammed together. The air was clouded with fog, or smoke – even inside the air-conditioned train I developed a tight feeling in my chest, and could smell oil or coal smoke, or industrial fumes of an uncertain and probably dubious source.

Although they were both large island countries, few people travelled from Salay to Dearth other than for business. There was the regular air route linking them, as well as a long sea crossing, notoriously prone to stormy weather. Not many islands lay between us: the Dream Archipelago in the southern hemisphere had many clusters of inhabited islands, but only a handful were in the deep, rough seas a long way to the south of Salay. There was a sense of emptiness and oceanic vastness between the two countries.

When Jo or I travelled we normally headed east or west, or sometimes northwards into the marvellous, sun-baked islands in the horse latitudes of the Midway Sea. Dearth had never attracted us. Apart from business executives and office workers, those who did travel to Dearth were mostly backpackers, bird watchers, rock climbers, loners, extreme sports enthusiasts, modern questors or adventurers, drawn by the wild, rugged and so far unspoiled terrain along the east coast of the island.

I remembered the plane I arrived on had flown low for several minutes above this sort of landscape. The pilot came on the PA and said that because of the weather over the sea we had lost more than an hour of flying time, but that Dearth was known for its gravitational anomalies and that we could take advantage of one of them. He advised us that we need not reset our wristwatches.

I hadn't the least idea what he was talking about: he delivered the message in the bland, supposedly reassuring voice that flight crew often use when speaking to passengers. Whatever he meant, it turned out that when the plane finally landed in Tristcontenta Hub, we were in fact about ten minutes ahead of the scheduled arrival time. I had no idea how that could have happened, but once I was inside the terminal I noticed that my wristwatch showed the same time as the clocks.

What did a gravitational anomaly look like, and how had the pilot found it? I had no background in science, certainly not physics. I fancifully imagined there must be a metal grid or a dome out there, or a series of masts with lights on. But there was nothing in the darkness. It could be anywhere. I was bored.

For a while I read one of the ebooks I had saved to my laptop, then I glanced through my speech again. I made a couple of small changes, improvements. I listened to music on my headphones, then because they isolated the sound I took them off. The train was moving faster now but there was still no sense of urgency. Marooned in my pod compartment, the only sounds I heard were the noises from the wheels and the track and it still seemed to me that I was alone on the train.

Dinner arrived without warning. Two young men I assumed were stewards brought a trolley and placed the food unceremoniously before me. Chafing lids concealed the dishes. There was a small bottle of red wine included. There appeared to be no choice offered by the chef of international repute, but by then I was glad of anything. One of the stewards released the catch on the sleeping bench, brought the whole thing down with a muted crash, then smoothed and straightened the sheet and pillow. Soon after this the train slowed suddenly, and came to a halt somewhere in unlit countryside. Total silence fell.

The dinner had left me unsatisfied. It was served dry, it was salty, the sauce had congealed and the portion was small.

The following morning I was awakened by the sound of voices in the corridor. I dressed quickly and opened my door. I recognised one of the stewards from the evening before. I asked him why the train had stopped.

'The track is the wrong gauge,' he said, walking on. 'Too narrow. We can't use it. Happens a lot. They'll fix it. We can make up the time later.'

I thought about that, trying to make sense of it. How could railway track used by trains every day, the permanent way, suddenly be the wrong gauge? And how could they 'fix' it?

I looked through the window of my compartment – a blizzard was blowing outside, and snow was already building up against the side of the train. It looked like we might be stuck there for hours. But then suddenly the train lurched into motion, slowly at first then with increasing speed. I returned to the pod. I read through the text of my speech again on my computer screen, then made sure all my tiny changes (emphasis, clarity, etc.) had been transferred by hand to the hard copy. The hours passed. I was fatigued by being on the train: the endless movement, the noise from the track, the dry heated atmosphere, the sheer tedium of being contained inside a bleakly modern capsule for nearly two days. Outside, we were passing through snow-clad scenery, much of it high and rugged, looming over the track. From the satellite map on my cellphone I knew this was the final stage of the journey. Dearth City was fringed by these peaks, but the mountains went on and on. The train was going slowly again, snaking between the peaks, labouring on the ascents.

I started preparing myself for disembarkation, glad of something active to do. I sent a message to Jo, telling her I would shortly be arriving in Dearth City. I hoped the reception party from the university would be at the terminus to meet me, as promised. I wanted to be driven to my hotel as soon as possible, take a shower, shave, put on some clean clothes, prepare myself for my speech.

I pulled on the arctic outfit, feeling as if I were wearing a spacesuit, and having a similar lack of dexterity. I put my smaller case, the one I would normally travel with, inside the now vacant larger one and slung my computer tote diagonally across my shoulders. According to my cellphone satellite map, we were now only a short distance from the terminus, so I parked my padded backside on the edge of the desk I had been using. Because of the sudden appearance of condensation I could see little or nothing through the window. I watched the map rolling slowly along.

The train made three or four more braking lurches. The last one felt definitive. Glad to be out of the sleeping cabin at last, I squeezed and manoeuvred my way through the narrow door and into the corridor. Here at last I saw several of my fellow passengers emerging from their own compartments. Everyone was bundled up in thick layers of padded clothing, and carrying or porting their luggage. One by one we waddled towards the outer door. It was then I felt the touch of the first tendrils of the sub-zero air of Dearth City. It was a profound shock. I had literally never felt anything as cold as that before.

2

The Mystery of the Two Keys

I clamped my gloved hand across my nose and mouth, trying to filter or slow the icy air. I could barely see. I managed to step down to the platform without falling, but other passengers, presumably more accustomed to the cold than me, pushed past. A wheeled suitcase ran over my foot, although because of my thick boots I barely felt it. The owner of the case looked back at me as if I had deliberately put my foot in his way. The platform had been freed of ice and snow in a narrow cleared passage alongside the train, but most of the platform was covered in old, compacted snow, uneven and dirty.

I followed the other passengers along the platform, tramping unsteadily. People in a hurry weaved past me, stepping off the cleared passage on to the hard-frozen snow because I was going too slowly. Several of them glared at me as they slithered past. The freezing cold air was now having a weird effect on my tongue and throat. I kept my lips pressed together as much as possible. My eyelids were starting to feel stiff.

I reached the station concourse. This was high roofed and ill lit, with the winds blustering in through the open sides. Loud music played constantly, echoing and distorted, even through constant station announcements. There was no sign of anyone waiting to meet me. I put down my bags and waited as the other passengers dispersed.

Then a quiet voice beside me said: 'Dr Fremde?'

I barely heard the voice because of my inner confusion, and all the noise. Someone had stepped up beside me.

'Yes, I am Todd Fremde,' I said.

So wrapped up against the cold was the figure that at first I had no idea if it was a woman or man. A long scarf and a tightly closed hood contained all but a small circle of face, itself mostly hidden behind protective glasses.

'Welcome to Dearth.' The voice, closer now, revealed its owner as a man. 'I am Soradauy Wendow, from the Historical Society.'

'Yes! We exchanged letters – you invited me.'

'I'm pleased to meet you at last, Dr Fremde. I hope you had a good journey.'

We made an effort to shake hands, but our thick gloves made it almost impossible. My teeth were suddenly aching from the cold, and breath was a drifting cloud of vapour around us.

'I'd like to go to the hotel before anything else,' I said.

'We might be able to take a taxi. But it's better we should walk. We can go straight to the venue.'

'I'd prefer to drop my luggage at the hotel first.'

'Not much time for that. You can leave your bags in the office.'

'You said you were going to meet me with a car.'

'That's generally in use by department staff at this time of the week. It's not too far to walk.'

'I'd prefer to hire a taxi,' I said. 'I will only be a few minutes at the hotel.'

'As you wish, Dr Fremde. But I think you'll find there's a long queue for the taxis outside.'

We made our way with difficulty across the concourse, having to step several times around groups of other heavily weather-insulated people.

Once we were outside the main part of the station there was indeed a queue, but I was determined not to yield. I did not want to walk an unknown distance in this freezing place, in these bulky clothes. After about five minutes a small group of taxicabs turned into the station yard, and we were able to hire the fourth one. We piled into the small passenger compartment, dragging my luggage in with us.

He gave the driver directions to the Plaza Hotel.

I said to Wendow: 'If you don't mind waiting I really will be only a few minutes. I just want to freshen up after the journey, and collect my thoughts before I deliver my speech.'

'Of course.' Wendow was peering ahead through the grimy front screen of the vehicle. 'As a matter of interest, Dr Fremde, we were wondering about your university career. Which is your alma mater, and where exactly did you gain your doctorate?'

'I'm an author, a writer. I'm not an academic. I write thrillers and mysteries.'

'Yes. We did rather gain that impression. Even so, you must have studied somewhere.'

'I have an honorary doctorate,' I said. 'It was given to me by the Citizens' University of Salay, awarded a few years ago. They like my books. But I never use it as an honorific, and in fact I'm surprised you even know about it.'

'We have ways and means of checking out our speakers,' Wendow said. 'A citizens' university, you say? How very fascinating. That would be a college for serfs, I take it? We don't have a system of honorary degrees on this island, so we're unused to the concept. Salay – you've had to come a long way.'

'Yes,' I said. 'It's a lot warmer than this place.'

'Of course, I was thinking about the university.'

'Culturally, Salay is renowned—'

But Wendow had abruptly lost interest. He began typing on his cellphone, having slipped two detachable finger covers from one of his gloves. He was holding the phone in his other massively gloved hand so I couldn't see what he was doing. He completed his message, then quickly slipped the finger covers back into place.

Soon afterwards the taxi arrived outside a large, concrete-built edifice, a rectangular block with small windows rising up in an orderly grid. The sign carrying the hotel name was partially obscured by grime, not snow. I noticed that Wendow was not readying himself to leave the taxi with me, and that the cab's meter was still running.

'I just need a few moments to dump my stuff. Will you wait for me here, with the cab?'

'No, I can't do that,' he said, and I sensed his impatience with me. 'I have to go straight to the conference hall. You should be with me. There are a couple of important guests I want to welcome, whom you should meet. However, we are now running a little late and I need to make certain our practical arrangements are in place. Because I've been on leave my assistants have been preparing the conference.'

'Then how will I get across to the hall – and where exactly is it?'

'I've sent texts to two of our History Society members asking them to collect you here, at the hotel,' he said. 'They will meet you in the lobby in a few minutes' time. They know what to do and where to take you.'

'All right,' I said. He was staring at me, waiting for me to leave. I opened the taxi door to a massive inflow of freezing air. I struggled past him, having to pull my bag past his legs.

'Should we exchange cellphone numbers, in case we need to make contact?'

My main bag fell on to the frozen pavement, and my computer tote was swinging down from under my arm and across my chest as I stepped, crouching and awkward, from the cab on to the slippery surface. I staggered to regain balance. Wendow reached across to the inner handle of the cab door, and slammed it closed with a forceful movement. The vehicle drove away moments later, while I was still straightening. I could barely glimpse even Wendow's dark shape through the condensation on the taxi's windows.

The moment I passed through the hotel's triple door complex I felt I was back in an understandable world. The doors closed swiftly behind me and streams of warmed air came down from ceiling grilles. The reception area was large and light-filled, soft classical music played unobtrusively. The atmosphere was fresh but overall maintained at a pleasant temperature. Lights were recessed, the carpet was thick piled. Close to a piano on a podium, not being played at that moment, there was a loose, informal arrangement of dozens of armchairs and long settees, clustered beside or around tables. Many groups of people were sitting about in the relaxed atmosphere, talking and drinking. Every table had a small, independent electric fan heater beside it. I could smell the appetizing aroma of well prepared food and saw direction signs to two separate restaurants. The reception desk was a long gentle curve following the back wall of the lobby, and was staffed by two young men and two young women.

I felt huge and disruptive in my heavy outside clothes, but I assumed the staff would be used to people moving in and out through the doors. I began unzipping my bulky padded jacket before I reached the desk and removed my hood. I pushed my protective glasses up my forehead. I felt the strap briefly adhering to the skin of my cheek.

I presented the confirmation booking I had been sent by the Historical Society several weeks earlier. The young man who was attending to me glanced quickly at it, typed something at his keyboard, then looked up at me.

'Dr Fremde?'

'Yes.'

'Welcome to the Dearth Plaza Hotel, Dr Fremde. I hope you will enjoy your stay with us, citizen sir. It is just for one night, I believe? And you are alone?'

'That's correct.'

'Is this the first time you have visited Dearth City?'

'Yes.'

He typed some more, then produced a room card and an electronic key. He wrote the room number on the card, made sure it was the same number he had seen on his monitor, and turned the card around for me to see.

'You are in Room 627, Dr Fremde. That's on the sixth floor. The elevators are in the corridor around the corner,' he added, pointing to the side. 'Are you familiar with the use of elevators in this city?'

'I assume so. Presumably—'

'You won't have any problems, Dr Fremde. All the elevators have printed notices reminding you what to do in an emergency. This is a period of vertical stability, so none of that will apply to you tonight. On the other hand, as this is your first time I have to inform you about mutability arrangements. I notice you are a citizen serf of the seigniory of Salay?'

'Yes,' I said, wondering how much longer this would take. I was anxious to go up to my room, take a shower, and so on.

A second electronic card had appeared in his hand and he was sliding it across to me. It was the same size and shape as the other one, looked slightly thicker, and was white all over with a bright red border. A computer chip was embedded close to one edge. Apart from a hotel logo, nothing was printed on the card itself.

'Again, you are unlikely to need this card tonight but the hotel rules insist you carry it at all times. Mutability is a problem many people who visit Dearth have never experienced before, but while you are staying at the Plaza Hotel we ask that you treat it with great seriousness so that you will fully enjoy your stay.'

'What exactly do you mean by mutability?' I said.

'You'll find all the information you need in your room. Always use the standard room key. That is the one for locking and unlocking your door.' He started speaking more quickly and insistently, as if he had recited the same words many times before. 'Under seignioral mutability regulations we have a legal requirement to provide you with a second key. This will also open your door, or any other to which you are directed. You must only use the second key if the first does not work properly. Hotel management are always on hand, here in Reception at street level, or in any of the Mutability Stations. There is a Mutability Station on every floor of the hotel. If you experience any difficulties at all, you can always find someone to help you. Both keys must be returned to Reception before you leave the hotel.'

'It sounds terrifying,' I said, trying to get an informal, unrehearsed response from him.

'A routine, sir,' he said. 'The last mutability crisis in this hotel was seventeen years ago – I had just started school. The incidence level is currently flagged at green. I hope you will have a most pleasant stay.'

The young receptionist turned away from me with a professional smile, to greet two more arriving guests. They were crossing the lobby with a slow walk, as thickly wrapped as I was. The man and the woman pushed up their protective eyeglasses, revealing their red-rimmed eyes and their eyebrows whitened by frost. As they passed me I felt the deep chill of the outside air still clinging to them.

I ascended to Room 627 and for a few minutes I was free of mutability warnings, inadequate doctorates, irritated hosts or mysterious keys. The room had an opulent feeling of luxury, cleanliness, privacy and comfort. There were flowers in a vase, a bowl of fresh fruit, and a notice that the minibar was fully stocked. A handwritten note from someone called Norie told me that she was my room maid, and that any requests I might have could be written on the notepad provided. The room, large and luxurious though it was, could not be described as a 'suite', as promised by the invitation letter, nor had I any idea if this really was the best hotel in Dearth City, also promised, but it was abundantly better than anywhere I had stayed before.

Warm air circulated gently. I stripped off my outer clothing with a sense of relief, tossing everything aside and making an untidy heap in the centre of the carpet. There was a radiant electric fire, programmed to pour out heat with fierce purpose for one minute at a time. I squatted on the stool that was provided, driving away the last vestiges of the sub-zero chill from my hands and face. I then used a second minute for my ankles and feet.

I ran a tub of hot water in the bathroom. I removed the rest of my clothes then stood in the warm and steamy bathroom while I shaved. Finally, I plunged into the tub and lay there for several minutes, glorying in the hot water. For the first time since leaving home I felt happy and comfortable.

I was dressing when my cellphone vibrated. I did not recognize the number.

A male voice said, but hesitantly: 'Is that Dr Fremde?'

'Yes, this is Todd Fremde.'

'We have come to collect you, citizen sir, and will be honoured to accompany you to the conference centre. We are waiting in the lobby.'

'I'm still getting ready. Can you wait another five or ten minutes?'

'We are already late, sir.'

'I'll be down in two,' I said.

I experienced a faint frisson of irritation. I had been through this before, the sudden requirement expressed by other people that I needed to hurry up. I had been travelling for nearly two days. What was I now late for? I was after all the main, the sole attraction that evening. What else is the role of a keynote speaker? I did not delude myself with self importance, but in every practical way the event could neither start, continue nor end if I was not there. For what other event that evening would I make them late?

Well, maybe there was a practical reason. A curfew, perhaps, that would define the finishing time, or an hour after which public transport no longer ran? But I have grown aware of this sort of possibility affecting other people's lives, and I try to allow for it when attending an event away from home. Wendow, in his various communications to me about this trip, had said nothing about a finishing deadline, but I supposed it was possible.

I completed dressing more quickly than I would have liked, aware of someone waiting for me down there in the lobby.

I did take an extra couple of minutes to leaf through the text of my speech again, pencil in hand. I always found something that could be improved or corrected. So it was that evening: a misspelling no one but me would even see, let alone take any notice of, but I made the correction anyway.

I then spent a few more seconds taking six deep breaths to calm myself (this always worked), and made sure my speech was complete and the pages were in the right order. Finally, I slipped my cellphone, the hard copy of the speech and a couple of pens into my computer tote.

On the interior of the room door was a printed notice I had not spotted before:

MUTABILITY AWARENESS

To all guests, when exiting your room ALWAYS be sure to turn off all lights and other electrical equipment. We have to remind you there is an extra charge if you ignore this rule. (See our standard conditions.) Thank you!

I read this twice, puzzled by it, but the hotel was an excellent one and I assumed there must be some reason. I quickly made sure everything was off, then let myself out of Room 627, took one of the elevators already waiting on my floor, and descended to the lobby area. To save time I had not put on my heavy outer clothes, and had everything bundled up under my arm. I headed straight for the reception desk, not glancing around to see if anyone was waiting to meeting me. The male receptionist who had checked me in was no longer on duty, but one of the women staff came forward immediately.

I held up my room card for her to see, and said: 'I have to be out of the hotel for most of the evening. Are there likely to be problems moving around the city later on?'

'No, sir. Public transport runs until one in the morning, and taxicabs can be hired all night.'

'Thank you. And if I should need a meal later, will the restaurants here still be open?'

'The grill room is open twenty-four hours. Snacks can also be obtained in any of the bars.'

I nodded to her and turned away, but immediately bumped into someone who had come up quietly and was standing right behind me.

'Doctor Fremde?' he said, from behind his mask and goggles. His voice made him sound nervous. 'We are from the Historical Society.' I realized then that another small person was standing close behind him.

'I'm ready to leave,' I said. 'Let me put on my warm clothes first.'

The one who had spoken to me took hold of my computer tote for me, while I struggled to pull on the thick garments. With two people watching I felt clumsy and self-conscious. One of the heavy sleeves made the arm of my jacket ride up inside, meaning I had to take the thing off and start again. Finally I had the top half in place. I reached down and wrapped the protective lower flaps around my legs and pulled the drawstrings. I put on my hooded cap and eye protectors, settled them around my head. Throughout all this neither of the students offered to help, but stood gawkily by. They were probably in awe of me, but I really wished they were not.

'I hope you've brought a car,' I said. 'I don't want to walk a long way.'

They glanced at each other.

'It's not far, Doctor,' said the one still holding my computer tote.

'The conference hall is in the next block,' said the other. 'Five minutes.'

'Ten,' said the other and handed me back my computer bag. 'There's a hill.'

Outside, deep night had fallen and a sharp wind had risen across the streets. The uncomfortable but warmly protective insulated clothing did what it was designed to do. I could soon see the conference centre ahead of us, floodlit in the night. It was true that there was a steep hill up to the entrance, for the last five hundred metres or so. We took it at a steady pace. The entrance to the hall was unostentatious. Its steps and pathways had been entirely cleared of snow and ice. As we pushed through the triple door system I glimpsed a poster announcing my speech. My name was prominently displayed. I was described as Dr Fremde. I decided not to spend the rest of the evening explaining I was just a writer.

3

The Lost Two Hours

As soon as I arrived I realized that everyone must have been waiting for me: a local courtesy? There was a concerted rush towards the bar. Rows of filled glasses were standing there waiting to be drunk. If the students who collected me had mentioned that there was a party being delayed until I arrived, I would have understood, hurried up, skipped the irritated feeling. Still, they were not to blame. Conversation roared around me. Waiting staff circulated with trays of canapés, from which I managed to extract a single bite: raw fish, cream cheese and some kind of vegetable. Later someone gave me a glass of wine, as because of the press of people I could not get to the bar. I did not particularly wish to see Professor Wendow, but if he was there he was keeping out of my way.

My hosts now were two graduate students, one male, one female, from the Revisionist History Department. In the noise I could not hear their names clearly. I liked them both and was attracted by their easy conversational style and, as an unsought-for bonus, by their apparent familiarity with several of the books I had written. Without going into my reasons in detail, I asked them both not to address me as Doctor, saying I preferred the use of my given name. They were fine with that. The ice was being broken in many different respects.

After another five minutes the woman disappeared from the party to return moments later. She said the audience was seated and ready for me to begin. It seemed the crowd of partygoers were not the audience, or not entirely. Several people were drifting away in the direction of the auditorium, but most appeared to be staying on at the drinks party.

The couple led me to the platform, where three red leather chairs and a lectern were waiting. There was a good if polite round of applause. I was introduced twice: the woman spoke knowledgeably of some of my books, and the man gave a brief summary of my professional life and various achievements and awards.

I stepped forward to the lectern. The remote control for the slideshow presentation was in place: I had forwarded the software a week earlier, and someone from the Society had replied to say that it had been tested and was working. It was too late now to make certain of that.

'*The Role of the Modern Crime Novel in a Crime-Free Society,*' I announced, hearing my voice amplified, but perhaps not by enough. I moved closer to the microphone. I took a pause, apparently to gather my thoughts, but in fact because I wanted to gain some idea of the size of the audience. This was not vanity. It is a mistake, I have learned, to think of an audience as a single entity. They are individuals spread out across the auditorium, an unmeasured space if the speaker has not been there before, and usually one undefined by limits if the place is not full. A speaker addresses them as a whole, sometimes in the plural, but they listen as single people. You need to know how best to address them. Some are further away than others.

The house lights were dimmed, but I could still see that the auditorium was large and banked, with an upper layer. No one was up there. The audience was spread all over the ground floor stalls, with at a guess about a quarter of the seats taken. A few more people were coming in, finding somewhere to sit. It struck me as a good-sized audience, compared at least with some of the ones I had travelled to in the past.

I pressed the remote, then turned my head to make sure the first image was up on the screen. It was, and in focus too. So far so good.

I launched into my lecture.

What did I say in my speech? If I were to claim that the whole thing was unique, inspired by the challenge of the occasion, it would be untrue. Every year I am invited to give about three speeches, talks or lectures. They are given in response to suggestions or requests from the group or organization inviting me, and most of them are informal in approach. Sometimes I am asked to speak generally about the crime-writing genre, and what I think about it. At other times people want me to talk about my most recent book, or about earlier ones. The talks vary in length and intensity, depending on what I expect, or hope, the kind of audience it will be. The main point is that because I am usually working on a new book I do not have the time or energy to think up something original every time. I recycle past efforts.

I therefore have a sort of template which I use as a basis for any talk. This makes certain points about thrillers and mysteries that I always wish to state, because I believe in them. I see them as a rationale not only for the books I have written but also as a way of evaluating the work of other writers in the genre.

The template is the bare bones for the rest of what the speech contains: I always reshape, sharpen, bring in ideas more directly relevant to whatever I have been asked to speak about. This is the difficult part.

In this case, the Historical Society had proposed an idea to me that I had not considered before: a crime-free society. Thinking about it I was struck not only by the possibilities but also by my ignorance of the subject.

While still at home I had tried to work this out calmly. I had never visited Dearth, had barely even heard of it. None of the reference books I usually looked in even mentioned the place. Online encyclopaedias were not much help. Dearth was treated as an anomalous island, secretive, run by a hardline seignioral family who were rarely seen in public. They encouraged industrial expansion and the performing arts, but restricted personal freedoms of both the vassal class and the citizen serfs. It was described as a stimulating but challenging place to visit. The mountainous wilderness on the eastern side was said to be ideal for activity holidays. The island was the site of several gravitational nodes which had erratic side effects. The idea of a crime-free state on the island of Dearth was described as 'alleged'. Alleged by whom? I wondered. There was still an active police force.

I sensed a risky subject.

One approach suggested itself. I could discuss the impact such a policy might have on my own work, whether it were real (I suspected it was not) or aspirational (more likely). I make no pretentious claims for what I do. I write crime fiction, pure and simple, and make my living from it. I am a commercial writer. I complete about one novel a year, sometimes with a couple of short stories written when inspiration on the novel temporarily fails.

Thrillers assume crime is a reality in the world, that murder is an intermittent but common event, that every killing or grand larceny needs to be dealt with firmly. A police force is therefore a requirement to catch the wrongdoer, as is a system for punishing or rehabilitating the offender. Crime should be discouraged. Mysteries need to be solved. Justice must be done.

But how would that sort of fiction work if the reader, as well as the writer, lived in a world without crime? What would be the point of fiction assuming the presence of something that no longer existed?

It was enough to suggest a few ideas for my lecture, and I worked them into the draft. With that done I set it aside and took another look at it a week later. This was about a month before I was due to depart for Dearth. During the remaining time I went back to it occasionally and gradually expanded it, changing the order of words a little, adding more ideas, deleting passages here and there, thinking up other examples to illustrate the theme. I read it aloud twice.

Then there was the visual presentation, the slideshow. Cause for much extra thinking and sighing! In recent years many audiences have grown to expect a slideshow of images, which ostensibly illustrate the talk but in reality either duplicate what the speaker is saying or distract from it. The software is widely available and easy to use, so no excuse there.

But I continue to dislike it. At one talk I gave three years ago I illustrated it with some stunningly graphic scene-of-crime images taken by police photographers. Halfway through I noticed that most of the people in the front row were staring glassy eyed at the screen, no longer listening to what I was saying. That was not the idea at all! Ever since then I have tried to assemble images that complement what I am saying, but are neither too interesting nor distracting.

The Historical Society said they saw a slideshow as an important part of my presentation, so I put together what I hoped would be some appropriate accompanying images.

I had timed my speech to last three-quarters of an hour. That was longer than I would normally aim for, but Professor Wendow insisted in one of his communications that the conference required at least that much material. The longer of my two practice readings had come in at forty minutes, so I planned to pause briefly between paragraphs, take sips of water, and so on.

I noticed that Professor Wendow still had not shown up, or at least was nowhere in sight of the podium.

So, I began. I proceeded slowly. I had removed my wristwatch and placed it on the lectern where I could see it. After twenty minutes I was halfway through, more or less on target. Once when I paused to take a sip from my glass of water I was able to half turn towards my two interlocutors, and received reassuring smiles from them both.

The next time I paused I glanced down at my wristwatch and was disconcerted to discover that in the few minutes since I had last looked the watch seemed to have stopped working. Although it has a quartz movement the display on the face is analogue sweep hands. The second hand was stationary. I shook the watch, in the way you are not supposed to shake electronic devices, then realized that of course I was being observed. I put down the watch again. I noticed that some of the people in the front three rows, the ones closest to me, were also looking at their own wristwatches, or in many more cases glancing at their cellphones.

I pressed on. Time was not of the essence. I had minutes to spare. Briefly distracted by the problem with the watch I read my speech more quickly, but soon realized what I was allowing to happen, and refocused. The slideshow was now two images behind the plan, so I swiftly brought that up to speed. In control of my material again I headed with a feeling of confidence towards the conclusion.

The applause at the end seemed genuinely enthusiastic. I smiled at and acknowledged the audience, sorted the pages of my speech into a neat pile, collected my wristwatch, and headed back to the red leather chair. My two introducers were on their feet, and they applauded and congratulated me as I sat down.

Questions and answers followed. A familiar pattern. While the third 'question' was drawling along (in reality it was, of course, a long and only half audible statement from someone in the audience, who would doubtless conclude with the polite challenge 'what do you have to say about *that*?'), I slipped my wristwatch back on my arm. I had time only to notice that the second hand was moving normally again, but that the time shown was more than two hours later than I thought. Two hours had gone by?

I essayed a brief answer to the statement-cum-question. The young woman sitting beside me called for the next one.

Three more questions followed, or it might have been four or five. My energy was low. It was hours since I had eaten a decent meal. I was having difficulty hearing some of what was being said: there was a local accent, or maybe people were shy of speaking up. My mind was starting to drift. I did not want to seem dismissive or rude. Somebody asked me about crime and religion, someone else asked about my feelings on capital punishment. While this continued several people in the audience left their seats and headed for the exits, their arms full of thick outer wear.

I turned to my interlocutors, hoping for a sign that they too thought we should wrap it up. To my relief the young man instantly sprang to his feet. He made a brief speech of thanks for my invaluable and fascinating speech, one which he was sure would provoke much discussion in the days ahead. There was another ripple of applause, the house lights came on and most of the audience began to drift away, pulling on thick wind-cheaters and hoods.

It was over.

Not quite. Four people came forward to the platform with copies of some of my books. Fatigue was blurring me. I signed these copies as quickly and politely as I could, answered some friendly questions, showed interest. These were people who actually bought copies of books: a small but valuable race of beings, in my view. When one of these people leaned forward to hand me his copies, I happened to notice that the wristwatch on his arm was showing the same time as mine, the wrong time, more than two hours ahead. I said nothing, but the next books came from a young woman, and making some kind of pleasantry I made a point of turning over her arm to see the time on her watch. It was the same. She appeared to understand my interest, and muttered something good-natured about not taking any notice of it. I was happy with these people and felt inadequate in the face of their encouraging and polite remarks. I wished I had the energy to say more, to find out a little about them.

Then it really was over.

Backstage I located my outer garments and my computer case, made myself ready for the cold dark outside. By the time I had everything ready to go I was just about alone in the place. I found my way to the main exit, and trudged slowly down the steep hill to the Dearth Plaza Hotel. It was further away than I remembered.

4

Lights in a Darkened Room

As soon as I was in the hotel elevator I began removing the
winter clothes, starting with the drawstringed leggings. I found
my room, entered, switched on some of the lights. It was warm
and well ventilated in there. I felt exhausted: the two-day train
journey, the stress of delivering a lecture and above all the lack
of food. I threw off the rest of the bulky clothes then lay down
on the soft quilt of the bed. I was on my side, stretching myself
in the way my cat Barmi often did – arms and legs straight out,
back arched, eyes closed. Then I rolled up into a foetal huddle,
making myself breathe steadily.

Five minutes later I realized that the tiredness was really a
result of hunger, which I could readily put right. It was a relief
to be myself again: not play the role of celebrated visiting guest,
nor a pseudo academic, nor a lecturer, and so on. I sat up, temporarily refreshed.

I booted my computer and logged on to the hotel wifi.
This was swift and painless, but I did glimpse a message that
appeared as a clickbox at the bottom of the page of Terms and
Conditions:

*I accept and understand the conditions of Broadband Mutability.
The risk level is currently 6 per cent. To proceed click here.*

I clicked there, and after a welcome screen and some options about long-term use, which I did not need, all went ahead normally. I glanced at incoming email, at the Salay news feed, at the web pages and social media I always scanned, then contacted Jo by email. I simply wanted to reassure her I had arrived and all was OK, but there were difficulties from the start. When I typed the word 'Dearth' the email server would not for some reason accept the letter 'h'. 'All OK, here in Deart,' I was forced to type, even after several attempts. Jo did not appear to notice, and did not comment in her reply. The letter 'h' appeared normally in 'here' and everywhere else I needed it. As I was signing off, the letters 'd' disappeared from my name: 'To'.

I closed down. I wanted dinner. I put my computer on to battery recharge. I freshened up, combed what is left of my hair after forty-seven years of male life, then left the room.

I was halfway along the corridor towards the bank of elevators when I remembered I had not switched off all the lights. I went back.

Inside the room I read again the message on the door. I wondered what the usual charge was they warned against, for breaking this rule. I also wondered how the hotel would know what I had done. Did they have a camera? A meter?

Next to the message was a special holder, containing a tall, narrow booklet entitled *What You Need to Understand about Horizontal and Vertical Mutability*. I riffled through it, thinking about dinner, but the print was small, there were words and phrases I did not immediately recognize, and the important stuff was summarized in big letters on the last page. These said in effect: always turn out all the lights and every electrical appliance when you leave the room. (The air conditioning and heating were specifically exempted.)

I took it literally. There was a master switch on the wall just inside the door, but I went around and switched off every light I had earlier turned on, and I disconnected the computer recharging cable. The television was showing a standby light: I turned that off too. I then used the master switch in case there were other electrical devices, such as timers, sensors or thermostats I didn't know about.

Whole plots can turn on details, or missed details. That was something I understood, even when I missed them.

I hurried down to the grill room. It was an airy place of subdued or indirect lighting, quiet background music and comfortable tables within discreetly lit booths. The menu was extensive and varied, the service prompt, courteous and helpful. The restaurant was not full. From where I was sitting I could see other diners at about six tables, small groups or couples. I was the only one eating on my own, but halfway through my meal a woman with grey hair came in by herself and was shown to a table on the far side of the room.

Not at that moment caring whether or not this meal was included in the cost of my overnight stay, I ordered three courses, appetizer, main course and dessert, taking my time, savouring the excellent cooking. I drank a half bottle of red wine, one imported from Salay Tielet, the third, the volcanic winegrowing island in my home group. I ended the meal with a small brandy and a cup of coffee.

I felt pleased and full. The only shadow that remained was the knowledge that I had a long return journey to start in the morning, two more days on the sleeper train back to the airport at Tristcontenta Hub.

I returned to my room, restored the lighting, put my computer and (now) my cellphone on to charge, and sat in the soft and enfolding armchair to pass what remained of the evening.

Ten minutes later I was bored. I switched everything off again, picked up my cellphone, and returned to the ground floor. I had noticed there was a bar.

I ordered another glass of the delicious Salay Tielet wine, and sat contemplating it pleasurably in a seat close to an immense wood-burning stove. Logs were smouldering steadily. My body glowed with warmth. Twenty minutes passed – I ordered another glass of wine.

Then: 'I believe you are Todd Fremde?'

It was a woman who had come up to stand beside me, holding a smaller glass that was almost empty. I turned, stood up.

'Yes?'

'I had the privilege of being at your lecture earlier this evening. I found it most interesting. I wonder – might I join you for a few minutes?'

Of course she could join me. I was glad of the company. I welcomed her to the table, signalled to the barkeep that her drink should be refreshed. I waited while she took the chair closest to the fire, then slid it a short distance further back from the direct heat. I remembered as she sat down that I had noticed her briefly during dinner: her hair was a splendid iron grey.

'I understand you have travelled here from Salay,' she said.

I confirmed this, and briefly described the long journey on the train.

'I was actually born on Salay,' she said. 'Salay Hames.'

'The fifth,' I said, the habitual way we had of confirming where someone meant in the island group.

'The fifth, indeed. My name is Frejah Harsent, which you will know is not a Salayean name. I was born Frejah Garten. Harsent is my married name. I left Salay Hames when I was six years old: for some reason my parents decided to move here to

33

Dearth. Because I grew up here I see Dearth and its peculiar-
ities as a kind of normal, and to me it has always been home.'

'Well, I was born on Salay Raba, the fourth, and still live
there. That also seems normal to me.'

'That's where the money is.'

'On Raba? Maybe – there's a huge financial centre, but none
of the money comes anywhere near me.'

'Then that's a peculiarity too, isn't it?' she said.

'I'm a writer. Money doesn't really come into it.'

She told me about her background, and the reason for her
interest in crime. 'When I went to university I began by reading social history,' she said, 'but after a few weeks I discovered
criminology, and switched courses. I gained a good degree in
the subject. After I left university I thought I should go into
law, since most of the books I read had been written by lawyers.
That didn't work out, though, so I moved into something else.
I'm still interested in crime, and read a lot of mysteries, the sort
of books you write.'

For someone I had only just met she was remarkably forthcoming about herself, and I began to wonder if I had met her
before. Maybe at the pre-lecture drinks party? I had not been
there long, but I had spoken to several people, a whirl of intro-
ductions and short conversations. I did not recall her, but then
I did not recall anyone else apart from the two young people
who were my interlocutors.

'No, I wasn't at the party,' she said, when I tentatively asked
her. 'I'm not a member of the faculty, and in fact I'm no longer
connected at all with the university. I saw your keynote speech
announced online, and because I had read a couple of your
crime novels I sent off for a ticket.'

'So there is still an interest in crime, here on Dearth?' I said.

'Very much so, but these days crime goes by another name.'

I waited for her to say more about that, but it was the end of a long day and I was tired of the whole thing. I did not press her. When she continued to tell me about herself I was content to let her.

She told me she was a widow – her husband had died nine years earlier. She said she read thrillers and mysteries for recreation, but not just those, she added. She described some biographies she had read recently. They were of Dearth notables, but I had not heard of them. I guessed she was about fifteen years older than me. She took her drink in small sips, but at frequent intervals. We ordered another round. I was impressed by her: she had a calm, steady manner that made her seem in control, but this was sometimes belied by the way she spoke. Much of what she said, at least in those first few minutes, was questioning, enquiring. I felt she was used to asking questions.

She asked me about my work. I was always guarded about this when meeting someone, but I told her a little, where I worked, when and for how long in a day, what I was writing at the moment. I told her something about Jo, the many years we had shared together, the contentment of a long relationship. I described where we lived: it was a large single-storey house on one of the coast roads to the north of Raba City. It was on the edge of one of the largest nature parks on Raba, a vast area of undeveloped tropical forest that spread across most of the width of that part of the island.

We ordered more drinks – she switched to the Salay wine, which she said she had not tried before. The logs in the stove settled, sparks flew, a feeling of relaxed ease came over me. I cannot remember everything we talked about then. It was just an agreeable conversation between two people who had recently met. I remember asking Frejah Harsent about her present life, but all she would say was that she was semi-retired, past the official age of retirement. There was a project she was working on that she wanted to see through to a conclusion. Something about a colleague. The seigniory was keeping her on until then. She gave no details.

The conversation drifted back to crime fiction. She wanted to know where ideas came from, how they could be constructed into a story. This is the question many writers are not only frequently asked, but often ask themselves. There is no easy or satisfactory answer. Certainly, in my own experience, working with ideas is a largely instinctive process, one you hardly recognize until afterwards. That isn't what most people expect as an answer.

I was worried that this was moving into chancy ground, somewhere by habit I trod carefully. Frejah Harsent had mentioned she had a degree in criminology − a warning sign. It sometimes happens that when meeting someone socially, and they discover what I do for a living, they start telling me stories of their own brushes with the law. A stolen wallet, an intruder into a neighbour's house, an unfair conviction for driving too fast. That sort of thing. Sometimes I heard about incompetent police investigations, or brilliant and effective policing. The unfairness of magistrates or judges, or an unexpectedly sympathetic judgement. Not uninteresting in themselves, these anecdotes are commonplace but they do not suggest a plot for a novel I might like to write one day,

I veered her gently away from that. But why did I write crime fiction? she asked

I said: 'Crime is something people fear. It's a low-level fear, because ordinary people, that is, those outside the criminal fraternity, never really believe it will happen to them. But it does strike, and seemingly at random, and it's always a disagreeable experience. Even what the courts treat as a minor felony can ruin your life. You hear about crime that happens to other people, or was witnessed by someone you know. Or you live in the same street or town where something awful takes place. It's ever-present, but largely invisible. And crime has mysteries. Who did this terrible thing? And why? What was the motive? Will whoever it was be caught? How should they be punished if so?

'Writing crime fiction is a way of trying to answer those questions. Most real crime is stupidly motivated, committed by unhappy or vulnerable people who have drug or alcohol problems, and often based on a grudge. Usually an unreasonable one. Many petty criminals have chronic mental health issues. This of course is not how most victims want to see it. They see crime as wilfully evil and they call for justice, when what they often mean is revenge.

'But the elaborately planned murder of a wealthy victim in the conservatory of a remote country house, or any of the other classic scenarios of mysteries and thrillers, are the fantasies of fiction writers like me.'

I was starting to talk too much, a sure sign that I should stop drinking. The time had gone steadily by, and now we were coming towards the end of the evening.

Because I believed my wristwatch had suddenly become unreliable I asked Frejah Harsent the time. Her watch showed exactly the same time as mine – the sweep second hand was even in an identical position. It was late.

I was astonished by the weird behaviour of my watch.

'It's a consequence of mutability,' Frejah said. 'A minor one. Everyone on the island is affected by it in the same way, so it never matters. Almost every clock, timepiece and digital gadget is synchronized to a central chronometer. They automatically update when it's needed. If you're ever unsure of the time there are public clocks in every street, but your watch is just as reliable.'

'How can the time on Dearth ever be objectively accurate? If it's constantly changing, does it fall out of synchronization with other islands, with other parts of the world?'

'Who knows?' she said. 'If it's out of synch with other places, it makes no practical difference unless you're actually there. But when you travel anywhere you always use local time.'

'I have to catch a train tomorrow morning,' I said. 'It's supposed to leave at 10.30 a.m. What happens if the clocks change between now and then?'

'That's the sleeper service to Tristcontenta? The changes in time have no effect. The train will leave when the clocks say 10.30.' She drained the rest of her glass. 'Just rely on your watch and turn up at the station in the usual way. You should be more worried about the food on the train.'

'The food is awful,' I said. 'A real problem.'

'It'll be worse tomorrow. Most of the train company's on-board chefs have gone on strike, and so are the people who refill the vending machines in the train corridors. If you want to eat, take your own food.'

'How could I do that?' I said. I was suddenly filled with dread: the two-day journey took on the aspect of a nightmare.

'The hotel would prepare some meal packs. The strikes are a regular problem on the trains, so the hotel has a carry-out service for travellers.'

'Expensive, though?'

'Without a doubt. But beautifully prepared.' She put down her empty wineglass and stood up. I did too, feeling unsteady. 'On the other hand,' she said. 'A thought has occurred to me. You're presumably heading for the airport. I'm planning to drive to the north part of the island tomorrow, and could almost certainly get you to the Hub the next day, in time for your flight. There are at least two flights to Salay in the evenings.'

'That would a terrible imposition on you,' I said. 'I couldn't possibly—'

'Of course you could. It's a long drive, and I'd welcome some company. Once out of the city and beyond the mountains the road is dull. I'd enjoy having a passenger. I know of several restaurants on the way, and there are a couple of good enough places to stay about halfway along.'

I continued to protest mildly, but also half heartedly, because an alternative to that interminable train journey was tempting.

We agreed to meet in Reception after breakfast. She added there would be no need for the bulky outer clothes. We walked together to the elevators – her room was on the fourth floor, while mine was of course two storeys above.

I had drunk more than I realized. I lurched against her as we turned into the elevator block, and she helped me back upright with a swift, strong movement. I leant against the wall while we waited for the elevator car to arrive, and I stumbled as we entered. I said sorry several times, I hadn't realized how long we had been in the bar, I didn't normally drink as much as this. She laughed. The metal walls of the elevator car, the carpeted floor, seemed to be circling. Frejah was not as intoxicated as me. I held the hand rail as the elevator swished upwards. On the fourth floor she bade me goodnight. I continued on up. Suddenly aware of being alone I leaned drunkenly into one of the mirrors, abashed at my grotesque and dishevelled appearance.

When the elevator stopped and the doors opened I made it out into the hallway without stumbling. I set off towards my room with a determined air, weaving from side to side.

Inevitably, I went wrong and had to retrace my steps. I returned past the elevator block, and this time found the correct corridor. I had to lean down beside each door to peer closely at the room number, inscribed in small letters beside the electronic lock. I was embarrassed by how drunk I had become. I was wondering what regrettable nonsense I might have been saying to that intelligent and interesting woman. I felt blank about her. For a few moments I could not even recall her name.

I found my door, rammed in the electronic key and lurched inside. Every light in the room was on. As I closed the door behind me, the television screen lit up with brightly saturated colours. Music was playing loudly, people were moving and laughing.

Befuddled, I stared around. I had a distinct, pedantic memory of switching everything off, and before closing the door throwing the master switch. I was confused, annoyed. Had I returned to the room at some point and turned on the lights again? A memory lapse? But once the woman had joined me, I had not left the table in the bar, beside the fire.

Something was buzzing irritatingly. I turned, tried to focus. There was a digital display embedded in the body of the door, next to the lock. I had never noticed it before, presumably because it had not been activated. I concentrated, leaned forward, looked closely. It said:

Exit and re-enter your room immediately, using only the authorized electronic key. Statutory penalty for improper use of mutability procedures: Th 100.

The key I was holding in my hand was the red-bordered white card, the one I had been instructed never to use except when told to by a member of staff. I felt momentarily resentful of the complication they had created, which I would be penalized for. Why did they make things so difficult for people late at night?

I swallowed, tried to take control of myself again. With deliberate motions I reached deep into my pocket, swapped one key card for the other, then returned to the corridor and closed the door behind me. I counted to ten, glancing furtively from side to side along the corridor. I was unobserved. I slipped in the correct key with precise, over-elaborate care.

Inside the room the lights were off again, the television was dark and silent, as I was convinced I had left them. I pushed my hand against the master switch, then I turned on the other light switches by the door. The room filled with light.

I was embarrassed by my blurry physical condition, but also vexed by this hotel and its weird systems and warnings. Was every hotel in town as obsessively, inscrutably, bizarrely restrictive as the Dearth Plaza? There must be a crummy one-star pension located near the train station, or the bus depot, where guests could come and go as they pleased, leave on the TV when they went to the bar. Maybe if I had owned up to Prof Wendow from the start that I was not an academic of his ilk, nor even the holder of a degree, I might have ended up in such a place.

I used the toilet. I filled the hand basin with clear, cold water, then splashed it over my head. I took off the rest of my clothes and stepped into the shower cubicle. I ran a warm spray over me. Across the bathroom space I could see myself reflected in one of the wall mirrors. With concentration I stared across at myself critically – I was looking overweight, unhealthy, my skin was blotchy. When I was at home I always thought I looked better than this. Maybe it was hotels with their unforgiving lighting, their mirrors in places you did not expect them to be. That was an excuse, I knew, but there was a tiny truth in it. I flexed my stomach muscles, tried to pull them in. I had eaten too much, but also drunk far too much. The words threaded repetitively through my mind. I stood there in the shower spray, staring at myself in the mirror and wondering what kind of impression I must have made on the Harsent woman. Harsent – Frejah! Her name came back to me now. She told me always to call her Frejah.

It was so late now, even by my unreliable watch. I towelled myself dry, then pulled on the flannelette robe the hotel supplied. I loved the feeling of luxury from the sumptuously soft robe, knowing the one-star pension located by the bus depot would not have such a thing.

I opened my laptop, connected it to the hotel wifi. This time I did not have to accept the Terms and Conditions, but a panel came on to warn of Broadband Mutability. During the evening it appeared that the risk level had risen from 6 per cent to 47 per cent. I logged on anyway. I was missing Jo.

I started typing a brief email to her. All I wanted to say was that I was at last about to go to bed, and that because the return train journey was affected by strikes I had accepted an offer of a car ride to the airport. I should be home as planned.

But the keyboard, or the software, or the email provider, was playing up again. The letter 'h' was still not registering normally, nor was the letter 's'. I pressed on, trying to find a workaround, other ways of saying what I meant. Soon the letter 'c' became unusable, and almost immediately after that the 'J'. I could not even type her name. When I looked up at the email address I had used, that too was incorrect. The letter 't' disappeared while I was trying.

I gave up. I glanced at the emails in the inbox, skimmed recent social posts, then turned off the computer and put it and my phone on to charge overnight.

I returned to the bathroom and brushed my teeth. I drank some cold water, climbed into bed, lay down, did not even try to read for a while. I turned out all the lights.

5

The Money Trap

Breakfast was a tentative matter. I chose carefully, took small portions, drank plenty of tea. I swallowed a paracetamol tablet. My head started to clear, but slowly. For a few more hours I would be suffering physical stiffness, mental sloth. This I knew. I did not see Frejah Harsent in the restaurant.

I returned to Room 627. Remembering what Frejah had said I packed my outdoor clothes into the larger case, put everything else into the smaller one. I exited the room, first scrupulously checking the lights to be sure everything was off. I threw the master switch as I left.

There were two short lines of guests queuing by the reception desk, so I waited my turn before requesting the account. The young woman at the desk ordered the bill from the computer and presented it to me without expression. I looked at it in horror and disbelief: it was immense, and ran to two pages. The total amount at the end was unbelievable.

I said: 'What currency is this?'

'Muriseayan thaler. Would you prefer it converted, citizen sir?'

I considered quickly. The currency used on Salay was the Aubracian talent, but the rate of exchange between the talent and the thaler was notoriously poor.

'Into simoleons, please,' I said. This was the currency used for general trade across the Dream Archipelago. It was the accepted currency within the publishing industry. All my book contracts were drawn up using simoleon amounts and rates, and the literary agent invariably sent me payment in that currency. I was used to it, knew instinctively what it was worth.

The simoleon was the old standard currency. It had been in use for centuries when most of the main clearing banks were established on the island of Muriseay, but in recent years, because of the flourishing finance sector on Salay Raba, the Aubracian talent had become the new standard for banking and trade. As a result the simoleon had evolved in effect into a virtual currency. I had never seen an actual simoleon banknote or coin – nor had anyone else I knew who used them. It was accepted as a universal legal tender, but only a handful of the more remote islands were thought to still use it as practical money.

The thaler, which also originated from Muriseay, was now seen as the currency for big businesses and high spenders. The fact that this hotel defaulted to the thaler was a clue to the status and wealth of the regular clientele.

The receptionist slipped the original account into a shredder, and moments later a new version came smoothly out of the printer. She turned it around and slid it across the desk to me.

The sums of money were now at least comprehensible, roughly understandable in comparison with the prices of other expenses that I might have to bear. The first price on the list, for instance, the overnight use of the room, was approximately three times what I had ever paid before, in any other hotel anywhere.

I said: 'My booking was made on my behalf by Dearth University. The Historical and Literary Society. Could you tell me, please, how much of this will be covered by them?'

She looked at her computer monitor, typed something. Still looking at the screen she said: 'That's correct, citizen sir. The information we have here is that the room was booked for you by the Revisionist History Department at Dearth University. A Professor S. Wendow. Is that name familiar to you?'

'Yes, it is.'

'The arrangement as set out by Professor Wendow is that the university will cover the cost of the room, and a two course dinner without drinks. Breakfast is not included. The instruction we have is that you will settle the full amount on departure, and the university will reimburse you in due course.'

'But I thought the account had been paid in advance—'

'No, sir. If you have a bank card I can finalize the account immediately.'

I said nothing to the receptionist, as it was none of her fault. But a leaden feeling was descending on me. This was the worst of all worlds, a situation I recognized from past experience. I had already spent unexpected money during this trip: buying the arctic outer clothing, being hit with baggage excess charges during the flights. The hotel bill alone was likely to use up most of what I had at present in my account. I rarely have surplus money, and this was going to clean me out. But also, a particular dread: from past experience I knew what the words 'settlement in due course' from a university meant in reality. Weeks and months of waiting lay ahead.

Then there was the honorarium. How and when was that to be paid?

'Do you have your bank card to hand, citizen sir?' the receptionist said, bringing forward the remote card reader.

'Of course. But I am trying to understand what I am being charged for.'

She leaned across the desk and indicated each item with her pen.

'We have listed everything separately,' she said, in a patient but noncommittal voice. 'This is the main charge, for one night in the room. This amount here is for your dinner in the grill room last night – each course is shown separately, as are the couvert, the drinks and the optional service charge. Then there is the bar bill. Again, everything you ordered is itemized. This amount here is the standard hotel wifi charge, based on your two accesses to the internet. You used your home island's protocols, not the Dearth defaults.'

'I didn't know there was a difference.'

'Dearth defaults would have been less expensive.' She indicated the bill again. 'There are two internet accesses under your home protocol. The second amount is higher because of the broadband mutability increase. From 6 per cent to 47 per cent, as shown here. You would have confirmed acceptance of that before going online?' I looked up at her, met her bland gaze. I nodded mutely. 'Finally, there is breakfast, normally included in the room charge, but the instructions we had from Professor Wendow were that breakfast should be an optional extra.'

Beneath all these were three extra amounts, each of them huge. I tried to make sense of what they might mean and why they had been applied to my bill.

The first two were identically described as *Standard Levy – electrical mutability abuse.*

The third was called *Seignioral surcharge – unauthorized horizontal prejudice.*

'What are these?' I said, already suspecting the worst.

'They are not hotel charges. We are obliged to charge our guests for them, and pass them on. The first two – it appears you exited your room without turning off the lights. That is a standard compensation fee set by the utility provider.'

'Yes, but only once, and I went back immediately to put it right. And the second time I found the lights had turned themselves on when I returned to the room.'

'That of course was related to the seignioral surcharge. You appear to have opened your room using the incorrect electronic key. That always turns all lights on as a reminder to the guest.'

'Compensation for what?' I said irritably. 'And how does the seigniory apply a surcharge to people staying in your hotel?'

'We have a contract with the electricity suppliers. If any of our guests interferes with the electrical mutability—'

'But I've no idea what mutability is!' I said too loudly.

'Citizen sir, there is an explanatory booklet in every room.' Her voice returned to its neutral note. 'If a guest interferes with the electrical mutability a spike or a surge in the current follows, and the utility provider has to adjust the supply to the whole hotel.' Her pen moved down to the third extra. 'This one is because you entered your room using the incorrect key. We post warnings everywhere about that.' She was still holding the bank card reader. 'Sir, may I go ahead and scan your card?'

I stared down unhappily at the account, still with a feeling of disbelief, and a certain amount of panic. How could I possibly pay all this?

The receptionist moved away to attend to two other guests who had approached the desk.

I was travelling with two charge cards. One did not have a sufficient credit limit for me to put the hotel bill against. The other did have available credit, but it ran up a punitive rate of interest if the entire amount was not paid off within three weeks. There was really no choice therefore, but I was reluctant to use the second card. The immense charge and the inevitable interest penalty that followed would jeopardize my presently stable but often fragile finances, simply because of Wendow's neglectful approach to my expenses. I could not imagine that he, earning a no doubt substantial professorial salary, would have the least idea of the trouble he was unwittingly causing me.

The receptionist returned, I proffered her the charge card, she ran it through the machine, she tore off a copy of the receipt. All was done.

'Thank you for choosing the Dearth Plaza Hotel, Dr Fremde,' she said. 'We look forward to greeting you again. Please be sure to deposit your room key in the slot provided at the front of the desk.'

She smiled professionally at me and turned away to deal with other customers. I reached deep into my trouser pocket, found the key and slipped it into the return slot. I heard it fall with a plastic clicking noise as it landed in the heap of used key cards already in the receptacle. I was glad to be rid of the thing.

It was approaching 9.40 a.m. I had less than an hour to reach the train if Frejah Harsent had changed her mind about driving me, or did not turn up. With my outer clothes packed away, and only the vaguest idea of where the train station could be found, I felt the first stirring of traveller stress. I knew there was a taxi rank outside the hotel, but when I went to the main doors and peered through the thick glass I could see no cabs waiting.

Then Frejah Harsent appeared from the direction of the elevator block, and strode towards me. The stress instantly fled.

'Good morning, Todd! I am ready to leave as soon as you are. I assume you have checked out. We have a long way to drive, so the sooner we start the better.'

We shook hands in a formal way. In the daylight flooding into the lobby she looked a taller, more formidable woman.

She had an erect bearing, and a manner that implied she was used to making decisions others would concur with. The relaxed drinking companion of the evening before was recognizable beneath this unexpectedly daunting image, but only just.

I gathered up my luggage, showing I was ready to leave immediately.

She led me to the elevators and selected the sub-basement level. The elevator doors opened on to a wide, sporadically lit parking area, with a concrete floor, concrete pillars, low concrete ceiling. Direction signs were everywhere, with arrows and stop signs painted on the walls and floor. The lot was about three-quarters full, most of the vehicles being of the large, off-road utility type. The cars shone under the overhead lights. A warm breeze fanned across the rows of vehicles and along the wide access tracks between the bays. I was certain I could sense a hint of blossom or spring flowers, wafting around in the artificially heated air.

She led me zigzagging between parked cars, aiming her remote electronic key ahead of her. One of the cars ahead beeped a loud signal response, its lights came on and the doors opened. This was to me an astonishing sight: the driver and passenger doors lifted upwards on hydraulic servos, folding into gull-wing shapes above the roof of the car. The trunk lid contrived to open fully, remain vertical and slide down half its length into a recess.

The car was a low-slung two-seat roadster, built for speed, painted a shining black, with steel-wire wheels, redwall tyres, aerodynamically perfect bodywork, deeply canted windshield, darkened side windows, a rear screen guarded by a narrowly slatted blind, a complete absence of chromium-plate trim. The roof of the car was not large, but it was studded with antennae: two short ones, three more presently retracted. They were positioned exactly to allow the doors to move into position when opened.

I recognized the marque instantly, and unbelievingly. It was a car for the car fanatic, the dream of adolescents of all ages. It was one of the road cars hand-built for supposedly advanced drivers by the engineering company who sponsored, manufactured and raced one of the most famous sports cars in the world. The company was based on one of the few commercially run islands in the Archipelago. This was the beach and mountain resort of Lillen-Cay, the playground of the super rich. No seignioral dynasty presided over the island. The only hierarchy was the scale of wealth, the size of private yacht, the speed of hand-built road car.

'There is room for your luggage in the trunk,' Frejah said. We walked around to it. The compartment was small. Her own bag was already there, standing tidily on edge to one side. I could get my larger one in by lying it down, with the smaller one on top. I made to retain my computer tote to have with me in the car. 'Everything must go in here,' she insisted. 'Space inside is restricted.'

I placed my tote on top of the other cases, but it was obvious that when the lid came down it would crush against it. I turned the tote around, tried to ease it, pressed down. That made little difference. I moved my overnight case out, then put it back in again at a different angle.

Frejah stepped around, perhaps to guide or supervise me. As she did so the shadow she had been casting from one of the overhead lights moved with her. The inside of the trunk was suddenly visible to me. There was a gun there, a large weapon, an assault rifle, attached to the back wall, close up against the passenger compartment. It was partly concealed by Frejah's own bag, partly by mine. It was disassembled, the parts mounted on a cushioned board: a snub barrel, metal stock, magazine, firing pin. I could see what it was.

In fact, I recognized it. For several years I have employed a technical consultant for my books, a retired police officer called Spoder, formerly a detective inspector with the Raba force. A few weeks ago I had asked him for advice on the type of gun one of my characters was likely to carry. Spoder had turned up at my house the next day with a portfolio of photographs and catalogue items. I recall the day was hotter than usual. I sat with him on the shaded patio outside my house as we went through them, eliminating the obviously unsuitable, until finally we settled on a choice of three. He left them with me, and I noted the details. As soon as I was able to do some more work on my manuscript after this trip I would select one and name and describe it in the book, cribbing all the technical detail some of my readers insist on. (I always suspect that many readers skip details like this, but if I try to omit them the publisher insists they must go in. I always snarl privately as I make the changes.)

What Frejah Harsent had stored in the trunk of her car was not one of those exactly, but it was similar. It was a semi-automatic compact rifle, with a snub-nosed barrel, self-reloading mechanism, and a multi-round magazine inserted into the grip. Assembled it would require both hands to fire it, with the weight cradled against one side of the body and braced against the arm that was firing.

I pushed in my computer tote against the top of the gun mount, and now there was sufficient clearance to close the trunk lid on top of it. As I straightened I looked towards Frejah, and she looked at me. I was thinking about the weapon. Our eyes met. She said nothing. I said nothing.

She touched her remote key and the lid silently raised itself out of the retaining recess, then swished down to close the compartment. There was a convincing sound of compressed air as it locked.

I walked around to the open passenger door. Frejah showed me the best way to enter: backside first, swivel my legs in, lean back and put weight on the back- and head-rest. 'You'll get used to that,' she said. She walked around and swung herself in one smooth motion into the driver's seat beside me, and brought down the doors.

Although I was reclining at near horizontal, the feeling of comfort, safety and control was total. I had perfect vision ahead, and could see to either side with ease. I have driven cars most of my adult life but I had never before experienced such a sensation of instinctive harmony between body and machine.

Frejah started the engine – there was an immensely satisfying roar from below and behind, and several LED instruments came instantly to life on the sculpted dash in front of the driver. After its first burst of power the engine settled into a potent idling, with barely any detectable vibration, a sense of energetic imminent release.

'Is this your own car, Frejah?' I said. I knew it was a stupid question even as I blurted it out, but I was overwhelmed by the discovery of what she drove around in. I felt something like an awestruck teenager finding himself materializing on the command deck of a spaceship.

'It's the car I use, yes,' she said.

'But do you own it?' That was too direct, too impertinent. 'I mean—'

'I think of it as my car. No one else drives it.' She revved the engine once, and a cloud of thin dark smoke billowed past the windows. 'Now – we need to get to the train station.'

I was surprised, but said nothing to that. She had said she would drive me all the way to Tristcontenta, and in the last few seconds I had developed and was relishing the expectation of a day or two speeding across Dearth's central plain in this extraordinarily lovely car. A short lift to the railway station was not what I was hoping for.

Frejah drove and controlled the car expertly through the parking lot access tracks. The highly tuned engine sounded awe-inspiringly on the point of erupting into devastating power. We approached the pay station and barriers, but Frejah made no attempt to slow the car. The barrier jerked suddenly upwards, almost as if in apology for having the temerity to be in the way. We swept underneath. After a long curving and ascending ramp we emerged into the cold daylight of Dearth City, a forest of tall buildings, with cars, buses and trucks everywhere, lighted advertising signs, a few pedestrians wrapped inevitably against the freezing air. None of them looked at us as we snarled past, presumably preoccupied by the need to arrive wherever they were going as soon as possible, not to gawp at passing cars.

I noticed that at every street junction, and jutting out at a low level from many industrial buildings, was a brightly lit digital display. The dazzling green image refreshed constantly: from the temperature (at that moment -19°C) to something called M per cent ('Mutability'? – anyway standing at 7.5 per cent, although on some displays it showed as 7.25 per cent).

Swerving efficiently but not dangerously between slower vehicles, Frejah soon reached the main entrance yard to the station. She pulled over into a zone clearly marked as prohibited for parking or waiting.

'Are you leaving me here?' I said, trying to conceal my sense of disappointment.

'Do you still have the return half of your train ticket?'

'Yes.'

'Go and claim a refund. You'll see several cancellation automats next to the ticket office. There's a machine readable code printed on the back of your ticket. Feed it into the slot, and collect the cash below. Or you can burn it into a charge card if you have one.'

'I didn't pay for the ticket myself.'

'Doesn't matter. Today's a good day to claim a refund. Because of the strike there's an element of compensation added to the ticket price, and because the strike has been going on for several days the railway company is obliged to refund an extra ten per cent, for tithes and commutations many passengers had to find.'

The door on my side of the car lifted effortlessly and silently. A blast of freezing air swept in on me. I had no outer protection! I levered myself out of the car seat as quickly as possible, and with a clumsy scrambling motion stood up on the concourse outside.

The car door whooshed down immediately. The engine was idling, the purring sound of a fantastically powerful giant cat, at the ready for a kill. I paid no more fanciful attention than that, and scuttled forward, crouching to try to minimize the impact of the cold.

The station entrance hall was not exposed to the outside air, but even so it was a chilly and draughty place. Music and announcements clashed on the overhead speakers, as before. The whole immense edifice was full of echoes. Three of the five cancellation automats were labelled as being out of service, one with a broken glass screen, but the first of the others I tried responded the instant I slipped in my charge card.

Within two minutes I had completed the transaction. My card was credited with the return part of the fare, also for the use of a sleeping compartment I no longer required, four pre-paid

meals I would never eat, cabin services I would not be bene-
fiting from. The compensation and refunded tithes Frejah had
mentioned almost doubled the total amount. Mutability dis-
counts added a few further cents.

The total refund was in simoleons, and as I hurried back to
the car I knew that the problem of the hotel bill was mostly
solved.

The car door opened. I swung myself inside. I was chilled
through. The door swished closed.

'Thank you,' I said to Frejah Harsent. She boosted the heater,
floored the accelerator pedal.

6

Strangers in a Car

The road leading out through the suburbs of Dearth City was narrow and congested with traffic, a steady uphill climb past long terraces of uninspired housing, industrial units and large complexes such as hospitals, schools and government buildings. Frejah drove patiently but the engine of the supercharged car was in a state of constant change, snarling then idling in turn, as it responded to pressure on the throttle. The forward motion of the car remained smooth and unaggressive. Only once, on a short strip of divided highway, did she give the powerful car its head. I felt the thrilling surge and pressure of the violent acceleration as we shot past a line of cars, trucks and delivery vehicles with almost insolent ease. But most of this early part of the journey was dull, giving me the chance to take in more details of the interior of the remarkable vehicle.

The dashboard was low and designed elegantly with both an eye to aesthetic appearance and functionality. There were no dials, merely a series of clear digital displays, more instruments than I had ever seen in any other car. Beyond even these were several other pieces of equipment, situated clearly but unobtrusively to each side of the driver's eyeline. None of them appeared to be in use, but they all had tiny pilot lights glowing.

A row of switches was on the door surround about Frejah's head.

Immediately behind the steering wheel, itself small, ergonomically oblate, clad in fine leather, were several communications boxes attached beneath the dash. I assumed at first they would be a radio, music player, etc., but as soon as the thought formed I realized that a car at this level of sophistication would not simply bolt on such commonplace gadgets. I had come to the realization that where Frejah was sitting was less the driving seat of a car, more the cockpit of a small plane.

The traffic gradually thinned as we reached the city limits. Frejah reached forward beneath the dash and pulled out a wireless headset with ambient-sound-cancelling phones. She spoke immediately. 'Ya . . . not until tomorrow . . . late afternoon, early evening, ya . . . I've got a 6/17 with me. Off-island, ya.'

By this time we had reached such an elevation that we were passing through intermittent low cloud, only glimpsing the great southern peaks rising around us snowclad. The land immediately to each side of the road was frozen, or had coverage of recent snow. The road surface itself, although recently ploughed of loose snow, and marked with the tyre traces of the traffic that preceded us, clearly bore large patches of black ice. Frejah appeared to pay them no heed, driving without hesitation, even through an increasing number of corners.

She took another headset call. 'Harsent . . . ya, send them in. Can't say – I'm with a 6/17.'

As she spoke she glanced away from the road, a mannerism, not a way of looking at where we were going. I was tense all over, rigid with anticipation of some catastrophic accident in this hostile and unpredictable landscape. I wondered briefly: she spoke in code. Was I the 'off-island 6/17' she was with? An instrument on the dash revealed the outside temperature to be -24°C. Neither of us spoke to each other. I felt incapable of words. Frejah was obviously not entirely concentrating on her driving, but appeared relaxed and expert. Something else was coming through on the headset. 'Ya, Harsent . . . no, I said no. Get it done.'

A few minutes went by, then she pulled off the headset and pushed it under the dash. Both hands back on the steering wheel.

Finally, she said: 'You haven't said anything since we left the city.'

'You've been taking messages.'

'There won't be any more until I decide. I can catch up later. Or this evening. What's on your mind?'

In fact, her hairline control of the car was what was on my mind. She exuded confidence, while I felt every muscle tensing.

I said: 'If this is your car, what do you normally use it for?'

'Watch this.' She reached forward to one of the gadgets attached to the top of the dash. 'See that truck coming towards us?'

In fact I could barely see it in the wintry haze, a dark shape in the distance ahead, lumbering up a long hill towards us. A head-up display flashed on to the interior of the windshield, almost like a three-dimensional image from virtual reality. It was a close-up of the truck. The licence number appeared superimposed brightly above the image, as well as the driver's name, his address at work, his goods operator licence number, the current tachograph data, the quantity of fuel remaining in the tank, the weight and axle distribution of the payload. The truck was travelling at just above seventy kilometres an hour.

'He has rear axle overload, and he's using an unregistered turbo booster to get up the hill,' Frejah said. 'Want me to haul him over?'

She touched another device. The truck disappeared from the HUD, replaced by an apparently close-up image of the car in front of us, travelling in the same direction, still some distance ahead. While I looked at the new image the truck with the weight overload and turbo booster roared past us. It was emitting a stream of dark smoke. Frejah said nothing about that. The image of the car ahead revealed the same sort of information as had appeared for the truck, but in addition there was a space for a list of existing driving misdemeanours against the driver. In this case the driver was a woman (I learned her name and address), and she happened to have a clean record.

Frejah turned off the image.

'You're a cop,' I said.

'I'm in semi-retirement. I told you last night.'

'You're still a cop. Is this car a police vehicle?'

'That is how it is registered. I don't own it, but I have exclusive use of it.'

She suddenly produced a slim leather wallet, with a warrant card visible in the front. She held it up so I could see it, but she whipped it away before I could learn anything from it.

'Let me see that again,' I said.

'That is your inalienable right as a citizen.' She intoned the familiar words, spoken in TV crime shows every week. They momentarily chilled me.

The warrant reappeared in her hand. She held it so I could read it properly. Her photographic image was a hologram. Her name was Commissioner Frejah Harsent. She was a detective in the Transgression Investigation Department, Dearth Seignioral Police.

'So you are a cop,' I said.

'Only on intermittent duty.'

'Are you on duty now?'

'Yes and no. Yes, because I'm investigating an open case. No, because at the moment I'm giving you a ride to Tristcontenta Hub.'

'Me being the 6/17 you're with?'

'You know what that means, or did you work it out?'

'I worked it out. Is giving a ride to a 6/17 disallowed by the police?'

'I *am* the police on this island.'

'Commissioner's a high rank on Salay,' I said.

'It's the same here.'

'You can't be the only commissioner.'

'No – of course not. There are five of us. We share responsibility across the island. But I am the senior commissioner. I report direct to the seignior's office. The other four report to me.'

'And that's how you were given this car.'

'The force gives you nothing,' she said. 'I had to argue for it for more than a year.'

She was overtaking an articulated truck as she said this. There was a turn ahead, from which an oncoming lorry suddenly appeared. Frejah put on a burst of speed, the car accelerating like a rocket opening up, and we slipped back to safety with a margin. The corner the truck had appeared from proved to be a sharp right hand turn lacking a protective crash barrier, with a drop below. The car negotiated the corner at high speed. My fingernails dug into the palms of my hands.

When I could breathe again, I said: 'Frejah – Commissioner. There's ice on the road.'

'We agreed. Call me by my first name. I'm not on duty when I'm with you.'

'OK, but the ice—'

'This car has the best anti-skid system ever devised. I know what I'm doing, because the people who built this car knew what they were doing. You want me to slow down?'

'Maybe a little, maybe not,' I said, because in spite of the frequent moments of hair-raising terror I was thrilled by her skilful driving, and the performance of the car. 'Do what's best.'

'What's best is to remember it's a long way to Tristcontenta.'

After another hour Frejah spoke again into the headset. 'Ya, Harsent. Off the road now.'

A roadside area of retail concessions was ahead, and we turned off for it. It had been snowing for the last twenty minutes and as we slowed down we could see that it was intensifying and wind borne, blustering from the south and east. Drifts were heaping up at the sides of the parking lot and against the body-work of many of the vehicles. Frejah ignored all directional signs and drove through an unmarked gated area – the barrier rose almost as we turned towards the ramp. We drove down to a small underground parking area. A place marked *Security* was vacant.

We left the car and ascended by metal steps to a refreshment bar. We were both peckish, not hungry. My hangover had all but vanished – the cold air, the adrenaline surges from Frejah's driving? We ordered biscuits and a couple of savoury pastries, with coffee, sitting side by side on tall stools at the counter. The guy who worked behind the bar stayed close to where we were seated, apparently searching through till receipts, moving glasses around. The bar stretched all the way to the other side of the room. Other customers were there. He could have stood on their side too.

Frejah kept glancing towards him, but said nothing.

Then she said: 'Would you give us some privacy, please?'

'Yes, ma'am,' he said. He moved away, but only as far as a

small counter at the rear. With his back to us he started folding paper napkins.

We picked everything up and transferred to a small table in a far corner.

'I've called in here a few times recently,' Frejah said. 'He's connected me with the car. I don't want him listening to us.'

'Could he be someone you've had to arrest in the past?'

'I arrest nobody. There aren't any criminals on Dearth. This you know by now.'

'No criminals, no crime. But you drive around in a pursuit car, armed to the teeth.'

'I'm not armed,' she said. 'Neither is the car.'

'There's the semi-automatic in the trunk.'

'That's true. But that's not part of the ordnance of the car. And it's not a pursuit car. It's C&C – command and control. We bought it secondhand from a force on one of the other islands.'

'We bought it?'

'The force did, yes.'

'So why do you need it?' I said.

'I wanted it more than I needed it,' she said. 'It's a car I dreamed about having. They saw it as a retirement gift, one I can keep until I really do retire.'

'When's that likely to be?'

'I'm on an open case. I'll retire when that's complete. Not until.'

'But there's no crime here.'

'True. Or true enough.' Music started playing from overhead speakers. Not loud, but intrusive. Frejah glared at the barkeep, but he turned away and the level of the music did not change. 'We'll drive some more as soon as we've finished these coffees,' she said.

Mine was still hot. Frejah was taking small, frequent sips.

'Last night at the conference, I felt I was floundering with this concept of a crime-free state,' I said. 'The Historical Society wanted it as the subject. All I could do was theorize about it. Once I started I felt I had been set up. The people in the audience knew more about it than I did.'

'I was there,' Frejah said. 'You didn't do a bad job. People on this island take it for granted, but they would never intellectualize about it. I think a lot of people were in the audience because they had read your books. Most of them enjoyed your lecture – you received more applause than many speakers do.'

'Some people rushed away the moment I had finished.'

'Some people had to get home.'

'Is intellectualizing what it sounded like? I was just pushing at a theory. Not even my own theory.'

'Pushing at a theory is what they wanted you to do.'

'I realized soon after I started speaking that I really had no idea what I was talking about. Crime is everywhere, whether you admit it or not. If somebody takes something away from me, or hurts me, or defrauds me, or kills me – that's a crime. It's a crime if the attacks are on someone I love, or someone I just know, or even if I don't know the victim. It's still a crime. It's a crime here as it is anywhere else in the world.'

'What if the law is different?'

'All laws in any civilized society are essentially the same,' I said. 'Only details are different. Different societies prioritize the matters that concern them most. Laws are a consensus – what ordinary people will put up with, and what they won't. If someone deviates from the consensus, they commit a crime and become a criminal.'

'I don't disagree with that.'

'So why do you say there's no crime?'

'Because on Dearth we have a civil code, not a criminal one. What you call a crime we call a civil transgression.'

'Same thing, different name. Is that all it is?'

'Perhaps . . . but most transgressions are not classified as crime, and the culprit does not acquire a criminal record. The outcome is usually compensation to be paid, or time spent working for the community without pay. A record is kept, but it is time-limited, and eventually scrubbed. The lower courts deal with almost all traffic offences, minor offences of violence, most thefts, most of the transgressions involving drug or alcohol abuse, many burglaries. These courts are set at serf level, but of course not all transgressors are serfs.

'More serious transgressions are dealt with by seignioral process. The procedures are set by whichever of their Lordships and Ladyships are sitting that day, so they are unpredictable. The penalties usually amount to the removal or denial of privileges and property, and the loss or partial loss of land. Some are sent for military service. Corvée is an alternative for those without land. Most serious transgressors are also reduced to basic serfdom, which is of course only what they deserve. It's the most effective deterrent for others.'

She was unsmiling, watching how I reacted. In fact, I was still persisting in thinking that the theory of a crime-free society was not mine.

Crime everywhere is the same, the law everywhere is the same. Only details vary. My books were published in many different island groups around the world, each one of which had its own penal code. The crimes I described were recognized and understood everywhere, or at least I assumed they were because no one ever complained that they didn't recognize the laws that my villains broke. How could they not? One human killing another is murder, whatever you call it.

But something she said was also sticking in my mind: reduction to serfdom as a punishment? That did interest me, coming from the woman who said she ran the police here. I thought about it for a while.

Then I said: 'Do you have something against serfs?'

'Nothing at all.'

'You said reduction to serfdom was a punishment.'

'It is.'

'And you agree with it?'

'It's never my decision. Police have nothing to do with sentencing.'

'But you just said you thought they had it coming,' I said. 'Vassals who transgress – they are downgraded to serf as a deterrent to others. So it's essentially about class and privilege.'

'Deep waters, Todd. Years ago, when I was young and still learning, I made a huge mistake. I'm not talking about police work now. It involved a couple of serfs – I thought I could trust them, and did so. They betrayed me. I've never forgotten that.'

'And they did this because they were serfs?'

'I couldn't think of any other reason.'

I was confounded by her prejudice, so openly declared. She was the top cop on the island. Shouldn't she factor out personal grudges?

I had finished my snack and I pushed the plate away from me. I drained my cup of coffee, which had cooled. I stood up, kicking back my chair. I was irritated by her. My situation as a member of citizen serfdom is irrelevant to me. I never think about it, not as a generality, not for any specific reason. She must have known: I am usually class-recognized wherever I go. Most people are. But now it seemed to me as if she was winding me up. Why should she do that? A long journey with this woman cop lay ahead. Within the first couple of hours of starting out everything felt as if it had changed. I was stuck with her.

We were by a window: outside, the snow was still falling, cold and hard, fine like drifting dust, but billowing in the wind, intense and accumulating. A small group of people crossing the yard from where they had parked their car had already picked up swathes of snow across their clothes and hoods.

Frejah stood up too.

I said to her bluntly: 'You know I'm a serf, don't you? A citizen serf. I thought you realized that.'

She reacted. 'I didn't know that, Todd. I'm sorry. Is that true?'

'Of course it is. Why should I make it up?'

'I'm embarrassed – I assumed you were a professional, a vassal.'

'That's just your assumption,' I said. 'Don't feel sorry for me. I'm a writer. All writers are serfs.'

7

The Enigma of Change

We returned to the car, Frejah leading the way. It was chill-
ingly cold in the basement because of the open entrance, but it
was sheltered from the worst of the icy wind. Looking up along
the ramp into the daylight I could see drifts and hummocks of
snow.

Frejah swung herself into the driving seat and started the
engine while I was still settling myself. The doors thumped
down. She turned on the heater.

We made it back to the road through standing snow so deep
I would have thought it would make driving impossible – the
powerful engine, temporarily held back by an inertial transmis-
sion system, sounded as if it was fretting at its containment. We
eased through. The wheels rarely spun. The road was narrowed
by the piles of snow on each side, but the surface was relatively
clear and soon after leaving the retail park we came to a long
downward stretch of the road, in the lee of the wind.

The headset reappeared. She took or made a long series of
calls and at first I listened in to them. I could hardly not. She
spoke cryptically, though – was that the way of police communications, or was it because she had a 6/17 with her? She
appeared to be working through a list of subordinates, checking up on them. I soon lost interest, watched the road ahead as

she drove swiftly through the bleak hills and undulating plains of central Dearth.

Against my own usual feelings, I had been provoked by her comment about serfdom. Of course I had an interest in the subject, but it was not a dominant one in my life. It had been, but only for a while.

My personal background, which she could not know unless she had somehow used one of her dashboard gadgets to investigate me, was that my parents came from solid vassal families. They were holders of land and obligations in fief, providers of corvée and tributes to the seignior, and were (in theory) military champions of his or her noble cause. In reality, they led unexceptional middle-class lives, enjoyed their house and small patch of land, brought up their children, worked hard, surrendered their tithes twice a year.

I turned my back on all that. It was not a deliberate rejection, but a sorting of my own priorities. As a child, a teenager, you care little for social systems. All I ever wanted to be was a writer. While I was in my late teens I wrote in my spare time: small articles and reviews for magazines, a few short stories. As my ambitions and skills steadily grew I decided to take a leap into the unknown, give up my steady but boring job in an office and become a full-time freelance writer.

Because of strict rules from the seigniory I knew that as well as taking on the uncertainties of being able to make a living I would be forced to abandon my status as the son of a vassal family. I would become a citizen, a non-manorial serf, a small step above a peasant, a small step below the administrative villeins with their zones of power and bureaucratic influence over petty matters.

In the eyes of society I would be permanently unemployed, a drain on public funds. The shift down to serfdom was theoretical but also practical. I had no land, no fief to a lord or landowner.

Writers never fit into a social system. It's the same for writers all over the Archipelago. I see it as practical and artistic freedom. Because we are independent we are not and cannot be treated as peasants, but as citizen serfs. Not much practical difference, but that suits me fine. The social structure means little to me – the lure of books and writing is a flame in me that I cannot extinguish. That is how it was when I started. It is still like that now.

Jo is also self-employed, an artist, a citizen serf. Technically and officially, according to the paperwork that turns up sometimes, we are both in fief to the Lords Seignioral of the Antient and Allodial Demesne of Sallaye, but as serfs we hand over our insignificant tithes every year to the villeins in the local administration office and remain effectively invisible to the system. In some of the past years, when earnings had been thin, my own tithes have been calculated as being no more than a couple of free copies of one of my books, to be donated to the local lending library. In those years I handed over more, because I know the librarian and she operates the library well. I have worked alongside the library for years. For instance, I have run writing workshops at the library once or twice, and would do so again if asked.

Being a citizen serf changed my social status, but it neither raised nor lowered me in any practical way: no one tells me when to work, how to work, what I should write in my books, where I might travel.

Some of my literary colleagues, the ones who make the most money, describe themselves as the new intelligentsia, but for me that is self-serving and vain. They write a best-seller, make television appearances, judge literary competitions, and as a result feel themselves elevated to quasi-vassalage, taking on airs and assumptions. But their fame, their money, their reputations, change nothing. They remain serfs for life, and so do I.

I continued to dwell on this as we drove north, the weather outside gradually becoming less horrible. The landscape remained bleak and wind-carved. I said nothing about what I was thinking to Frejah Harsent. I did not want to seem defensive about serfdom, because I was not. I did not want to seem obsessed with the subject, because again I was not and in fact I took it so much for granted that my social condition rarely impinged on my awareness. On the other hand, she clearly had some kind of attitude that she had never dealt with. That was of interest for another reason. I wondered briefly what those two serfs, long ago, had done to her to warrant her antagonistic feelings?

At least an hour passed in silence, all but for the growling of the engine and Frejah's intermittent remarks. Then, unexpectedly, she twisted the headphones away from her and pushed them back beneath the dash.

She said: 'Someone on the staff of the hotel mentioned you had problems overnight, with horizontal mutability.'

'The hotel was mad and unforgiving!' I said at once, because this was something else that had been passing through my mind as we drove along. I gave vent to my feelings. 'They charged me a pile of money, and I didn't understand why. When I asked for an explanation the receptionist told me I should have read a booklet in the room. The only warnings I saw were opaque, and the cost of the penalties was undefined.'

I had been wondering privately about trying to find out who owned or managed the hotel, and sending some kind of protest to them. However, the unexpected and profitable refund of the train fare had taken the urgent edge off that need.

'It's not the hotel's fault,' Frejah said. 'Dealing with mutability is a problem for everyone, but it's worst of all in the south. Every home and office has to take similar precautions. It's more acute in a big hotel like the Plaza. Because they take in visitors from islands all over the world, people like you, their infrastructure is much more vulnerable. They have to account for everything that happens.'

'Well, their warnings are not clear. I accidentally used the wrong key—'

'It happens in hotels all the time. Late at night, dimly lit corridors, people leaving the bar, in a hurry to get back into their rooms for whatever reason. Wrong key goes in. Easily done—'

'It sounds familiar,' I said, remembering my erratic meandering back to my room. 'Maybe they shouldn't give everyone two keys.'

'Well, they have to. But if several people make the same mistake at the same time the whole building can be immobilized. That's difficult to fix, and expensive.'

'I had no idea what the risks were, or even what was happening. Why do they hand out those keys if they can cause so much trouble?'

'It's a safety law. Used properly the key can't do any damage. You were assumed to know what to do, or at least that you would have read the information in the room.'

'I was hardly in the room. I didn't have time to take it all in.'

'Then I suppose you could say that's the reason for the surcharge. You'll be certain not to do it again.'

'It sounds like the Dearth penal code,' I said. 'Deterrence for others.'

'You might be right. We hand out a lot of fines.'

'I still don't know what mutability is.'

'I'm not the person to tell you.'

'You're the only one I can ask,' I said.

*

Frejah said: 'All right – if you ask the mutability specialists they will tell you it is a natural phenomenon, not a science. They say mutability is best understood as existing somewhere between quantum physics and psychology. That means two kinds of perception, outer and inner, both of which are difficult to grasp. What ordinary people say is that the effects of mutability are real, and also unreal. Something happens, but later you only think it happened. That doesn't help much either, but at least I can follow it.'

'It still doesn't make sense.'

'That's what I'm trying to say. Mutability makes physical changes. Most of them are minor changes, not even noticed, but others can be drastic. You can see the changes, be affected by them, but afterwards you can't be sure they happened. What the hotel worries about is the safety of their guests, because they lose their licence if they fail. A mutability event could change the physical shape of the whole building. The room doors might warp and not be openable, or there could be an electrical fault and a fire, or a flood. The building would become unsafe. That's why they have extensive precautions. In time, the mutability would stop, things return to normal, and the people involved would start questioning if the event had really happened.

'About a month ago, there was a serious mutability event in Dearth City. The people who monitor the phenomenon warned that one of the mountains on the outskirts of the city was about to undergo a change of dimensions. Because of the snow coverage, this meant there would be an increased risk of avalanches. It's happened before. People living in the affected zone were evacuated from their homes, roads were closed and the rescue services were put on alert. Twenty of my officers were involved in that.'

'A change of dimensions?' I said, incredulously. 'You mean the mountain physically changed size?'

'It changed shape as well. Within a few hours a major avalanche and landslide came down. Three people were reportedly killed. Two of my officers narrowly avoided being overwhelmed. The event was filmed, shown on television. You can find the footage on the internet. My officers were working with the mountain rescue people, and they had cameras monitoring the gully where it began. There's no doubt it happened.'

I said: 'How can a mountain change shape? That's unbelievable! I mean – the avalanche would have been a real event, but not for that reason.'

'The gully was in an area of the mountain which had developed a measurable bulge. It was surveyed from the air – the survey was still going on when the slip started.'

I said nothing more, it being a subject about which I had zero knowledge, and, in fact, had even less belief. I doubted what I heard. Frejah sounded serious, though.

Eventually, I said: 'So is the bulge still there? Couldn't it be geologically investigated, explained?'

'The bulge is not there. It was caused by mutability. It was a real event, witnessed and recorded, but afterwards most people seemed to doubt it had happened at all.'

'What about the victims?' I said. 'The people you said were reportedly killed. Was that imaginary?'

'They died. Their identities are known. Two of them were from Dearth City; the third was a visitor from one of the other islands. The avalanche was a real event, but the cause of it is in doubt. Now, a month later, most people accept that it was imagined.'

'Mutability can change physical dimensions? I can't believe that.'

73

'Nor can most people here. We have to live with the phenomenon.'

'All this is new to me – I had never heard of mutability until yesterday.'

'You told me you're from the Salay Group?'

'Salay Raba, yes.'

'Salay's an interesting case. According to the mutability experts Dearth is not the only island that experiences the phenomenon. There are thought to be between two and three hundred islands in other parts of the Archipelago where there are gravitational anomalies. The vast majority of islands are unaffected.' Frejah was driving noticeably more slowly as we talked about this. The engine was making a distinctive back-burning hunting sound as we gradually decelerated. 'But there are a few islands, several hundred, which are described as poten-tially vulnerable. They are classified as Mutably Incipient. Some islands in Salay are included in that. Salay Raba is one of them. In fact at a high level.'

'I've lived on Raba all my life. I've never experienced any-thing like it, never heard about it and I don't know anyone who has.'

'I was born on Salay Hames, the fifth. That's even higher on the scale of incipience, but until I moved to Dearth as a kid I'd never known it either.'

Again I was silent, trying to work out what to believe, and how much of it. I glanced at my wristwatch, moving normally – it was an hour or so since I had last looked, and it was show-ing what felt subjectively still the correct time. The tiny digital clock on Frejah's dash confirmed it. Mutability affected even the flow of time on this island? Somehow that was easier to be-lieve than that a mountain could temporarily produce millions of tonnes of bulge – but isn't time also immutable, an absolute?

If that was so, then it must be the clocks, the chronometers, the cellphones, which drifted away from true?

Then I remembered the train – still only the day before. It had braked to a sudden halt, because, the crew said, the track was at the incorrect gauge. An impossibility! The track was a permanence. What must have happened was that the engineer, the driver, or one of the control instruments in the cab, had perceived a change in gauge.

I mentioned this to Frejah, but she said immediately: 'That's a regular occurrence on the trains. The tracks are often out of true. It's extremely dangerous. Especially on that line, because it passes one of the main gravitational nodes. There have been several accidents.'

'Caused by a perception?'

'The problem of mutability. It is both real and unreal, it happens or it is only thought to happen.'

'I still don't get it,' I said.

'No one else does.'

She started fingering one of the touch-enabled instruments beneath the dash, glanced at a graphic that instantly appeared on the HUD.

'We're approaching another off-road area,' she said. 'Are you ready for lunch yet?'

'Getting that way, yes.'

Ten kilometres further along we drove off the highway and into a cluster of low-level modern buildings. As before, Frejah ignored the directions about where and where not to park, and headed for a subterranean garage. It was marked *Strictly Private – Authorized Vehicles Only*. There was only one space vacant – Frejah took it.

A long lunch followed.

8

Sad Story of the Death of Kings

By the time the food was brought to our table we were both hungry, and while we ate we said little to each other. I still had at the back of my mind Frejah's remark about serfs, but I was hoping the subject would not come up again.

The feudal system, still almost universal in the Archipelago, was the subject of an extended debate going on in political and seigniory circles: it was one of those subjects that kept cropping up on news broadcasts, whenever someone else had an argument to make about it. The debate was beyond me – I understood it, but it was a subject that you could not help feeling was seized on by opportunistic politicians and administrators, trying to make their name. The needs or wants of ordinary people were disregarded, except in some general way. The arguments were based on theory, not the reality of everyday life in the islands as known to millions of islanders.

The debate was about social change, the governance of the islands.

A handful of islands, after losing their seignioral succession, had experimented with democracy. The results differed. Two mainland countries in the north provided examples, good or bad, depending on your point of view. The Republic of Glaund was in theory a state founded on revolutionary and enlightened social principles, but it was now inflexibly ruled by a military junta, the result of a coup in the previous century. Glaund's bitter rival, Faiandland, a liberal democracy and the world's most militarily powerful country, was known and feared as a colonizing power with territorial ambitions. Neither of these alternative systems of government was attractive to islanders, the military régime for reasons that were obvious, democracy slightly less so.

The instinct amongst most islanders was the wish not to change a system that had survived for many centuries. For all the many annoying faults, freely admitted and often complained about, the feudal systems on each island had led to the present state of independence, stability, peace and a general sense of well being. But of course there were populist and fringe groups campaigning for change, any kind of change. And ambitious young politicians who wanted to make a mark. There always were people like that, and always will be.

While we were waiting for the coffee to be brought, Frejah took a call on her phone and left the table to speak. When she returned she of course said nothing about it, but the call had somehow lightened her mood. She smiled as she sat down again.

She started asking questions again about my writing. I had already tried to divert her on this. Today she ran through familiar questions: where do ideas come from, how can an idea be turned into a plot and from that into a book, did I work with a pen or a typewriter or a computer, did I use a literary agent, who chose the cover illustrations? And so on. She said she had read two of my novels, and questioned me about them, although not closely.

One of them was my only attempt at a police procedural. Since discovering what she did for a living I had been secretly hoping she did not know about it. I was defensive about it. A police procedural is an unusual kind of novel because it is in effect about a job, and the people who work in it. The novelist is a novelist, not a police officer, but the result is a novel about police days at work.

Do we write procedurals about the daily work of a butcher? A landscape gardener? An accountant? Some occupations might lend themselves to narratives – a spy, an adventurer, a doctor, a film star – there are books about them all. But the work of police as they go about investigating a crime is of endless fascination to both readers and writers. Dozens of police procedurals are written and published every year. I have often wondered how many of them are read by police officers, and what they think of them. But I wasn't too keen to find out what this police officer thought of my novel. Not that one.

The Tanglewood Mystery was not my first book, nor my second, but it came early in my career. I now thought the title was dull and unoriginal: 'Tanglewood' was the name of a business complex where the murder took place. A detective serjeant was given the job of sifting through the evidence to establish how the killing had happened. Meanwhile, his career was in jeopardy because he had a secret and uncontrollable addiction to gambling. His move towards an answer to the murder mystery ran in parallel to his coming to grips with his addiction. The idea, the secret method of the killing, was good, as was the way the detective arrived at the solution by calculating odds and risks, but the telling was pedestrian. I've written better since.

'I liked *The Tanglewood Mystery*,' she said. 'Clever and original.'

'You didn't find it a little slow? Did it seem unconvincing to you?'

'Not at all. I wanted to find out what happened. The only thing is – have you ever worked with a forensic police team?'

'Not directly. Actually, no, not at all.'

'Have you ever thought of working with a police adviser?'

'Was the book that bad?'

'No,' she said. 'There were no serious mistakes. But there were other possibilities which would have made the story more interesting. An adviser would have been able to suggest them.'

I said: 'Whatever's wrong with the novel is my responsibility, and if I left out anything like that it was my fault. But I did have a consultant.'

I then told her about Spoder, who had advised me ever since I wrote my second novel.

'I don't think I know him,' Frejah said. 'Which force was he with?'

'Salay Raba Police. He retired a few years ago.'

'I never knew the Raba force well. What's his full name, and what rank was he?'

'He has never told me his given name – I don't know why. I know him only as Spoder. He was a Detective Inspector before he retired. I don't collaborate with him. I pay him a retainer, and on my behalf he browses for old files, cold cases, newspaper cuttings and so on. He leaves the stuff with me, and then I write the novel. If I miss anything, that's my mistake not his.'

'And you say he's still working with you?'

'I wouldn't be without him.'

'Does he ever suggest story ideas for a book?'

'Not so far.'

'Have you asked him?'

'No! I would never do that.'

'You surprise me,' said Frejah. 'Any experienced detective will have come across many great stories in the course of their work. We don't solve everything. Even when we work out who the perpetrator was, there's always something that doesn't quite make sense, some remark that one of the people involved happened to make that didn't fit with the facts. I've been involved in several cases like that. I could tell you some of them—'

The coffee was at last delivered to the table. I took hold of mine at once, and applied myself busily to the task of adding cream and a little sugar. I stirred the cup with intense interest. I did not look up to meet her gaze.

'Wouldn't you be interested in hearing some of them?' Frejah said. 'I'm sure you could write a few books based on them.'

And there it was – the suggestion novelists never have an answer for, and try to avoid at all costs.

Everything we write as fiction is based ultimately on story. In some novels a storyline, the narrative, is virtually all there is, in others the story is deeply or subtly woven into the language, the mood, the characters, the setting, and so on. But fiction always directly or indirectly relates the movement of events and decisions that amounts to a story.

Story is what many readers remember about a novel long after they have read the last page. Story is seen as unique to each novel.

We all involve ourselves with story. Most people who read books love to think about 'what happened next?', or if they read mysteries 'whodunit?'. They follow the story, enjoy its twists and turns, wait for the final revelation.

Sometimes readers feel let down by the way the author has tied things up. People want stories to work properly, as they see it, to give a kind of satisfaction. It makes them dream about what they think would have been a more gratifying ending: the hero didn't die after all, the business didn't collapse, the couple married and lived happily thereafter, and so on. Or, getting further into the spirit, they think up a whole new plot, one they have never read anywhere or heard about from anyone (they believe). Or they are told an anecdote by a friend, or there is a court case they read about some years ago in a newspaper, or there was some unusual event that occurred in the locality whose details have never spread into the wider world – they all seem obvious material for a novel.

This to me is a natural part of the enjoyment of reading. Reading is a stimulating experience, suggesting ideas and situations and stories. We read partly for that pleasure. The instinct to remember stories and re-tell them is innate. We learn to love stories as children. When we've heard a good story there's a real pleasure in narrating the sequence of events again, especially if it contains a surprise, or ends in an unexpected way, or is funny or shocking. From this instinct, many a successful novelist has emerged.

The creation of a story, though, is not simply a matter of re-telling a sequence of events, however embellished those events might become in the process. Writers do come across unusual or interesting stories in newspapers and magazines, they watch television and take ideas from odd moments in news bulletins, they do listen to what they happen to hear strangers talking about. Some even carry notebooks and jot down snatches of random overheard conversations. But all this is the minor raw material for stories.

Other more complex and undefinable sources exist. Personal experience of things that went wrong, or for that matter went well, or living their own lives as they grew up, taking risks, suffering blows, achieving and surviving. Or there is a need felt by the writer to make a certain point or argument, and then will construct a story to illustrate it. Or one of the great classical works, drama, a major novel from the previous century, will suggest a theme that is still relevant in the present day and can be reworked imaginatively.

There is no rule about this. Where writers find inspiration and develop their ideas is not a practical or literal exercise – nobody can truly describe it because to a large extent it is an internal, organic process.

In all innocence, and with the best intentions in the world, readers will often say to a writer something similar to what Frejah was saying to me: 'I know a great story. If I tell you what it is, you can write it into your next book.'

Because I did not wish to seem rude or arrogant, but partly because I could not forget she was a cop and I was nervous of the underlying differences that were emerging between us, and also because I was going to be in her company for at least another day, I could not, would not, say any of the above to her.

But I really did not wish to listen to several hours of her case histories.

I said, weakly: 'Maybe we should be getting back on the road?'

'There's no hurry,' Frejah said. 'We've made good time. I think you'll be interested in some of my experiences. One of the first cases I ever dealt with—'

'Frejah,' I said. 'You should never tell story ideas to a writer, a novelist. We steal everything we write about.'

'That's the idea! When you hear the story, it will give you scores of ideas for material. You have your cellphone with you? Why not make a recording, and then when you feel like it you can transcribe it. If I've left anything out, you can check with me later. The case I'm talking about was years ago, it was a sensation at the time, but almost everyone who knew about it has died since and no one else remembers it.'

'I think you shouldn't tell me confidential details of a police case.'

'This is a cold case, probably no different from what your research colleague turns up for you. The murder was fifteen years ago, and the file has been closed for years.'

'Yes, but—'

'You've never heard anything like this, I promise you. It was a case of murder, and the killer confessed to it, but in the end the case had to be closed because nothing could be proved. It remains a mystery.'

We argued to and fro for a little longer, but in the end there was nothing I could say that would stop her. I yielded to what felt like the inevitable. I took my cellphone from my pocket, switched on the voice recorder and laid it on the table between us.

I listened to what she told me, although at first I was feeling resentful that I was having to. It was noisy in the busy restaurant: there were voices calling, doors opening and closing, piped music, a deafening coffee-making machine with constant loud steam release, interruptions from the waiting staff, and everything else that was going on around us. I had transcribed interviews in the past, and knew how difficult ambient noise could make them.

Frejah was not a natural storyteller. She often repeated herself, or added later something she saw as important but had missed out. She sometimes turned away expressively, causing her voice to drop. She mentioned names I was unfamiliar with: I assumed they were Dearth names. I took a few notes on these, intending to check them with her later.

I watched her, at first only half listening to the story she was trying to construct. Her body language was not confident. She seemed half-guilty about the story, also proud of it, almost playing a game. I had the unmistakable feeling there was some agenda larger than just the telling of her ideas for a plot. Was it a confession? A way of sharing the events so that in some way I would become complicit in them?

My interest increased.

Then she finished. The story came to something of an anti-climax, I thought. It was a police case, not a narrative.

Police cases end in one of three ways. They do not end, because the matter cannot be solved or enough evidence cannot be found, and the case becomes 'cold', remaining technically open. Or they end with a successful prosecution and a culprit who is sentenced. Or they end because after investigation of the evidence it becomes apparent there is no point in taking it any further – another kind of cold case. Frejah's story was of the third type.

I switched off my voice recorder. Frejah ordered more coffee.

9

Dreadful is the Checking

Frejah drove on for another two hours until we came to a small hotel she said she had stayed in several times before. There were still about five hundred kilometres between us and Tristcontenta Hub. From my point of view the hotel was agreeably old school. There were no warnings about mutability, and the one key to the room was conventional.

That evening, when I was alone in my room, I made internet contact with Jo. The broadband was strong in the hotel room, and we spoke for a long time.

I told her about my meeting with Frejah Harsent in the bar.

'She latched on to me,' I said. 'At first I was glad of the company. I was feeling tired after the speech. She said she had read one of my books. Later on, she told me that the trains here are running a reduced service because of strikes, and offered to drive me to the airport instead. It turned out she is a senior cop on this island. So now I'm being driven at high speed across the island, but I'm starting to feel a bit suspicious of her. I'm not entirely sure why.'

'You sent me some weird emails last night,' Jo said. 'I couldn't make sense of them.'

'The internet was unusable. It kept dropping characters as I was typing. I was trying to tell you some of this, but I was exhausted and gave up – I couldn't cope with it.'

'So what's wrong with this woman cop? Do I need to ask? A cop's a cop.'

'I know – I had no idea at the time she was a cop. She acted like a normal member of the audience, someone who was into crime novels. That was fine. She's obviously highly intelligent and I liked her. I only found out today what she does. I saw her ID card: she's at commissioner level. It turns out she has a big grudge against serfs. She implied she wants them locked up. She said she was betrayed by a couple of them some years ago. When I told her that you and I are serfs she hardly spoke to me for another hour. And she packs a gun.'

'Cops carry guns,' Jo said. 'Or some of them do.'

'This gun is a *big* one! A military grade semi-automatic, with a huge magazine. It's hidden in the trunk of her car. I think I wasn't supposed to see it. The weird thing about this is that Dearth is supposed to be a place where there's no crime. That's what the conference was about. So what does she need a gun like that for? And she calls me a 6/17.'

'A what?'

'A 6/17. I think it's police radio code for a lowly serf. Or a hitch-hiker. Or someone they're suspicious of.'

'She's dropping you off tomorrow at the airport?' Jo said.

'Yes.'

'Well, you won't see her again after that.'

'Jo, there's something you could do for me before I get home. She told me a story this afternoon about a crime she covered up. She seemed proud of it and insisted I had to hear it. She said she thought it would make a good plot for a novel. You know how badly that idea goes down with me.'

'But you listened anyway,' Jo said. 'Of course you did – you always do.'

'It was difficult. I didn't have much choice.'

'Would it work as a novel?'

'Probably not even as a short story. But I found it interesting. She made me take a recording of it, which I'm glad now I did. It was a murder that happened on Salay Hames, the fifth. About fifteen years ago. Someone had his brains bashed out. I had never heard about it before. I can't find anything on the internet about it. I looked just now. I'll get Spoder to look into it for me, of course, but before he does I'd like to know if this murder has made it into the literature. Is there any chance you could have a quick look through the indexes of my reference books and see if there's anything about the case? Only if you have the time, of course.'

Jo would know the books I meant. I had a small shelf next to my desk: encyclopaedias of crime, transcripts of trials, notable police failures and successes, miscarriages of justice, and so on. All with accessible and useful indexes. They were published for a general audience, but for me they were a first reference source.

'I don't mind looking,' Jo said. 'But wouldn't Spoder have access to the police files?'

'I don't want to activate the Spoder machine until I'm ready! You know how he rushes around, piles stuff on me, always more than I can manage. Then he comes through with even more. Before Spoder gets interested, I'd like to know what is already known, at least to criminologists. There's probably nothing about it I can use, but you never know.'

I gave Jo a list of the relevant names I had noted. Frejah's of course, but also the name of the cop she had been partnered with in Dearth City, the murdered man, and the alleged murderer.

I spelt them to Jo phonetically. The victim, for instance, was called Woller (or perhaps Waller) Allmann (or Alman or Almann).

'I'll have a look for you,' Jo said. 'That's possibly enough to be going on with.'

'Tomorrow I'll check the spelling of the names with this woman. Perhaps you should wait until I have those.'

'I'll make a start,' Jo said.

I would not normally ask Jo to begin my research for me, but there was something about Frejah's story, or in particular her defensive body language when telling it to me, that gave her account a certain extra interest. I was certain it was to some extent confessional, suggesting she was involved not so much in the investigation, as she claimed, but in the crime itself. For now, that hunch was enough to give me the feeling I should listen properly to her account as soon as I was home.

'So when do you think you'll be back here?' Jo said.

'I'm hoping to catch the evening flight tomorrow, but if not I'll be on the first one the next morning.'

Jo then started telling me about a new job that might be coming her way: a design commission from a major theatre on the island of Muriseay. She would have to fly across there sometime soon and maybe stay a few days, depending on how it worked out. I knew this was the sort of chance she had been hoping for, and I was happy to hear her talking excitedly about the details of the producer who had contacted her, the theatre, the time deadlines, the probable fee. It could be a big break for her.

10

Presumed Guilty

Frejah Harsent and I met for breakfast in the hotel bar, then continued our long drive northwards across Dearth. We were soon passing through another grim industrial area. We saw open-cast mine workings, steelworks and gigantic windowless factories sealed from the world. Tall chimneys gushed white and black smoke. Smaller ones expelled worryingly coloured fumes. Vast estates of dull housing were spread across the undulating landscape. There was a shroud of smoke or fog in the air, low and gloomy. The temperature remained below freezing. Pedestrians were few, but the highway now was cluttered with many vehicles. Frejah drove with her usual sense of dash, but we were always being held up by the slow-moving trucks travelling in both directions. I was used to her adventurous driving by then, and lay relaxed in the contoured, semi-reclined passenger seat. I was glad not to be on the train.

Frejah took more of her cryptic calls on the radio headset, leaving me the space to think about my plans for the days ahead. After three nights away I was beginning to miss home comforts, the routines of my ordinary life. And I had work to do: the proofs the publisher had sent me needed to be checked soon, not a difficult or unpleasant chore but still a chore. I had had to set aside writing the first draft of my next novel to make this trip.

89

I wanted to get back to that as soon as possible because a first draft, if left unattended, starts looking unsatisfactory. And I wanted to have some time with Jo, who would be going away in the next few days.

We passed out of the industrial zone – the road climbed for a while, bringing us to a high, wide plateau. Ice was thick on the road surface once more. The few trees that clung to the soil were wind-carved, their branches reaching out like desperate arms, south to north. After about forty kilometres the road descended again. The distances of Dearth felt interminable, the terrain a constant horror.

I kept looking at the recessed digital clock display on the dash, wondering what time we would arrive at the airport. The Historical Society had sent me a ticket for the Salay flight taking off in the early evening. That was the plane scheduled for passengers arriving at the airport on the train. I might or might not still be in time for that, but the ticket was an open one so if necessary I could catch an earlier or later flight. I had no idea how many more flights there were.

I thought of looking at the online airline schedule on my cell, but I was nervous of using it in this place. The coverage would undoubtedly be on the wrong protocol. I did not want to reset to Dearth defaults.

We stopped for lunch. I was impatient to carry on to Tristcontenta Hub, but Frejah said she wanted a proper meal.

While we were at the table we worked out how much further there was to drive, and what time we would arrive at the Hub. Frejah was convincingly optimistic. Even if we stayed in the restaurant for another hour, she said, it would still be possible for me to catch the plane on which I was booked. She checked on the internet and said there was another plane two hours later. The one after that took off early the next morning.

She dawdled over her cup of coffee and began asking me more questions about the books I write. I was thinking ahead about getting to the airport, flying home, and anyway I felt I had said enough about that. She asked me if I wrote any other kind of fiction, or if it was just crime fiction.

I said nothing to that, trying not to glower, even mentally. *Just* crime fiction?

I changed the subject, and told her I had been interested in the story she told me. I asked her if I could check the spelling of some of the names she had mentioned. Even then I was anticipating having to transcribe what she had said. I was guessing that the name of the older cop she had been partnered with was called Jexid or Jeskit, but she put me right on that: Jeksid. I mentally noted it, as I did the name Waller (my guess had been 'Woller') Alman. I like to get details right.

I made a mental note to pass on the correct spellings to Jo, if she was looking through crime reference books for these names.

We returned to the car. It was still freezing cold but now it was raining, a hard, clamant downpour, a roaring noise against the frozen ground, with flecks of ice or snow bouncing and shattering on the car's shiny surfaces. Frejah rejoined the traffic, driving swiftly once more. The road was slippery in many places.

I could not help it: I was in fact brooding with irritation about Frejah's 'just crime fiction' remark. It was like a casually delivered stab.

I know I am over-sensitive about this. Like all categories of fiction, crime is misunderstood and underrated by those who never read it. Within the reasonable limits of the genre it is possible to take on numerous subjects as well as the crime in question, and narrate them in different ways. There are many tones and moods and approaches possible within the genre, from the slight, repetitive and mechanically plotted, to the well imagined and technically accurate modern mystery, to the deeply researched, well thought out and psychologically plausible. There is almost no such thing as a generic or typical crime novel. Thrillers occupy a literary house with many different rooms.

Some of the crime writers I was acquainted with made a career out of the repeated activities of a single sleuth, who from one book to the next encountered and eventually solved one seemingly mysterious crime after another. I recognized the attraction of that kind of story, for the writer as well as the reader, but I had tried it in three of my early books until I realized I was becoming dissatisfied with it, and also bored. Since then my novels have been increasingly concerned with the psychological nature of crime, the criminal instinct and the buried motives of the criminal.

What, beyond a sudden insane impulse of rage or desperation or a misguided sense of grievance, would drive one apparently normal person to kill another? It is such an irreversible step into the dark night of the soul that few people would venture into it. That strikes me as a valid enquiry for a novel. Many of the great classic novels of the past, now accepted as general reading, were in effect crime stories. Few of us can write classics, but they provide a standard of excellence. Some writers excel at the genre, but in truth the plots of many modern thrillers are based on straightforward or banal motives, trivializing this grim psychological territory.

Although there have been honourable exceptions, most killers in books develop an acute need for money, or they want revenge for some real or imagined grievance, or they wish to receive a legacy that would otherwise go to a sibling or a disliked cousin, or for various reasons they feel they have to get an unwanted spouse or relative out of the way. They try to cheat insurance companies. They think they can elude the police, or the private detective hired to trap them. They remain, on the surface, civilized and articulate, and in some cases see the evasion of justice as a game.

Several thriller writers have an interest in psychopathy, the motives of a maladjusted serial killer, but as far as my own books were concerned I felt there were only a limited number of ways that could be used as material for a novel.

I was increasingly interested in the ordinary person, one who is invisible in the context of normal society, who ventures for some reason into that dark world of the soul, who then tries to be released from it, or who rejects it, or who dangerously embraces it.

My recent books therefore depended less on plot, murderous gimmicks or a twist ending than they did on character, circumstance, background. I wrote about the conflict created when the protagonist (or the person driven to murder – not always the same) sets up boundaries, or a context within which the crime will take place, but overlooks a crucial fact that will ruin everything.

Sometimes my books ended without the solution the main character was looking for – the crime is unsolved, the murderer gets away with it. A few of the reviewers said they disliked that. I was scolded because crime must not pay. Every puzzle must have a solution, they would sermonize in their reviews, perhaps overlooking the fact that there was a different kind of mystery leading to another sort of outcome, one which I intended to be read as more human, more plausible.

I found it difficult to describe my recent books to anyone, like Frejah, who was curious about them but was not familiar with the overall genre. I knew I could easily sound difficult, ambitious in the wrong way. I had heard that said about me several times. I never liked it! So I would normally stick to describing my half-dozen first books, the ones which were conventionally plotted and narrated straightforwardly, knowing that what I was saying was no longer true about my current stuff, but it was not important. Readers who had kept up with my later books did not need to be told.

In any case, it seemed the only book of mine Frejah knew well was my old police procedural. No more questions came from her now. I wondered if she was thinking I was pretentious, or perhaps, because she viewed me through her many years of being a police officer, believing that I had an unhealthy interest in crime, what she called transgression, and was sublimating it into what I wrote.

We were now closing in on the north of the island. I saw a sign announcing that Tristcontenta Hub was a further 75 kms. The next sign said 42 kms.

I began wondering what I should say or do when Frejah deposited me at the airport. She had done me a big favour by offering me the car ride, and I did find her company interesting. How often does one get to meet a semi-retired police chief in a souped-up roadster with a military grade semi-automatic stashed in the trunk? Maybe there would be a story in this experience one day?

I am always curious about motive and outcomes – there was something about Frejah that did not fit. For example, was our first meeting in the hotel bar entirely by chance? That is how it seemed to me, but it turned out she had known who I was, and had found out or already knew where I was staying. It made me think.

We arrived at the Hub about thirty minutes before my flight was due to take off. Frejah pulled the car, engine growling, into the passenger drop-off area, and for the last time I levered myself into an upright position and swung out of the passenger seat. The bitterly cold air chilled me at once. The walkways had been cleared of snow, but big patches of ice remained.

Frejah released the lock of the seamless lid of the trunk. It opened with a muted click, a sound of suction. She left the car and walked around to the other side. She had halted the car directly beneath a high lamp shining down on the area, so that the interior of the trunk was brightly illuminated. With swift movements she pulled out my computer holdall, my overnight bag, and the larger case which was holding my padded outer clothes.

The automatic weapon was in clear sight. The constituent parts were clipped securely into the shaped and customized recesses of a cushioned board. The inner working surfaces were bright – the rest of it was matt black. The barrel was short, the magazine at least a third of a metre long.

'That's an assault weapon,' I said. 'Is that standard police issue?'

'Command and control,' Frejah said, intoning the form of words. 'I am licensed to carry it, and my authority is renewed every seven days. I retrain every month.'

The lid came down swiftly.

'I was just asking,' I said. 'You still claim there are no crimes on Dearth?'

'Asking is your right as a citizen serf.' She held out a hand, and gave me an unforced smile. 'Well, this is goodbye. It has been most interesting to meet you, Todd.'

We shook hands, then we kissed lightly on the cheek. We muttered conventional thanks and farewell. We had made no plans to meet again, nor was there ever any expectation that we might. I said something about the fact that I hoped the case she was working on would soon be resolved, and she replied to wish me well with my writing career.

Then she added something odd: 'Closing the case might be something you can help with. I told you how it began.'

She moved quickly to the car door. We were both under the insistent freezing rain, and unprotected against the icy temperature. I gathered up my stuff and dashed towards the terminal building. Before I had passed through the automatic triple doors I heard the now familiar roar of the roadster's engine.

I missed the boarding gate closure by three minutes. I walked slowly back to the main part of the terminal, making a swift decision: rather than hang around for another two or three hours in the terminal, waiting for the next plane, which anyway would land me back in Salay in the early hours of the morning, I decided to go to an airport hotel.

Once I was in my room (whose door was opened with an electronic card, but the room was otherwise free of warnings about mutability), Jo and I exchanged messages on the internet for half an hour. She said she was still looking through the reference books, had found a couple of possible mentions. I confirmed the spelling of the names with her. Then I went to the hotel restaurant for dinner.

In the morning I caught the first flight out, landing on the island of Salay Ewwel, the first. After a short internal flight to Raba, the fourth, I was home in the early afternoon.

The house, the beach beyond, the surrounding forest, were bathed in a balmy heat. The sounds of insects and birds, children on the beach, the scent of trees.

11

Questions, Questions

I sprawled on the decking of my patio outside my study, Dearth already a bad and chilling memory. I was born to be a warm climate man.

It was great to be home again, a place I left as infrequently as possible. The house I lived in with Jo would possibly seem to many people to be too big for only the two of us. It was long and low, single-storeyed, shaped like a capital E, with wings at each end and the kitchen/diner and other rooms sticking out in the middle. The rest of the living and bed rooms were arranged along the central section, which Jo and I always thought of as the useful corridor that joined us. Our work rooms were sufficiently far apart that we did not disturb each other, but sufficiently close together that we could when the mood took us wander along to see each other.

Roughly aligned east/west, the front of the house became a natural suntrap during the long summers on Raba, and we made constant use of it. When Jo and I first moved in we loved staring out across the sea – the view was one of the main reasons we bought the house. Gradually, though, as the years went by and the house became more intensively a place of work, we neglected the garden. Thick undergrowth grew up to hide the view. We encouraged that: most of the bushes and young saplings that sprang up were natural to the forest, and we planted a couple of other trees as well. We were not alone in doing this: many of our neighbours also encouraged a natural screen. A road ran past the house, between us and the beach. It gave the harmless impression to anyone walking or driving along the road that the beach was fringed with forest greenery. Very few of the houses could be seen from the road, but most of them, like ours, had rough-hewn paths through the trees that were kept open down to the road.

Jo's studio was in the wing at the western end. It was a huge room, cluttered with art materials, canvases, sketchbooks, film and video projectors, bottles, huge coils of rope, plastic fishing nets and driftwood salvaged from the sea, dozens of pieces of work, some unfinished, some early efforts. The studio had a specially strengthened concrete floor, overhead in the re-inforced roof space was a pulley used for lifting and moving heavier pieces into place, and one of the exterior walls had been entirely replaced by sliding doors. Medium-sized trucks could squeeze alongside the house and reach the studio, bringing in or porting away the largest pieces. Recently, Jo had been spending less time in her studio, and instead was now pursuing a more lucrative career in freelance theatrical design.

My own study, occupying a large room at the opposite end of the house, was a more austere place, and tidier. Dark stained bookshelves lined two of the walls. The books that stood there, randomly acquired over the years and added to slowly all the time, constituted my primary research source. Apart from my immediate reference shelf, next to my desk, I had accumulated hundreds of books directly or indirectly concerned with true crime. Many of them were transcripts of significant criminal hearings, some were the memoirs of eminent jurists, private detectives, criminal lawyers, journalists, and so on. A few described the political or social ramifications that followed the conviction of certain criminals. But the majority of the books discussed my own area of interest: alleged cases of wrongful conviction, imprisonment or execution, and the loosely connected similar matter: the cases that remained a mystery, where the perpetrator was never identified or arrested, or which had baffled the police and all other investigators.

Only a few of the books on my shelves were fiction – thrillers or crime novels. Some of them were gifts from friends or colleagues. I kept most of those. Others were sent to me by publishers or the writers themselves, in the hope of a favourable endorsement that might be quoted on publication. I kept only a few. I was always nervous of inadvertently 'borrowing' an ingenious idea from other writers' novels, so I was not an enthusiastic reader of my colleagues' works. Every year I would hand out a few of these books to the local library, and pass on the rest to a secondhand shop in Raba City, from which they were quickly sold.

Copies of my own books were sent by my publishers to other writers, for similar reasons. No doubt these too ended up a year or two later in the same sort of bookstore.

My desk, with both my laptop and desktop computers, stood in the centre of the room, with a secondary table placed behind for the printer, a box of paper, and so on. When I worked at my desk I faced north towards the sea, but because of the trees in the garden and the steep slope down to the shore there was no distracting view. During the warmest months I worked with the large picture window open, and a sun shade pulled over the decking outside my study. If I sat outside I could hear the breaking of the waves on the shingly beach, and the happy cries of children. When the weather was hottest I would go out to the deck to read or doze, cooled by an electric fan, but the sunshine was too annoyingly bright for me to work for long at a computer monitor.

Once I was home from my four-day trip to Dearth I relished the return to my normal daily life, seeing Jo again, catching up with news and gossip, sitting at my desk and browsing online at the sites I visited most frequently. I was always surrounded by books, not just the ones on the shelves, but the loose and unstable stacks that stood on the floor near where I worked. Every few weeks I would tidy these up, transferring them to shelves or to another room, but the stacks would soon rebuild themselves with new titles.

On the evening of my first day back Jo and I drove into Raba City and indulged ourselves in an expensive dinner and a movie. She told me then that she had come across a few possible mentions of the case Frejah had described – she had put the books on the floor next to my desk, with paper markers tucked in. A new, lower stack. I had noticed these, and guessed what they were, but not yet looked at them.

The next morning I slept late – Jo had already been up for two hours before I was awake. She was due to visit a stage designer in Chor, a town on the other side of the island, and had her own preparations to make for a trip. I pottered around slowly, feeling tired, listless in my body. People who invite you away to a function where you are to appear or speak, or to take part in a workshop, or simply to be a guest at some celebration or other, do not realize the collateral loss of time and energy that is involved.

My trip to Dearth, for instance. I more or less stopped work on my current novel about three days before I departed. I was distracted then by the thought of the long journeys ahead, the unknown venue and what would be expected of me. My speech too was a problem. I kept looking at it, fiddling about with details, worrying about what it would sound like. And the mail-order company from which I had ordered my arctic outer wear alarmingly delayed the delivery. It all worked out in the end, but in essence those three extra days were lost to me.

Then came the four days on Dearth – closer to five, in fact. They made me feel like an alien, a visitor, someone who did not understand and therefore had to have everything explained or translated. I met a senior cop. I was calmly reminded of my serfdom.

Now I was home, but I was dragging around in memory a large shadow. All that stuff I had heard about crime-not-actually-crime, the weirdness of the mutability effect, the serf-loathing cop who had befriended me. It had left me feeling vague and undirected, but I was relieved it was not happening any more and that I was at home. Two more days had slipped uselessly into nowhere.

Jo departed for Chor the next morning. I was up in time to see her leave. Soon after her car drove away I made myself a large mug of coffee and went to my study, feeling purposeful once more. I caught up with several unanswered emails, visited my usual social media sites, checked my bank. All the normal routines of a morning.

At last I opened the document where I had been working on the first draft of my next novel. I had reached page eighty-six, well into it but a long way from the end. I read through recent pages, remembering writing them, of course, but I had trouble recollecting what I had had in mind. Back then, a week ago, pre-Dearth.

I closed the document. I needed time to reflect.

I looked at the small stack of my reference books that Jo had put out for me. I moved them to my desk. Each one had slips of paper marking certain pages. I opened the top one, and immediately found a handwritten note from Jo:

Hey Todd – in case we don't get a chance to talk about this before I leave:

Here is what I have found for you on the murder case you told me about. It's not much and everything might be referring to another case entirely. I drew a complete blank on the name Waller Alman, or any variant of that. I tried the other spellings you guessed at. You said it had happened about fifteen years ago. As you know, there haven't been many murders in the Salay Group, and there was only one in that time frame, but it was in fact on Salay Hames, as you said. I felt it was probably the right one? The victim was called Lew Antterland. Nothing like 'Waller Alman'. The police thought Antterland had been murdered, but later it was judged by the inquest court to be a suicide case, so the file was closed.

But listen to this! Lew Antterland had a brother who WAS murdered five years later. This happened on Salay Sekonda. His name was Dever Antterland, but he was also known as 'Willer'. Coincidence, or what? There isn't much about him in the books, but I've marked every mention I could find from the index.

Why not see what Spoder can turn up? He happened to phone while you were away – he said it was not important. Maybe you should call him?

See you back here soon, I hope.

Jo XXX

I looked at the pages Jo had marked for me, but as she had warned me there was not much there. Lew Antterland committed suicide, his brother Dever was murdered a few years later.

The file on Lew's death was closed. Dever's murderer had never been identified or caught, and after a long delay the inquest court on Sekonda had declared a verdict of unlawful killing. That file remained in theory open, but there had been no further investigation for ten years.

It was a strange surname: Antterland. I had never come across it before on Salay. Two people dying on Salayean islands, two Antterlands? My crime writer's antenna briefly twitched with interest.

I thought I should call Spoder back, but then I remembered that I should be correcting the proofs for my publisher. I had not started on them before I went to Dearth. There were nearly three hundred pages to read and correct.

I looked briefly at them, put them aside. I decided to call Spoder instead.

As I had mentioned to Frejah Harsent, I did not know his first name. He always said it was unimportant. He had been Detective Inspector Spoder of the Salay Raba police, but he had left the force before I had any contact with him.

I met him when he answered an advertisement I placed, hoping to find a technical consultant for the crime novels I was writing. He was eager for the job, and had decided before we even met that he was the ideal applicant. There were no others, so Spoder became my police consultant and had been for several years. He worked hard, and sometimes the exactness of his memory surprised me.

He was not forthcoming about his past experience in the police, although he had certainly risen to the rank of DI, and was still well connected with the Raba force. He had proved useful to me, and I had learned to trust most of the information he passed to me.

He retired from the police early – why? That was a question you never asked a senior police officer who took early retirement. In fact, I did ask Spoder that question at our first meeting, and that was the answer he gave me. I never asked again, although of course I continued to wonder.

He had his weaknesses. One was that he was out of touch with many of the minutiae of current police procedures, which he said were constantly changing, and which did not matter. I had discovered this shortcoming of his when I wrote *The Tanglewood Mystery*. However, he still had many contacts and he remained informed about personnel, policies and new initiatives. Best of all, from my point of view, he was still able to access police files, although mostly on cold cases. I was never sure how he did this, whether it was legal or not, but thought it best not to ask.

He also had odd quirks. He travelled around on an elderly motorcycle, which I put up with but which Jo detested because of the noise. He was over-effusive about some of the subjects I asked him to look at, urging me to use everything he had found, no matter how trivial. Sometimes his enthusiasm for the work wore me out. We usually communicated by landline. He did have a cellphone but rarely used it. He often called me 'sir', which I found slightly uncomfortable, but I had grown used to it. We met irregularly, usually when he had papers he wanted to pass to me in person.

I paid him a monthly retainer, and considered it money well spent. I had grown to like Spoder, and he did good work for me.

On the phone I said to him: 'Spoder, I've heard about a sudden death in Salay Hames, the fifth, about a decade and a half ago. I believe it was a suicide. A man named Antterland. Would you know anything about it?'

'I was never involved with suicides. They are not usually a police matter, unless there's something suspicious when the body is discovered. Anyway, Hames was not my area.'

'I know that – but it was linked to a murder on Salay Sekonda, not long after.'

'Same again,' he said. 'I rarely went off-island, and I never went to Sekonda for a case.'

'Can you try to find out what happened?' Spoder said nothing. He was silent for about a quarter of a minute, until I said: 'Spoder?'

'I'm trying to remember.' He was silent again. I had learned about his occasional silences, so I waited. Then he said: 'These two deaths, sir – you say they were connected. Is this the case of the two brothers? The name Antterland rings a bell.'

'There were brothers involved. That's what I'd like you to check for me.'

'I might have something for you. I wasn't involved myself – I think I was on some other case at the time. But I remember now that it was something the guys used to chuckle about, in the squad room. I assumed it was some kind of private joke, the way Antterland had killed himself. Is this for a new book you're planning, sir?'

'I think it might be,' I said, not wanting to go into the whole background. 'Yes.'

'I'll get on to it as soon as I can. It's starting to come back to me now. The brother who was murdered – he was the twin of the brother who killed himself.'

'A twin? An identical twin?'

'I think so,' Spoder said. 'It wouldn't change anything, would it?'

After we had hung up, I thought: Identical twins? That wouldn't change anything. Not in the real world it would not.

★

I was getting interested.

It became urgent to listen again to what Frejah had told me. She had described it as a murder, not a suicide. The name was different, very different, but as Jo had pointed out there weren't many murders to choose from. Salay is a relatively peaceful place. Murders were rare. Frejah had said nothing about a brother, any kind of brother. Twins: Waller and Willer? Maybe I had mis-heard, or my attention had wandered? Were they identical?

I had been dreading the thought of transcribing her long story. Transcription is slow, difficult and tiring, an expert job usually handled by professional agencies, but I did not want to pay an agency to do the work for me. With the other tasks I was already late completing it seemed like something to postpone for a while.

But I had remembered that morning that my cellphone came with an app I had never actually used. It claimed to convert the spoken word into written text, with an accuracy of some 90 per cent. I thought it might be worth a try. Even at that level of accuracy it would be short work to check back to the recording for omissions or mistakes, and make corrections.

I found the app on the phone, clicked on the icon, then went through the usual process of registering myself as user, waiting for the latest upgrade to be downloaded, and so on. When the program was ready, I ran it against the recording I had made. After ten minutes it declared itself finished, and the first page appeared on the cellphone's monitor.

It was indecipherable: an alphabet soup of letters and weird symbols, not even an occasional identifiable word. I scrolled through the rest of the pages, but the constant background noise in the restaurant had obviously interfered with the recording.

When I listened to it on the speaker, I could fairly easily make out what Frejah was saying.

I settled down, transferred the recording to my desktop, loaded my word processor, and started the transcription. With several breaks it took the rest of the day, but by the evening I had what I was sure was an accurate copy of the story she had told me.

12

The Death Club

Transcript of the account of Commissioner Frejah Harsent, Dearth Police:

After a long wait I had recently graduated from uniformed police work to plainclothes investigation. I was partnered with a slightly older but more experienced detective called Enver Jeksid, a detective serjeant. Jeksid also acted as my mentor and adviser. I was unusual on the force because I was not native to Dearth. I was born on Salay Hames, the fifth. Jeksid claimed I still had a Salayean accent, and sometimes teased me about it, but any trace of accent must have been lost years before. I was six years old when my parents moved from Hames.

Most of the transgression work we did was in Dearth City itself. Neither of us was senior enough to be a given a police mobile unit of our own. To get to any incident we normally had to beg a lift from one of the other teams we worked alongside. Resources were always a problem at that time. It slowed our response, so Jeksid and I had probably the worst clear-up record on the force, but apart from that we were no different from the other detective teams. Most of the transgressions we investigated were minor.

I enjoyed the work and felt a growing commitment to policing, but it was a slow progress. Detective work is usually routine and uncontroversial, and when we were in the station house we spent our time peering at computer databases, making endless phone calls or completing by hand the case and information forms demanded by the seignioral management of the force.

In those days, we were expected to carry a certain hand-held device called a 6M8. It was designed to reverse or suppress temporarily the effects of a mutability event. The reason for that was because in the past defence lawyers had frequently argued in court that our investigation of an incident was inadmissible, because a mutability event might or might not have taken place since the alleged incident. This would make forensic evidence unreliable: measurements, placement, movement of evidential objects, and so on.

We were therefore issued with the 6M8, a battery-powered wave generator which had the effect, for a short time and in a restricted area, of reversing any recent mutability event. Its total range was no larger than an average room in a house. We called it, unofficially, the mute-muter. Most of the time it made no difference at all, but occasionally it had the dramatic impact of restoring the scene to the condition it was in when the transgression took place.

We used it a few times and so did the other cops, but in the end it was taken away from us. The same lawyers who had argued that mutability might have interfered with evidence since the transgression now argued the other way: that our little wave generator was contaminating evidence. We haven't been allowed to use it for years.

I mention this because I was still routinely using the 6M8, the mute-muter, when I was asked by my department head if I would be prepared to investigate an off-island incident that involved someone born on Dearth, but living on Salay. I would be working alone. The trip would run up travel and hotel bills, and for that reason they could not afford to send two officers. The case was straightforward: I was to check the detective work carried out by the local force. It was well within my ability level. I leapt at the opportunity.

The detective interviewing me said: 'We understand you were born on Salay Hames. We thought if there was any difficulty with local patois . . .'

'I don't think it will be a problem,' I said.

Because I was thrilled to be offered this solo job I wanted to maintain the belief that I was ideal for it. I therefore did not add that I had never spoken patois at any time, and that Salay was a modern, civilized island group with many trans-island connections. The speaking of patois was a thing of the past.

I departed the next morning. In those days, now long gone, there was a small, privately run airfield that linked Tristcontenta Hub with Dearth City, so the first part of the journey was a mere two hours in the air. I had a few hours to wait for the flight to Salay at Tristcontenta, but I had brought the file on the case. I found a quiet corner in one of the transit lounges.

I learned the details. A man named Waller Alman had been savagely murdered in his home. His full name was Lew Waller Alman, but he never used his first name. He was a Dearth citizen, vassal to a manorial landlord in the Dearth City, but he had been resident on Salay Hames since childhood. As an immigrant he had been removed from the vassalage and reduced to serf status while he remained on Salay. However, his birthplace and fief heritage made it mandatory that the investigation into his death was overseen by a member of our force.

Waller Alman's body had lain unnoticed until a friend or acquaintance had called at the house and made the shocking discovery. Because Salay Hames is a warm island with a humid climate the body had started decomposing rapidly, and the forensic pathologist had used the method of blowfly hatching as a means of establishing a time and day of death. The Salay Hames police had immediately set up the SCI – Serious Crime Investigation – and as far as I could tell from the file they had done a good job.

The body was swiftly but provisionally identified as that of Waller Alman. He lived alone in a large house in a wealthy area of Hames. There were no signs of other occupants anywhere in the house. A driver's licence found in a pocket of the dead man's clothes confirmed the name and address. The victim was believed to have a brother, but he could not be traced any-where in the Salay Group. Eventually a neighbour was able to identify the body.

The likely murder weapon, a wooden bat or club, presumed to be a baseball bat and marked with the badge of the sport-ing club Waller Alman played for, was in the room close to the body. There were abundant traces of blood and flesh tissue on the club which matched Waller Alman's own. These traces were consistent with a massive impact wound to the back of his head.

There were no witnesses to the killing, but there were exten-sive interviews with Waller Alman's neighbours, his manorial landlord in Dearth City, and his non-manorial landlady on Hames. Attempts to trace his brother remained unsuccessful. Telephone calls and text messages made and sent by Waller Alman had been logged, and the names verified. His internet activity was examined and found to be unexceptional. None of the interviews produced any hint of the possible identity of the killer.

Door-to-door enquiries elicited several mentions of a home-less man seen sleeping rough in the area. Few people knew who he was, but he was believed to be known as Stud. He was often seen in the streets, and when drunk he could be aggressive.

The local police rounded up Stud and he was taken in for questioning. At first he denied all knowledge of the murder, but the interviewing officer noticed flaws and contradictions in his story. Questioning was intensified. After two days Stud suddenly surrendered resistance and confessed that he had done it. He said that he had broken into the house in search of alcohol or money, but he was discovered by Waller Alman. He said he panicked, seized the baseball bat and beat Waller Alman to death. Afterwards he fled the scene. At the time he was arrested he was trying to find some way of moving on to another part of the island.

Stud was in custody, awaiting a court date for the evidence to be confirmed, and for dates to be set for trial and sentencing.

Waller Alman's body was in the mortuary. All witnesses and pieces of evidence would be available to me. My job was to satisfy myself that the local investigation had been thorough, that the dead man was indeed who they said he was, and that the man held in custody was the likely perpetrator. Because this was a case of murder the forensic evidence had to be of the highest standard. With that done, Waller Alman's body could be released to his family.

From the information on file it appeared to be an open and shut case.

After the long wait in the transit lounge I caught the trans-island flight to Salay. All trans-island flights land at Salay Ewwel, the first. I stayed one night in an airport hotel, and the following morning took an inter-island shuttle flight from Ewwel to Salay Hames, the fifth. I was welcomed by the police on the island, assigned a car and a driver, and a young detective constable. He had no part in the enquiry but was there to act as liaison to the force, should that be necessary.

I went first to the mortuary, where I was able to confirm the body had been correctly identified and labelled. I approved the release of the body to the family, who would have to arrange for transporting it back to Dearth, if that was what they wished. The mortuary assistant said they were still trying to trace any family member who could make such decisions, otherwise the body would be interred in a serf grave.

I then went to see the man called Stud, on custodial remand, awaiting sentence. After this I was taken to the station house where I was shown the police paperwork, including several pieces I had not seen in the file I had been given in Dearth. Finally, I was driven to the house where the murder had taken place. It was indeed an impressive and in my view ostentatious house. I made a close examination on my own for nearly half an hour.

I returned to the station house, where I formally confirmed the papers were in order, signed the necessary release, thanked everyone I had met for their help and cooperation, and after a quick lunch I was driven to the airport. Once I was back in Dearth City I filed my report and returned to normal duties with Serjeant Jeksid.

There it could have ended, but there were several inconsistencies I had noticed. I had either been discouraged by the Hames force from investigating further, or for various reasons I felt the anomalies were beyond my jurisdiction.

Firstly, there was no evidence that placed the prisoner, Stud, inside the house at any time, let alone at the point when the murder happened. There were, for example, no signs of a forced break-in. Stud's fingerprints were not found on the murder weapon, nor indeed on anything else in the house.

But Stud had confessed to the murder. In fact, he had confessed twice – the second time it was written down and he signed his name. He incriminated himself and although he was given several chances to withdraw the confession he re-affirmed it. The police in Hames maintained that it was inescapable proof of guilt.

However, the interview in which Stud made the first confession was videoed. There is a gap in the recording, both sound and vision. Before the gap he can be seen repeatedly being threatened and bullied by the interviewing officer. Stud appears confused and sounds incoherent, frightened. He is complaining of a pain in his side, asks to see a doctor and says that he has been repeatedly kicked. There are traces of blood on his face.

When the recording resumes, the scene has changed. The interviewing officer is no longer visible on camera, but he, or someone like him, is in the room and questioning Stud. There is still blood on Stud's face, and some of it has seeped into his shirt. Stud is lying back on the bench, his arms over his head. He is largely inarticulate. He is crying.

Then he says: 'Yes, I killed that man. It was me.' He goes on to say more.

It has all the appearance of a coerced confession, forced out of a vulnerable suspect after a long period of rough interrogation. If presented to a seigniory panel on Dearth there is little doubt that it would be deemed inadmissible.

However, for all that it was a full confession. Stud's version of events aligned almost exactly with what the other evidence showed happened. Most compelling of all, no other suspect had been found or charged. Waller Alman did not kill himself – someone else was involved. Stud was the only possible killer in the frame.

My training had already made me familiar with certain attitudes held by police officers, and I had sometimes been aware of them myself – usually off-guard remarks while investigating a transgression. It amounted to this: when there is unchallenged partial evidence, and if it is supported by circumstantial evidence, and there is only one suspect in the case, there is a strong temptation to ignore everything else. The known or assumed facts are then fitted to the person they are questioning. It is known as confirmation bias.

If I had not already been suspecting it in the case of Waller Alman, everything was made clear when the young constable who was in the car with me said informally, as we drove away from the custody remand building: 'As soon as Stud was brought in we all knew for sure that we had the right man. After that it was just a question of waiting for him to confess.'

There was a third evidential problem, one the local police were totally unaware of. This was not their fault as they had little or no experience of mutability, but it was one of the procedures I was tasked with carrying out. I was to try to establish if there was a mutability element to the killing, because if there was it could affect the quality of the forensic work. In the past Salay Hames had known few mutability events, but was considered high-risk on the scale of Mutability Incipience.

While I was in Waller Alman's house I made a visual examination of the room where he had been murdered, comparing what I could see with police photos taken shortly after discovery of his body. I then routinely took a reading from the mute-muter, which recorded a major incursive event: horizontal and vertical mutability had occurred immediately after the estimated time of death of the victim. The latter reading was off the scale of the device. What could this mean? I stored the results. I then followed another standard procedure, in which it is possible to reverse engineer the mutability effects: I selected the day before the attack. This should have restored the 'normal' state of the room, but the readings again were much higher than anything we had been trained to accept as normal. I had never encountered anything like it before.

It meant, in short, that no evidence taken from the scene of murder could be used in court. That also meant that Stud's confession was unchallengeable. There was no evidence that anyone else might have been the murderer.

Two weeks after I arrived back in Dearth, news came through that Stud, still being held in solitary confinement while waiting for sentencing, had hanged himself in his cell. The police files on the murder of Waller Alman were later closed for good, both on Salay and Dearth.

13

The Riddle of the Hands

Why were there differences between Frejah's story and the relatively superficial accounts Jo and I had dug out of the reference books? The entries were short and synoptic, but all of the four or five mentions Jo had found in the books of lists, the court records of crime, tended to agree.

There was in fact a murder, or a violent death, recorded on Salay Hames about fifteen years ago. Murder was unusual on our islands – it must be this one. Why had she changed the name of the dead man? She called him Waller Alman, and at one point on the tape she said his full name was *Lew* Waller Alman. According to the references Jo and I had found, the victim was called Lew Antterland. (Had Frejah actually said 'Antterland', and slurred the word, or I misheard it? When I played part of the tape again, that was unlikely. She said the name several times. Anyway, I had checked the spelling of the name with her. No mistakes.)

Lew Antterland's brother, himself later murdered, was called Dever Antterland, and was sometimes known as 'Willer'. A reference in one of the books gave his full name as Dever Willer Antterland.

What were Frejah's motives for telling me the story?

This was itself a mystery if I accepted that our acquaintance-ship had started casually, but I was no longer so sure. Belatedly it appeared otherwise. She had meant to locate me and in some way had engineered our meeting. So this deepened the mystery. Was part of her purpose in approaching me with the intention of telling me this story? It was hard to see why, unless it was, as she had said, a wish to pass on an anecdote in the hope I might turn it into a novel. That seemed to me a trivial reason.

If not trivial, then there was something contained in the story, or perhaps omitted from it, that was intended to get my interest. She had certainly succeeded in that. While I pondered all this, the unchecked novel proofs were lying on my desk, a silent rebuke.

I alleviated the guilty feelings by spending an hour checking the proofs, then set them aside. It was now evening. I turned on the lights in my study, and closed the windows against the large and sometimes aggressive insects that I knew would otherwise fly in. I made myself a meal. I played with Barmi the cat, then fed him. I read a few more pages of the proofs while I ate.

I switched on my desktop computer and began a systematic internet search for any information that would confirm, en-hance or explain Frejah's story. Of course, many of the results were much the same as Jo had found for me in the reference books. But I had a range of specialist websites I often looked at when researching, and I had subscriber access to several privately maintained archive sites.

There was nothing at all about anyone called Waller Alman in the newspaper archives, TV news channel archives and the usual news pages. I looked up the police gazette and court rec-ords without success. The subscriber websites returned nothing.

To be sure, I ran similar checks on 'Willer Alman' and various spelling changes of the surname. Nothing at all.

With that established, I turned to checks on the name Antterland. Here I was more successful, although I was soon aware that too much time had passed for complete reliability. Files were closed or sometimes lost, or had been moved to another archive under a different name. Even so, a few facts emerged. Facts are for me the core of a story.

Lew Waller Antterland lived alone in a large house on Salay Hames. He was believed to be wealthy. In interviews after his death several neighbours said that he appeared to live well but not ostentatiously, and he rarely spoke about himself. He was polite, but seemed secretive.

His death was caused by a heavy blow to the back of the head. Next to the body was a baseball bat, badged by a local sports club, bearing blood and hair traces that were consistent with the wound. The only fingerprints on the bat were his.

The house was locked, with no sign of a forced entry. The body was found by a neighbour who had a spare key to the house, normally used at times when watching the house if Antterland was away. This woman noticed that mail deliveries were being left outside the main door.

Two features of the death could not be explained.

The time of death had been calculated with an error allowance of about one hour on either side. However, the neighbour who held the spare key, and another woman who worked in a local restaurant a couple of hundred metres along the road, both reported seeing Antterland leaving the house and locking it up two hours later. That is: he was seen between one and three hours *after* he was killed. He was carrying a large shoulder bag, one they had seen him using before. He did not speak to either of them, but this was not at all unusual. (Frejah's account had not mentioned the singular fact of Antterland being seen alive after the murder.)

The other feature was that when Antterland's bank and other financial records were examined he was found to have virtually no money. Audits of his accounts discovered that all his wealth had been converted to cash on the morning of the day he died. There was no trace of the cash, either inside the house or anywhere else that it might have been concealed. The large shoulder bag he was seen with was never located. (Again, Frejah did not include this in her story.)

Because of these unexplained and inconsistent matters a murder investigation was launched.

A vagrant who had been seen in the area at the time of Antterland's death, name of Stodson, known on the street as Stod, was arrested and held on suspicion. When questioned he boasted unconvincingly but also unwisely that Lew Antterland was a friend, his best friend. He maintained his innocence even under sustained questioning. A heavy drug user and an alcoholic, Stodson was in poor physical and mental health and while being questioned about Antterland's death he collapsed. He died later in hospital. There was no evidence to link him to the crime.

With no other possible suspect, and all the evidence pointing to Antterland's injury as self-inflicted, no matter how extraordinary the circumstances, an inquest court found the death to be occasioned by suicide while the balance of the mind was disturbed.

Because Lew Waller Antterland was a manorial vassal in fief to a demesne lord from the island of Dearth, two detectives from that island arrived to oversee the investigation.

But Frejah said she was sent to Salay Hames alone. Two separate archives reported in factual terms that two Dearth officers went to investigate. Who was the other? Frejah's partner and mentor, Serjeant Jeksid?

At least I could forget the name 'Waller Alman'. 'Stud' was Stod, or Stodson. Stod maintained his innocence throughout, he did not break down and confess, he was not put on remand in prison, he died of ill-health and, perhaps, police maltreatment, but he did not kill himself.

The more I considered it, the more the post mortem verdict on Antterland of suicide seemed increasingly perverse. The mere thought of someone picking up a baseball bat as a suicide weapon defeated all logic. The bat, admittedly an efficient club should one want to use it as that, held behind with both hands then swung against the back of the head? With enough strength to crush the skull and inflict deadly pressure on the brain? And just one swing?

So it had to be murder as Frejah had said, and perhaps more sinisterly, as she actually knew. She still seemed to me complicit in some way. Who then might have committed it, and why?

The fingerprints on the handle of the baseball bat were the only hard evidence, but they did not incriminate anyone else and revealed nothing of how the murder was carried out. The disappearance of Lew Antterland's money established a motive, but not the method.

If Antterland was a member of a sports club, or played for a local baseball team, then the fingerprints found on the handle were likely to be his. That assumed he did not wear protective batting gloves when playing, which he probably did. Alternatively, if he only used the bat as an exercise aid of some kind, or if he simply liked picking it up from time to time, then he would probably not wear gloves at all.

The killer might of course have been wearing gloves when he or she smashed the bat against the back of Antterland's head, but the pressure and gripping action of the gloves would almost certainly have removed or blurred patches of the existing prints. Salay Hames was hot and humid at the time of the crime, a summer month, so gloves would not naturally be worn – unless the murder was planned and premeditated. If no gloves were worn by the killer then there would be plenty of traces: humidity makes hands sweaty, which will leave clear fingerprints as well as DNA.

The report I read said that there were fingerprints and palm prints all over the handle of the bat, many of them obscuring others, or blurring across them. There were few blank areas. All the prints were the same: Lew Antterland's.

The other mystery was the reported witness sightings of Antterland leaving the house after the time of the murder. Assuming the witnesses' statements were accurate, this raises two questions. Firstly, how reliable are the timings, and secondly, if it was not Lew Antterland himself seen leaving the house, who was it?

The importance of the exact time of the death of a victim often comes up in crime fiction. In reality, it is an imprecise science. Forensic pathologists invariably warn that their opinion is only that. Many different factors can affect the way a body reacts after death: position, body weight, clothing, ambient temperature, and so on. Frejah in her story mentioned that the pathologist on the Antterland case had used blowfly measurement to try to establish the time of death. This method works from the knowledge that within minutes of dying, carrion blowflies arrive on the scene and lay their eggs. By measuring the developmental stages of the larvae or young flies, a pathologist can estimate the time of death with greater accuracy than with more conventional methods. That time was recorded in several accounts of the investigation.

The observations of Antterland leaving his house were also narrowed down to more or less exact times: between one and two hours after the murder. This was of course a significant mystery.

Even if the timing was wrong, both by the pathologist and the witnesses, Antterland was definitely seen leaving the house and locking it up. No one saw him returning later to meet his end, and for that matter there was no other person, the possible murderer, spotted hanging around outside.

But mysteries are there to be solved, and I believed that Spoder had already supplied the explanation. Lew Antterland had a brother, a twin brother, quite likely an identical twin brother, Dever Antterland. He must have been the killer.

Why one twin should murder his brother was something I would never understand, but it seemed there was an overwhelming circumstantial case against Dever.

Dever's plan. He could enter his brother's house without breaking in – possibly he had his own key. After he killed his brother he would exit from the house in a normal seeming way, locking the door behind him, presumably hoping this would provide an extra delay before the discovery of the body. Whether or not he intended to be seen by witnesses and mistaken for his brother was a matter of speculation, but if this was what happened then from Dever's point of view that would be so much the better. If they did not see him, then he had made himself briefly invisible.

The problem of the fingerprints would also be explained. Identical twins do *not* have identical fingerprints. However, in some cases the fingerprints of identical twins are alike in appearance, with minor distortions, slight differences in size. They are not similar enough to be wrongly identified by a fingerprint expert, but in certain circumstances they can be easily mistaken for each other. It seemed to me that the ungloved hands of the murderer on a humid day, seizing a baseball bat in a fierce grip, using it violently, would leave behind several blurred or smudged fingerprints, looking little different from the ones already there, the ones they partially obscured.

Motive? Not all brothers love each other. Families are complex and dynamic, often riven by jealousy, ambition, perceived betrayals, a sense of unfairness. Just because Dever and Lew were twin brothers did not mean they were incapable of murdering one another.

And there was the matter of the missing money. How could that be explained? There was a chance that it was not the immediate motive for murder. Perhaps Lew, sensing his life was in danger, converted his wealth into cash that morning, concealed it somewhere he thought would be safe, then met his nemesis later that day.

Another possibility: Dever, his identical twin brother, posed as Lew. He made false use of identity papers, faked his brother's signature, converted the wealth into cash, hid it temporarily, then went to his brother's house and murdered him. After that he locked up the house, returned to pick up the money from where he had stashed it, stuffed it into the large shoulder bag he had taken from his brother, then caught the next inter-island flight to wherever he lived on Salay Sekonda.

It was late. I went to bed.

14

Half Answers

Spoder phoned. It was still early, a peaceful time of quietude and warm air, before the sun rose high enough to bake the land. The road was virtually free of traffic. The cicadas stilled long before the sun rose. I had woken early and was on my recliner on the decking, the remains of an early breakfast around me. I was holding a mug of coffee.

'Sir, I have found out almost everything you need to know about Antterland's murder,' Spoder said. The cable of the land-line was stretched from the connector on the wall of my study, through the open windows. He went on: 'I have access to the file, photos of the body, plans and more photos of the crime scene.'

'Is this the murder on Salay Hames?' I said. 'Lew Antterland?'

'No – he was the suicide. I'm talking about his brother Dever.'

'I think Lew was also murdered.'

'No, sir. Lew killed himself. I have a copy of the inquest report.'

'OK, Spoder. Tell me about Dever.'

In the past I had learned that Spoder did not like discovering I was already ahead of his researches, seeing himself, justifiably, as my professional consultant. The internet had made access to documentary information so widely available that sometimes he and I followed parallel routes to similar pieces of information. Whenever that happened and we duplicated the effort, or as in this case I had gone more deeply into the story than him and worked out what had probably happened, I chose to stay silent, as now.

I needed Spoder's input, though. He had access to internal police material that I could not get hold of otherwise, and his outlook on crimes and the mentality of criminals was usually different from mine. He challenged and refreshed me when he passed material on, even when we had doubled up our searches. Even when his sometimes manic attitude alienated me. As often it did.

Apart from my certainty about his role in the death of Lew, I knew nothing about the events surrounding Dever Antterland.

'I'm still sorting through what I have,' Spoder said. 'I wanted to tell you it's all here.'

'Could you bring it over later?'

'Tomorrow would be better.'

'I'm thinking about what happened to Lew, his brother,' I said.

'Is there a story or a novel in that?'

'I don't know at the moment. It probably depends what you have on Dever.'

'I'll come to the house tomorrow morning.'

In the middle of the day Jo contacted me from her hotel room in Chor. A business meeting was going on which did not involve her. We spoke online for half an hour. After she had told me about the work she was being offered, she asked what I had found out about the Antterland brothers. I told her how grateful I was for the research she had done. I said I thought that as a result I had solved one case, but Spoder and I were still working on the other. I told her my theory of the murderous twin.

Relating the events aloud made me think again about what I had deduced, what I was saying. I had not consciously thought about this before, and suddenly I opened up to Jo about it. Was there still an allowable, plausible way of plotting a crime novel that involved identical twins?

I voiced this aloud to Jo, putting into words the concern that had been lurking unsaid. Impersonation as an attempt to conceal a murder was an old story device, over-used by thriller writers for decades.

I told Jo I was inspired and excited by the idea of the Antterland case, because it was a real one, not a story some-one had made up. I had worked out the modus operandi of a murder, one thought by officialdom to have been a suicide. Then every few minutes I would resile mentally from it, reject-ing it because it was so familiar, almost obvious.

I anticipated the embarrassment of putting the Antterland killing into a story or novel, modified and fictionalized in some way, only to have the publishers tell me that I could not get away with such a clichéd idea: not now, not these days, not another one of those identical twin plots. Worse, perhaps, further on down the line having the reviewers and readers say much the same thing.

I knew what a standard trope it was for a crime novel, one that had fallen from favour because of over-use, exactly like locked room mysteries and attempts to commit the perfect murder. They too were classic stories of the past.

But my position kept shifting. I would recover my confi-dence and something about Lew Antterland's death would grab my interest again.

Jo listened, then said: 'Maybe this means there was more to the murder than you've realized.'

'I've tried to see it that way.'

'This woman cop you met on Dearth – she told you that long story. There must have been a reason.'

'An ulterior motive?'

'I don't know,' Jo said. 'I haven't read it, of course. But was she trying to tell you something else?'

'I thought that too. I simply didn't know her well enough to read her intentions properly. At the time I wasn't paying attention, mentally fending her off because I'm fed up with people trying to describe their rotten ideas for books. I was listening to her but not paying proper attention. It was only yesterday, when I transcribed the recording, that I began to wonder what was going on.'

'You always say that's where the real interest of a crime story lies. Not in the mystery the plot seems to be about, but what is *not* being told, the undercurrent. You once described it to me as the darker world of unadmitted motive. The story the killer didn't intend to reveal, the one the detective misses, and only spots belatedly.'

'Yes,' I said, suddenly alert again. I needed Jo to remind me of these things.

'That's what makes your novels different, Todd. But this Antterland murder has made you think like an amateur sleuth, isn't that right? You always say you shouldn't do that. It's the wrong way to make crime interesting.'

'Yes,' I said again.

'Now you've solved a mystery from fifteen years ago, one few people have ever heard of, let alone will care about. What's the real story behind it? The one you should be interested in. The one you might be able to write?'

'I suppose that's what I've been looking for,' I said, feeling chastened. Jo knew my work better than I did.

'Your last novel broke new ground,' Jo went on. I glanced across at the page proofs, about a third read so far, the rest of them yet to be checked. 'You said that book, when it comes out next year, will move you further away from the standard genre stuff, and the new novel—'

'I'm still working on it. I'd be writing it now if I hadn't had to go away for a week.'

'OK,' Jo said. 'Then can't you forget this old stuff and get back to it?'

'I will,' I said. 'I haven't lost interest – it was just that going to Dearth was a huge interruption, and I was distracted by what you call the mystery from fifteen years ago. I'm beginning to realize there wasn't a mystery at all – just the usual story of the police not doing a thorough job.'

'Good.'

'I'll get back to the new book tomorrow.'

'After Spoder has been to the house and given you a new mystery to solve?'

'No – I want to carry on with what I was doing. I'll throw him out as soon as I can. And the proofs are here of the last book. I have plenty to get on with.'

'So you'll do it?' Jo said.

'I will.'

Jo suddenly said: 'You haven't mentioned those newspaper links I found. Did you follow them up?'

'No – not yet.'

I had noticed them, but I skipped over them without searching for them online. They were old URLs that I would have to enter manually, and most of them in all likelihood would have been closed in the years since they went up.

'There was one that ran an article about Dever Antterland. At the time he was killed he was working as a magician.'

'What?'

'A stage magician. He had his own small theatre and ran shows in a holiday resort. I thought that might interest you.'

I loved Jo for the mischief she often played on me.

'I didn't see that!' I said, rising to the bait. 'Where was it?'

'I have to go. Their meeting has finished. Get on with your new novel, Todd.'

We said goodbye, broke the connection.

I looked at the first draft of the new novel, but once again it felt arid. I had learned the hard way not to force myself to write when the inner chemistry was wrong. Not an excuse – a pragmatic decision. I read through all the pages I had written before I went away, made some handwritten notes on what would come next, then put it aside. I would try again the next day.

I took a break, walked through the garden, crossed the road and walked down the sward towards the beach. It was mid-afternoon and the sunshine was broiling. I had left the house on an impulse so I had not brought my hat. I stood for a few minutes regarding the familiar scene of the shingly beach, the shining sea with its gentle waves, the tiny offshore islands almost invisible in the glare from the sea, then I turned back and went to the house. I made myself an iced drink, returned to my decked patio and turned on the cooling fan. Later, Barmi joined me, sitting so that his fur was lifted by the flow of air.

I had been thinking about what Jo said, so as soon as I was settled I pulled the page proofs towards me and began reading and checking them in earnest. I completed them within an hour and a half.

In the evening I felt a return of the restlessness that the Antterland story had induced in me. I had a spurious feeling of triumph: I had worked out what had happened the day he was killed. I was sometimes able to anticipate the revelation in someone else's novel, but that was not the same as this. Lew Antterland was real, his death came about through a violent attack.

I read Frejah Harsent's account again. It seemed increasingly unreliable every time I looked at it or thought about it. As I read the words I had transcribed I remembered the noisy restaurant where she had spoken them, the semi-guilty way she had looked, my own feelings of uncertainty about what she was telling me and why. The coldness of print both smoothed those impressions away, but also revealed more and more duplicity.

At the end of her story Frejah had drawn attention to what she called three inconsistencies in what she had experienced. These were: the lack of evidence at the murder scene of Stud's (Stod's) involvement, the dubious quality of his confession leading to the way the investigating police officers had tried to fit the available evidence to him, and the effect of the mutability she had detected within the house. (Of this last one, I had no opinion.)

As a police officer, Frejah had a duty to report these findings, but instead she signed off what she had investigated, adding nothing to the file compiled by the police on Salay Hames. At the very least this indicated incompetent police work, but as Jo had said to me, the duplicity hinted that Frejah knew more than she admitted. That in turn suggested she might have been somehow involved with the crime, and/or was covering something up, and/or that she had pre-knowledge of it.

Now that I had been able to compare her account with what was objectively recorded in the media at the time of the incident, I could see several more 'inconsistencies', to use her word.

The most glaring of these was that she had said she was sent to Salay Hames alone, whereas the record showed two Dearth detectives were there. Frejah seemed certain to have been one of them. Detective Serjeant Jeksid would be the obvious companion. What then was his role in checking the facts of the murder? Was he also somehow involved with the crime itself?

While she was working with the Hames police, Frejah must have seen or been shown the witness accounts describing how Antterland, or someone who looked just like him, was seen leaving the house after the murder. She must have been told about the missing money – a clear motive for the killing. And if fifteen years later, my contact, Spoder, then an officer on another force, could remember the story that Lew Antterland had a twin brother, she would surely have been told, or found out about it. Those details were memorable, unusual, not easily ignored.

I added these thoughts to the pages of notes I was taking of the Antterland case.

But then, with a feeling of guilt, I put everything aside. Jo's remarks to me had been important. She was not a writer, and lacked any need or aspiration to be one, but channelled her artistic abilities into the design and sculpting work she did. However, she had an uncanny awareness of and sensitivity towards what I tried to do in my books. We had been living together for many years. Jo knew more about my writing than I ever liked to admit. I had learned to listen to her.

She was right about the Frejah story: I was obsessing about a minor mystery from fifteen years earlier, of no lasting interest or relevance.

★

Once again, my absorption in the Frejah story had made me un-aware of the passing of time. It was now close on midnight. My eyes were tired and I knew I should not have wasted most of the evening on this. I closed down my study, switching off all the equipment and lights. I headed for the bedroom.

While undressing I noticed that the clothes I was wearing while travelling on Dearth were still lying in a heap on the floor. It was time they were laundered. As I checked that the pockets were empty I found, to my surprise, deep in one of the back pockets, a stiff plastic card.

It was a clean, brilliant white, with an embedded computer chip in the centre. Apart from a small hotel logo printed in gold in one corner, and a border strip coloured bright red, there was no identification.

I placed it on my bedside table, then went to the bathroom, dumped the clothes in the laundry basket, took a brief shower and brushed my teeth. I was expecting Jo would be home again the next day, giving us a few more days together before her trip to Muriseay.

15

A Detective Inspector Calls

I was awake, eating breakfast on my patio decking, reading my emails. The main one was a terse one that had just arrived from Jo – she said she was being delayed, and would not be returning until the next day. I had written back straight away, because I was concerned about her upcoming trip to Muriseay. The delay would mean there was only a day and a half at home before she had to travel again, and the Muriseay visit was open ended. She had warned me she would have to be there at least five days, maybe a week, maybe two, depending on how well it went. I did not mind and said so, but I knew how wearing these trips could be. Jo was younger than me, but not by much.

We were both at an age of denial: we wanted to act as we always had from the time we met, denying the two decades we had put behind us since, but we now appreciated comfort and the pleasures of idleness and early nights more than we would admit.

Jo replied to say all was well. She would be back early, we'd have time before she had to leave again. She had already pre-packed her bags for the longer trip.

We agreed to make contact by internet that evening.

I was still browsing through the other emails when Spoder arrived at the house. I was not expecting him because he normally turned up in the middle of the day. I knew it was him as soon as I heard him: he always arrived on his motorcycle via the narrow access road behind the house, then scraped and scuffed noisily across the gravel of the short drive, leaving tyre grooves.

He marched through the house without preamble, wearing his crash helmet. As he came on to the patio he lifted it off and tossed it aside. It landed on the edge of the table, toppled over and rolled noisily but harmlessly over the planking.

'Sorry, sir!' he said, when he saw my reaction. 'I didn't mean to drop it like that.'

I stood up and faced him. He was wearing bright blue shorts, a yellow T-shirt with the name of a rock band printed in gothic lettering on the front, and sandals. He threw down a pile of papers on the table next to my laptop, then picked up my electric jug of coffee and looked around for a spare mug. I went into the house and found one for him.

'Help yourself to some breakfast,' I said, indicating the small plate of rolls and croissants I had put out.

'Thanks, but I never touch food at this time of day,' he said. 'Sir, you know what a pleasure it is to act as your researcher, but this time you have excelled. I am in debt to you. This is the sort of case I have always dreamed of.'

I am slow to respond in the mornings. I like to wake up and bestir myself in small steps. It's a gradual process, slow and if performed at the right pace pleasurable. I suspect 'perform' is an appropriate description, since the possibility of dynamic action is always available as an option, but one I rarely select. Jo has been accustomed to my withdrawn morning state for many years, and leaves me to it. We hardly ever meet for more than a brief hello in the mornings. Light food, dark coffee, social media and the online newspapers are all part of the steady adjustment to the new day. Barmi the cat likes me like that – he often curls up on my lap at this time. Today, he had torn himself away from me as soon as he heard Spoder's motorcycle,

Spoder was the antithesis of a gentle awakening, with his noisy motorbike, his clattering around, his loud voice and the immediacy of his expectations about my response. I could cope with Spoder at midday, but at this early hour he was a challenge.

'I need to finish what I'm doing,' I said, returning to my chair in front of the laptop. 'Sit down. Wait. Drink coffee. Tell me about the case in a few minutes.'

'I need to tell you now. We have to go somewhere.'

'Is it a murder?' I said. 'Not a suicide that is mistaken for a murder?'

'No – this is the real thing. But it is not without a few strange features. When I read through the file yesterday my first thought was that you and I should travel immediately to Salay Sekonda, the second. There are several shuttle flights this morning, so we can leave now. The crime scene can still be visited. Once you know the details you will feel as anxious as I am to see where it took place.'

I thought: No more travel. At least not with someone like Spoder. The luxury of sitting around at home had not started to wear off yet.

'What would be the point of visiting a crime scene so many years after the event?' I said.

'It's still there to be seen. More or less untouched.'

'Spoder – I've other work I must do.'

'This is work too.'

'The crime scene can wait.'

'Sir, I have to say you are disappointing me. You would be investigating an extraordinary crime.'

'What are the unadmitted motives?' I said, thinking of Jo and what she said about my acting like an amateur sleuth. I was also trying to change the subject.

'This was almost certainly revenge! A classic case of one person settling an old score against another.'

'That is the admitted motive,' I said. 'But there would have been more to it than that. There always is.'

'I think so too. This is why we must visit the scene.'

Spoder had started pacing impatiently around my patio, his mouth full of the croissant he had lifted from my plate without my noticing. He advanced towards me.

'I think with respect you should get your priorities sorted, sir,' he said. He leaned towards me, hands resting on the edge of the table, still chewing. Flakes of fine pastry floated down.

I said: 'So how long ago was the murder? If I'm right, this person, Dever Antterland, killed his brother Lew about fifteen years ago. If the crime scene is still intact, and we're talking about someone killing Dever in revenge, it can only have happened recently.'

'The file says it was about ten years ago.'

I was aware that Spoder and I had been duplicating our research efforts, at least in part, but it sounded as if he had turned up rather more, as often happened.

I said: 'So Dever was killed, what, about about five years after Lew died?'

'Yes. I heard about it at the time. The Salay forces talk to each other, you know. I wasn't involved in the case, no one on the Raba force was directly involved apart from having to file paperwork and copies. But in the police stories are passed around all the time. The main thing I remembered about it was that the victim, Dever Antterland, had a twin brother who had committed suicide by somehow managing to bash his own brains out.'

'He was murdered,' I said. 'By Dever.'

I assumed that after Dever killed his brother he made good his escape, either carrying all the cash he had stolen, or making some arrangement with a bank on Hames to transfer the money to an account he controlled. He would then have laid low while the Salay Hames police fumbled around, failing to solve the case. But I also assumed that people other than the police would be looking for him. Whoever they were they eventually caught up with him and delivered swift rough justice. But for some reason that took another five years.

'Tell me more about the crime scene,' I said. 'Are you saying it has remained untouched for ten years?'

'It is apparently still exactly as it was on the day the body was found. This is why we must visit it.'

'Murder is always messy,' I said. 'You know how disgusting crime scenes can be. No one could leave the place exactly as it was.'

These thoughts were discordant while breakfasting at the beginning of a day that had promised to be peaceful and lovely. I decided against eating the rest of my food.

I had never in fact visited a real crime scene, but had seen many photographs and reconstructions. Of course I had written about them. It was always tempting to over-describe the chaos and horror of the aftermath of a murder. I had succumbed to that temptation when I was writing my early books. Spilled blood and dismemberment, dropped weapons, cartridge cases, blood-covered knives, deadly clues, all these were interesting to write about and brought a sense of visual excitement to a story.

Thrillers are for much of the time internalized: the characters wonder and speculate, hide secrets, worry about what will happen next, form suspicions. The sleuth theorizes about motives and methods, calculates who was where and when, notices

accidental revelations of clues, carries out interviews with recal-
citrant witnesses, obsesses over railway timetables. Thrillers are
not especially thrilling.

'On this occasion I understand the crime scene has been pre-
served, almost exactly as it was discovered,' Spoder was saying.
'Whatever mess there was has been cleaned up long ago, of
course. But the place, the scene of the murder, is as it was on
the day. I assure you this is a truly unusual and astonishing story.
I am indebted to you for bringing me in on it. All will become
clear as soon as we reach Sekonda.'

'Spoder, if you go to Sekonda you go without me.'

He took one of my bread rolls, split it in half and smeared
some fruit preserve across it. He took a huge mouthful. Then
he licked his long fingers and ferreted around inside the file.
He pulled out what looked like two pieces of card. He slapped
them down on the table and covered them with his free hand
before I could pick them up.

'Here is the proof of twin brotherhood you have secretly
been worrying about,' Spoder said. 'This is a photograph of
Lew Antterland, taken in the same year he died.'

He turned over the first picture. I had not formed any kind
of mental image of the dead man, so the head and shoulders
photograph that Spoder now showed me was a revelation. Lew
Antterland was a young man, in his mid-twenties. He had a
rather square face with noticeable jowls, pale blue eyes spaced
well and with a direct look. His short hair was combed forward.
He was clean-shaven. His face was unlined.

'Now look at Dever. This was taken about five years later.
Again, I think this must have been not long before he died.'

The second photograph that Spoder turned over was just as
clear, taken from a different angle, a studio portrait. The physical
resemblance between the two men was immediately obvious.

Dever looked older than his brother, but not greatly so – the picture was obviously taken later. Dever appeared to be in his early thirties. His hair was longer than Lew's and combed differently, but the similarity was striking. He had the same jowly face, but wore a narrow, well trimmed moustache and a goatee beard.

The principal difference between the two was that Dever was wearing a silky top hat, with a narrow line of reflected light down the vertical crown. In his left hand, held up for the camera to see, was a tall wine glass with two white and black dice lying at the bottom. In his right hand, Dever was holding a short wooden stick, a magician's wand, painted black with white ends. Somewhere behind him, obviously superimposed after the picture was taken, there were a number of glittering stars, in different colours.

'Dever was a well known illusionist on Salay Sekonda,' Spoder said. 'He performed in clubs and theatres all over the island, as well as sometimes visiting schools where he had an act suitable for children.'

'And he performed as Dever Antterland?'

'His stage name was Willer the Wonder. There are several newspaper reviews in the file, if you'd like to read them.'

'Willer the Wonder!' I suddenly wanted to laugh aloud.

'Yes.'

'So – when Willer the Wonder was murdered, did they ever catch whoever did it?'

'No, but this is one of the extraordinary features of the case. The murderer was actually seen and spoken to at the crime scene!' Spoder's voice was raised with excitement. 'Several witnesses saw him and spoke to him after the killing, but no one knew who he was or what he had done. Because Dever's body was not discovered straight away, they didn't realize a murder had taken place. By the time the body was found, the killer had made a clean getaway.'

'There must be descriptions of him.'

'There are some in the file, but you'll see they are not specific enough. Average build, no distinguishing features, dressed in the same clothes you might see every day in the streets. There were no other clues, no other suspects, no known motives. It is a cold case, still unsolved.'

I thought for a few moments.

Then I said: 'If the killer was disturbed at the scene, and people saw him leaving, why did it take so long for the body of the victim to be found?'

'Ah,' said Spoder, taking the last of my croissants, and crushing it into his mouth. 'This is why we must go to inspect the crime scene ourselves. The murder was carried out inside a locked room. There was no way in or out.'

I said: 'That's it. You can forget the whole thing, Spoder. I'm not going to believe in a locked room mystery. It's a hoax of some kind.'

'I promise you this is serious. Look – I only downloaded the file last night. It is exactly as I found it.'

'And I promise you that locked room mysteries are entirely a figment of the imagination of crime novelists. And even then, only from a small minority of crime novelists. Impossible crimes don't happen in the real world – they *can't* happen in the real world. Murder is brutal, irrational, usually impulsive. Murderers don't hatch complicated schemes to baffle people who come along later. They are out to kill. They kill, then they try to get away. If it is planned at all, a murder is worked out in the vaguest way. To the typical murderer preparation and planning mean finding out when the victim routinely comes home from work.

Or the licence plate number of the victim's car. Or the lonely walk the victim takes every weekend. Other than that the motives are basic: money, sex, revenge, and so on.

'Locked room mysteries are planned meticulously, often with almost mathematical precision. They are contrived, made up, invented, they have outrageous and insanely complicated explanations. Bullets shaped from frozen blood taken from the victim earlier under a pretence, clocks with microscopic poisoned darts that shoot the victim on the stroke of midnight, icicles that can be shot from hidden crossbows. That sort of thing. The locked room mystery depends on intense and detailed planning, logistics, exact timing of both the weapon and the behaviour of the victim. Everything has to happen precisely according to the plan. For that reason alone the entire subject is nonsense. The real world is too random and unpredictable. Things go wrong.'

Spoder listened to this in silence.

I went on: 'If it's recorded in the police file that Dever Antterland was murdered inside a locked room it means some hoaxer has accessed the file and made changes. Perhaps it was meant as a laugh. If the police actually found the room locked with Dever's body inside, it can only mean the room was locked after the crime took place. Or it means they made a mistake and the room wasn't locked at all. Or Dever's body was found somewhere else and the file is wrong.'

'I think the file is genuine,' Spoder said, sounding crestfallen. 'I recognize some of the names of officers who worked on this. In Raba as well as Sekonda. They weren't the sort who made simple mistakes, or who would put false material on file.'

'Well, I don't want to be drawn into this. If you want to go over to Sekonda and see what happened then of course you'll get your usual hourly rate.'

'This locked room was different,' Spoder said. 'Really different.'

'They all are,' I said. 'Every impossible crime is a novelty. It has to be.'

'I think you should see this, sir. The room that was locked was part of a museum, a museum of magic. The magician's apparatus was used in the crime. It's still there.'

16

The Temple of Wonders

I rode pillion on Spoder's motorbike, wearing his spare crash helmet, a size too large, loose on my head and hurting my neck, the strap too tight and chafing beneath my chin. At the last moment I had conscientiously stuffed my laptop into my computer tote, slinging it diagonally across my back, but already I realized that it was going to be a day dominated by Spoder and having to make this sudden journey. He was not going to stop talking long enough for me to do any reading, let alone any work, now or ever. He was talking as we roared down the road following the edge of the forest reserve in the zone beyond my house. He kept swivelling his helmeted head a quarter turn, shouting at me incomprehensibly as we rushed along. I don't know what he was saying.

We soon came to the part of the freeway skirting around the edge of Raba City, the tall shining towers of the renowned financial quarter basking in the hot morning sun. Raba was officially the clearing centre for most transactions and banking investments in this part of the world, but its reach was extending ever more widely. Financial institutions even in Muriseay, largest island in the Dream Archipelago and de facto administrative centre, were now said to be routing transactions in increasing quantities through the Raba fund houses. The Raba bourse had been the focus of share and investment dealing throughout the islands for several decades.

The activities of the finance houses brought incredible wealth and monetary power to the Salay Group, or so it was popularly believed. The reality, as I saw it as a long-term resident of Salay Raba, was that little of the wealth created in the tower zone of polished steel, mirrorglass and aluminium leaked out to the island itself. The more cynical islanders sometimes referred to the place as Robber City.

Many social problems beset Raba. There were beggars in the streets of Raba City and homeless people were found in most of the smaller towns along the south and eastern coasts. Many families lived in poverty. Disaffected minorities, originally transported in for manual work and service jobs, existed in an extensive area of poor housing on the edge of the city. Crime rates were high. Alcoholism and substance abuse were worsening problems for the civic authorities, whose offices, situated within sight of the skyscrapers of the financial district, were permanently underfunded and ill equipped.

On the western coast of the island, on the far side of the forest reserve, was a place called Ocean Domaisne, an immense concentration of neo-vassalage. It extended some fifty kilometres down a reconstructed shoreline largely reclaimed from swamps and tidal basins. This was where the wealthy bankers, brokers, fixers and entrepreneurs lived. In effect gated and managed by commercial security operatives, it was a long strip of luxury hotels, mansions and skyscraper condos, with marinas, sports arenas, casinos, golf courses, private airstrips and retail malls. (To my certain knowledge from the trade there was not a single bookshop anywhere along the strip.) Some of the territory had been extended out into the sea on artificially built islands and peninsulas. The largest of these used as foundations the rubble from the demolition of several centuries-old fishing settlements which formerly worked the coastal shallows, and was constructed in the shape of the thaler sign.

Ordinary residents of Raba knew of these places, these sumptuous resorts and palaces of leisure, but few of us ever went there. I was one such. I had seen photographs and images on television, but I had never yet had direct contact with anyone who was resident.

The freeway at Raba went nowhere near Ocean Domaisne, which was on the coast further to the west, but ran alongside the cluster of towers in the financial district. Spoder speeded up and we were past it within a minute. The airport was not far beyond – the constant movement to and fro of money operatives meant that there were regular shuttle services to the other Salayean islands.

We bought tickets for the first available flight, and an hour later we had landed on Sekonda.

Spoder wanted us to rent another motorcycle, but I insisted on a car. He had no licence to drive a car – I did.

It was several years since I had visited Sekonda. As we drove out of the airport I was looking around with interest. Although there were major industrial towns in the interior of the island large sections of the shoreline had been left undeveloped. Sekonda was famous for its deep-sea fishing and scuba diving. On the eastern promontory, close to where a meeting of two oceanic flows created cross currents, rough water and high waves, there was surf riding and a variety of other beach pursuits.

Over the past century five separate areas of the coastline had been developed as holiday resorts, catering for all. It was possible to find inexpensive camping grounds or pensions close to the sea, but also mid-price hotels, holiday let cottages and houses, as well as more expensive rentals and luxury hotels. In the interior of the island there were several designated nature or wilderness parks. Sekonda was now a popular holiday destination, and in the five coolest months people travelled great distances to stay there.

There was little of interest to see while we were close to the airport, but Spoder directed me to the coastal freeway and I drove towards the holiday town of Corlynne. After thirty-five kilometres we turned off the freeway and began following a narrow road with breathtaking sea, forest and mountain vistas. A blend of flowery scents rushed in through the open car windows. This still being the out-season of intense heat and tropical storms, traffic was light.

Spoder refused to say anything in detail about what we would find when we reached Corlynne. He had only read police reports and old newspaper accounts and wanted to see the place for himself, discovering it at the same time as I did. It hardly silenced him, though. He regaled me with his views on everything else, looking down from time to time at the road map on his lap. I said little, trying to seem interested while in fact relishing the scenery, the mature broadleaf trees of the Sekonda forest, the rocky coastline. I kept glancing at my wristwatch. Spoder had said we could do this trip within the day, but it was already past noon. The occasional signs indicating that Corlynne lay ahead gave no indication of distance. I kept up the speed.

Eventually we started passing small houses built close to the sea. Not long after that we were driving slowly through the centre of the town, which Spoder confirmed was Corlynne. He put aside the map and opened the police file, riffling through the pages.

'We're looking for a place called Bonnzo's Carnival Sideshows,' he said. 'On the other side of the town, but not far. It says here it is open all year round, although out of season some of the rides will not be in use.'

'Bonnzo's Carnival?' I said. 'Are you certain that's right?'

'I'm just following the notes, sir.' He was looking from side to side as we moved away from the main part of the town. Three minutes later, in an area of dunes and scrubland, he pointed forward and past me, indicating an untidy shambles of old-looking carnival rides and sideshows. Although other cars were parked outside it did not look as if it was open. There was a kind of portal with a painted but faded sign overhead, announcing Bonnzo's Holiday Park. Ghastly clown faces had been painted around the words.

I halted the car. 'And this is where Dever Antterland was murdered?'

'It's described in the file as Bonnzo's Carnival Sideshows.' He held it up for me to see. 'It's obviously the same place. Police officers writing up notes at the end of the day don't always get every detail right.'

We left the car and stood on the scorching, sandy ground, regarding the holiday park. Close to the road and to our left were two rows of sideshow shacks. All the ones we could see had their shutters drawn down. Immediately to our right was a large wooden building, painted off-white, with lurid, brightly coloured images of ghosts, vampires, skeletons, witches, scary black cats, and so on. This too was closed, with a green water-proof sheet pulled down across the part of the building where the ticket office and ride entrance were located. There was a carousel, not shrouded or covered, and a race track for electric cars.

Immediately next to the carousel was a burger bar, offering soft drinks, ice creams, hot dogs, pizzas. The lights were on, radiating bright and blinking messages about prices and meal deals. A young woman was standing behind the counter, watching us expectantly.

Beyond, with curving and geometric lines crossing against the sky, stood a traditional wooden rollercoaster. I could see workers on various parts of the track, high on the structure, hammering and drilling. One was in a suspended cradle, painting. At the base of the structure a man in a metal face guard was welding one of the support girders – a brilliant blue flame, a cascade of scattering yellow sparks. Further on, and to each side of the rollercoaster I could see other high rides, some more modern and technological in appearance than the old coaster.

Spoder and I had continued to walk slowly into the park, beneath the arch. Suddenly, loud pop music came on, over-amplified and screeching, and the lights of the carousel flashed into life.

The woman selling burgers and drinks came out of her concession and approached us.

'May I help you gentlemen? We're closed for maintenance right now, but we can start up any of the rides if they are not being worked on.'

'Thank you,' Spoder said, glancing at me as if for a decision. I shrugged. He had the file, he knew what he was looking for and I did not. 'We're interested in the magic museum you have here.'

'Willer's World of Wonders? Sure thing. It's closed at the moment, but I can open it up for you. You do understand there is no magic show these days? When the season begins we're hoping—'

'We'd simply like to see inside.'

'No problem. These days we maintain it as a museum, an exhibition of magical history. You can go in and look around, but it's also a memorial to the magician who built the museum. All his apparatus is still in there. There's a case of his magical props, and several working illusions children can try. I'll have those switched on for you.'

'Did you know the magician?' I said.

'Willer the Wonder? No – he was here before my partner and I took over the place. He died while performing a trick, or so the story goes. There are many stories about him. He left detailed instructions about maintaining what he called his temple of wonders, which we try to follow. As far as we know it is exactly as he left it. The guys service it every year. I'll come with you. We can't let anyone in there without supervision. Willer was adamant about that. His cabinets can trap you inside if you don't know what you're doing.'

'Yes, we'd be grateful if you'd show us around,' I said.

'I have to run the concession,' she said. 'But – are you gentlemen hungry? If you'd like to have lunch now I could close up afterwards and take you down to Willer's.'

One of the guys high on the rollercoaster began noisily banging a wooden slat. The pop record came to an end and another one started immediately.

'Would you like to ride the carousel before you eat?' she said.

'No, thanks.' Spoder and I exchanged a quick look. 'But we'll have something to eat. Thank you.'

She went behind the counter, threw a hidden switch and the lights and music from the carousel instantly died.

Spoder and I took a table under the shade of an awning, perching on unsteady little stools. In a while she brought us burgers with onion rings and salad, a huge plate each of curly fries, iced fizzy drinks in plastic beakers with lids and coloured straws, and afterwards two cups of extremely weak coffee.

'Delicious!'

That was Spoder, not me.

17

Into the Cabinets of Death

She told us her name was Ketty. She and her partner owned and managed the park together. No, neither of them was called Bonnzo – they didn't know where the name came from, but the park had been here for many years and that was what it was always called.

She walked us through the heat of the unshaded aisles between the sideshows, past several children's rides and other food concessions. All closed. There were several larger rides. They were compactly arranged to save space. For instance, built between the main supports of the wooden rollercoaster, which Ketty told us was more than fifty years old and still in working order, was a compact modern mini-coaster, with a steel skeleton and several terrifying twists, turns and sudden plunges. The cars would pass with minimal headroom beneath the wooden trusses of the rollercoaster. Many of the other rides were positioned close to each other, ingeniously taking up a minimum of space.

One of the largest rides was called the Scrambler: mobile cars, circulating on metal tracks, were spun by the turning of the main platform, moving speedily across several gradients. Next to this was a square building, painted red all over. The lintel carried cursive lettering painted in gold: *Willer's World of*

Wonder and Magical Memories! There were three steps up from the ground, a narrow walkway and a solid door.

'We have retained as much as possible of Willer's original scheme,' Ketty said, as we paused beside the door. 'He operated it as a theatre while he was still alive. Inside he had a small auditorium with three rows of seats, and a stage with lights and curtains. We removed the stage so visitors can walk around and look at the exhibits, but the seats are still there. In the season we often arrange with magicians on the island to come here to put on magic shows.' She banged her fist against the door. 'This is Willer's famous unopenable door.'

There was no handle.

Spoder reached past me, and pushed a hand against it. It did not shift. I pushed too, but it seemed pointless to try. It was jammed tight.

'This door is the only way in and out of the building,' Ketty said. 'There are no other exits at all, not even secret ones. It can't be opened from either side.' Then she said, without having seemed to move, or have touched anything: 'The door is now openable.'

It swung freely with a fingertips touch. From the darkness within a long gust of moist air was expelled. It felt hot and humid, even as we stood in the sunlight. The door swung slowly back to the closed position.

'I'll put the ventilators on,' Ketty said. 'There are no windows.'

She threw a switch on the wall beside the door.

I tried the door again with my hand. It opened smoothly. Lights were now on inside the building. Fans could be heard.

Ketty said: 'We'll give it a couple of minutes to cool off. We normally do not allow the public in here unaccompanied. The door is still a problem for us. We have a concealed override outside, which only I and my partner, plus a few members of the staff, know how to use. Willer left explicit instructions that there must be none inside. Although this is not the original door, which at one point was damaged, it was rebuilt exactly to Willer's own design. But the door itself is separate from the switching. Willer devised a clever system – when he was inside the building he had secret switches for both opening and locking the door. Two of them were concealed on the stage, and we found and removed them when the stage was taken down. But we know there are others because Willer's instructions warned against touching them – we've never been able to locate them. Obviously, if the public has access we can't take any risks, which is why we have the override. The visitors can handle and manipulate the illusions on display, but we always warn them never to touch anything else. The other switches must be somewhere inside – the kids love knowing that, and they run around putting their hands on everything they see.'

'Do they ever find them?'

'Not yet. We ransacked the place when we remodelled. This was a secret system designed by Willer. He knew exactly how to hide something like that.'

'Did Mr Willer lock the door on the day he was murdered?'

Ketty looked sharply at Spoder. 'Why do you say he was murdered?'

Spoder held up the file. 'I'm a former police officer, ma'am. Some of my colleagues investigated Willer's death.'

'Does this mean the police are re-opening the case?' Ketty said. 'We should have been warned. We're running a business here.'

'It's nothing like that,' I said quickly. 'We're just here out of interest. I wanted to see the place where it happened.'

'Willer died a decade ago. It's in the past, forgotten. Few people have ever heard about what happened. We don't want to lose business. Most of the people who come here are families.'

'On the other hand, you might get an extra boost,' Spoder said. 'Kids love macabre scenes. Mine certainly did.' This came as a startling surprise. I had no idea Spoder had children. How little we sometimes know of the people we work with! While I was still digesting this thought, he went on: 'We have a professional interest in this. My companion here is Todd Fremde, the novelist, the thriller writer. You possibly know his books? I retired from the police years ago, as I told you.'

'Then what's that file you're holding?' Ketty said. 'Is it something connected with the police? Is it for a book?'

'Some notes I made,' Spoder said. Then he added untruthfully: 'Directions on how to get here from the airport, mostly.'

I said, intending to change the subject: 'What we'd be interested to hear is anything you know about the day he died. Was the park open to the public that day, for example?'

'Are you really a writer? Would I know your books?'

'Look, my books aren't important to this. Please tell me about the day Willer died?'

'There were people here, I believe, but at the time it happened Willer was alone in the museum – the theatre as it was then. It was the end of the day and the park was about to close. I don't know much about it. I wasn't involved in the park at the time – I was still at school ten years ago. Vejo, that's my partner, Vejo and I bought the rights to the park about four years ago. I found out about Willer's death from a few things people said to me.' She indicated the interior of the building. 'Let me just check the atmosphere in there.'

As soon as she was inside, I said to Spoder: 'I didn't know you had children.'

'Yes sir, a boy and a girl.'

'Do they still live with you?'

'No – they're long gone. They're twenty-five now, and left Salay after university. I see them two or three times a year. The boy's on Muriseay, and the girl works on Paneron.'

'They're the same age?'

'Yes.'

'So they are . . . twins?'

'Yes. Fraternal twins, not identical, of course.'

'Of course,' I said. 'Spoder, I'm really glad you told me that.'

'They're the love of my life, sir.'

Ketty appeared at the door, indicating we should enter the building. Spoder walked ahead of me.

Like the exterior of the building, the walls inside were painted a deep red, giving a muted feeling to the place, crypt-like. The lights were against the walls, throwing indirect illumination below. Under most of the lights were the showcases, and some working examples of apparatus.

There was a large glass case with several familiar pieces of magical paraphernalia: opera hats, decks of cards, red and white billiard balls, wands, handkerchiefs, candles, cups, and so on. A plaster clown stood in one corner – when you walked towards him his face creased magically, and horribly, into a broad smile. There were two weights you could not pick up separately, but which became inexplicably lighter when you lifted them together. Inside one long glass case was a display of dozens of books about magic. Some of these were open at pages showing the way tricks could be prepared and performed. One of them was a large, authoritative-looking tome in solid binding. My habit on seeing a book, any book, is if possible to turn to the front pages to see what inscription is there. Ketty was not watching me. This volume had a handwritten dedication: *To my dear son Willer on his sixteenth birthday*. The handwriting was squarish, unremarkable, and there was no signature.

Mounted on the walls above and beside the cases were several posters advertising magicians or magic shows from past decades. There were also several photographs of Willer, Dever Antterland, in the middle of his act or posing for a publicity shot.

I regarded these with interest. I still could not help thinking of him as the certain killer of his twin brother, Lew Antterland. From that point of view his work as a magician, entertaining children and families on holiday, was difficult to reconcile. Before seeing this I suppose I had imagined he retreated into the fairground life as a way of cleverly reinventing himself, hiding away in plain sight. Yet as I wandered around the little museum it struck me with some force that Dever Antterland had devoted much of his life to magic. Two large photographs showed him surrounded by smiling and laughing children – one of them was holding a glass tumbler in which a pencil had been mysteriously thrust through the side. Another picture was of three adults sitting around a baize-covered table, watching with rapt attention as he manipulated coins. One of the coins appeared to be hovering above his hand.

Performance magic takes years of dedication, endless hours of rehearsal. You do not take up magic on a whim: it is a lifetime commitment. What was the powerful change that overtook him, I wondered, that converted Willer into a murderer, that made him take the irreversible step into the dark night of the soul?

Ketty was waiting by the door.

The stage on which Willer performed had been at the rear of the room. All trace of it was gone, but the overhead runners where the curtains or stage lights had hung were still in place.

Two painted wooden or metal cabinets stood close to each other, where the stage had been, with their doors open. There was a third one behind them, slightly larger, set close against the back wall. I walked over and looked at the nearest of them. A showcard on the door said: *Willer's famous vanishing cabinet – see if you can detect the false door.*

I peered inside, reaching in with my hand. All four of the internal walls were painted matt black, and felt solid and un-yielding to the touch. I stepped a little nearer and pressed more firmly, trying to find any weakness, or joint, or part of a wall that felt different from the rest. Before I realized I had found the key, the cabinet wall on the right slid swiftly to one side, mar-ginally narrowing the space inside the cabinet but making extra room in a triangular cavity that had opened up. Any young or slim person could easily be concealed there. From even a short distance away the interior of the cabinet looked exactly as it had before.

The cabinet next to it used a different system for concealing someone. The doors front and back both opened fully, revealing an indisputably vacant space inside. This cabinet was mounted on castors. Photographs showed that the magician could rotate the cabinet for the audience to see through to the other side. He could even walk through it himself to 'prove' that there was nowhere for anyone else to be hidden. But the secret here was not a mechanical device. When both doors were fully open the magician, with perfect timing and a trained assistant, could rotate the apparatus swiftly, while the assistant moved nimbly from the concealment of one open door to the next, ending up inside as the doors were closed, ready for a magical production moments later.

Ketty was standing next to me, observing everything I did.

I indicated the slightly larger cabinet, at the back. Its door was closed.

'May I have a look at this one?' I said.

'I can open it and you can inspect it. But don't touch anything. This one has a self-operating mechanism, which goes suddenly into action. Three years ago a child, brought in by one of the visitors, had an accident. Since then we always have to supervise.'

At that moment the door to the museum opened, admitting a shaft of brilliant sunlight. One of the engineers I had seen earlier was standing there. The welding mask was tipped back above his head.

'Ketty, a big party of visitors have arrived,' he said. 'They would like you to open up the Scrambler and a couple of sideshows.'

She responded immediately.

'I'll be right there, Vejo,' she said, and the welder withdrew. Ketty turned to Spoder and me, looking indecisive. 'I have to go. You ought to wait outside – I shouldn't leave anyone alone in here.'

'We're just looking around,' I said.

'All right. I'll come back shortly. If you want to finish in here, let yourselves out and I'll close the building later.'

She took a key from her pocket, an ordinary key, the sort used to open house doors. She slid it into a recessed lock on the side frame of the third cabinet, and the front screen of the cabinet opened silently. She passed the key to me.

'The important thing to remember is that the front screen of this cabinet will close automatically after three minutes. It's designed to do that, but the hydraulics are powerful. Be careful not to have your hand or anything else in the gap. It's safe only to look. When the screen closes you can open it again as many times as you like with the key.'

Then she hurried away.

Spoder walked across to the door of the building and made sure it could still be opened from inside. I would not have checked that myself, but I was glad he did. He went to stand beneath one of the wall lights and pulled some papers from his file.

'I think I understand how Antterland was killed, sir,' he said. 'There's no mystery about the actual cause of death. His assailant shot him using a semi-automatic pistol, a handgun. The bullet went into his chest, close to his heart, and death would have followed almost immediately, within ten to fifteen seconds. There's a full autopsy report here. The weapon was found: the killer had cleaned off all fingerprints, and left it behind in here when he was eventually released from the building.' He licked his finger and thumb, and pulled another sheet of paper from the file. 'Ballistic evidence established beyond doubt that the bullet had been fired from the gun found in here.'

'It was a simple shooting?' I said. 'You made me think it was more complex than that. And what do you mean, the killer was eventually released?'

'The shooting was the cause of death, but there are extra features which make this murder exceptional. The killer having to be released from a locked room is part of that.'

'So what else haven't you told me?'

'Two matters are unusual. The first is that no body was discovered. The building was locked, the killer was inside, but there was no hint a murder had taken place. The people who were running the park ten years ago discovered the building had self-locked with someone trapped inside. As they were opening up the park the next morning they heard shouting and banging coming from in here. In those days there was no override on the door lock, so it had to be broken down with physical force. They found a man trapped inside. He was distraught. He claimed he was an ordinary visitor who had been accidentally locked inside. He said he had been trapped for several hours, and had gone all night without food or water. The park owners were obviously alarmed that they might be sued by this man, but his main concern appeared to be to leave at once.'

While Spoder was speaking he had to raise his voice. The screech of over-amplified pop music started up again, from close to the museum. There was also a grinding of machinery and metal wheels grating on metal runners. After a moment people started to shout and scream with excitement. I remembered that the Scrambler ride was positioned against the side of the museum.

Coming closer to me and raising his voice, Spoder went on: 'At first no one realized a murder had taken place. The noise of these rides is deafening – even if you were close to this building it would be hard to notice the sound of a shot inside. The Sekonda police eventually realized that this unknown man must have shot Antterland, but they weren't on the scene until a few hours later. Once the staff forced the main door, but long before the police were involved, the killer departed. No one realized what he had done. There is a receipt from a taxi company in the file – it looks as if the park owners were so eager to placate the man that they paid for him to take a cab back to town. Afterwards, people tried to describe him, but their memories were dominated by the fact that he looked wild, untidy and unshaven. When those were factored out he answered to a general description that would fit a hundred thousand other men.'

'So when was Antterland's body discovered?' I asked.

'The notes here say that it was later the same day. It took them all that time to realize that Antterland himself was missing.

'This is the second unusual feature. There were no reports of suspicious activity, no hint of trouble, no dead body, no sign of a weapon lying around, a trapped man who claimed to have been accidentally locked in – who would suspect a murder? But after the man had made his getaway it was soon clear Antterland, Willer the Wonder, was nowhere to be found. Once the police started searching it took another twenty-four hours before they found his body. It was discovered in what they describe as the basement area of the theatre. He had been shot in the chest. They launched a search for the weapon, and it was eventually discovered stuffed inside the cushion of one of the audience seats.'

I said: 'He was found in a basement? Here – in this building?'

The layout of the room was plain: the four walls, a carpeted floor. There was no sign of a staircase, or any other way down.

'Somewhere here. Probably beneath where the stage used to be.' Spoder walked across to where I was standing by the cabinets. 'There must be a secret hatch of some kind.'

First glancing back towards the main door, presumably wary of Ketty returning, he bent low and looked carefully at the base of all three cabinets. He rolled the one on castors a short distance to one side. He tapped the floor hard, listening with his head pressed against the carpet.

As he was doing this the screen door on the cabinet I was standing next to silently closed. It was in the under-lit part of the museum, and it gave me an uneasy feeling that some hidden supernatural power had moved the screen.

'If there's a basement, it must be beneath that cabinet,' Spoder said. 'Open it up again.'

I used the key and the cabinet screen door instantly re-opened.

Spoder said: 'The pathology report says that when he was shot, Willer, as they call him in this report, Willer stumbled backwards. The impact of the bullet alone would have thrust him violently back. There were impact bruises on his head, on one of his arms, on his back. So he crashed into something, or fell heavily. He was shot at close range, from the front. There was evidence of powder burns around the entry point of the bullet. He was in deep shock, on the point of death. So how did he manage to get to the basement, and where is it?'

He moved forward excitedly, shoving past me. He leaned forward into the cabinet, his weight on his hands, gripping each side of the entrance.

'Spoder, be careful! You heard what Ketty said.'

'I'm just looking. If he was thrown or he collapsed back into this cabinet, then there must be some sort of concealed entrance to the basement.'

His voice was muffled, and because of the noise coming from outside I barely heard what he said. He stepped further forward, one foot balancing his weight inside the cabinet. Then he took a second step and was completely inside.

The music from the Scrambler changed abruptly: a heavy rock number began, with a screaming, insistent lead guitar. A singer yelled out vocals. The shouting and whooping of the people enjoying the thrill of the ride increased by a decibel or two. The racket of their fun was barely diminished by the wooden walls of the museum.

I moved back a little, watching what Spoder was doing. I knew the front screen of the cabinet would be closing again soon, but I did not know how to prevent that. All I could do was re-open it once it had closed.

'There's nothing to see here,' he said. I leaned forward to

hear him better. 'I thought there might be a way of triggering the mechanism. Some hidden pedal, or a switch—'

He had turned around, facing away from me. His hands were reaching up towards the top of the cabinet, where there appeared to be some soft material where the wall met the internal ceiling of the cabinet. I saw him pressing against it.

The front of the cabinet closed silently. There was a sudden thud, and I sensed a heavy movement as well. I grabbed the key, thrust it into the lock. The cabinet opened again. In the space of two or three seconds Spoder had disappeared.

In the indirect light at the back of the museum the black-painted inside walls of the cabinet gave away no details. I knelt down and reached forward, groping for some clue as to what had happened. This cabinet was slightly more spacious than the one I had investigated a few minutes earlier, but felt just as solidly, unshakably built.

'Spoder?' I shouted, feeling foolish because I was certain he must be concealed somewhere behind a false, movable wall. 'Where are you?'

I heard a voice, but with the music still throbbing in from outside I couldn't make out what he said.

'Say again!' I shouted.

'Down here, sir!' I heard him gasping. 'It was a trapdoor – I fell through. I've hurt my leg, my ankle. I'm in the dark – let me out!'

He started banging on the base of the cabinet, from below.

'I can't see how to open it!' I said loudly.

'There's no air down here. It's as hot as an oven. I'm having to crouch and I can hardly move my arms.'

'The trapdoor must slide,' I said. 'Try moving it to one side.'

'Which side?'

'Try them all. I will too.' I was still on my knees, at the wrong attitude to exert much force, but pressing and pushing I tried to shift the wooden floor. Or the trap cover, as I had to assume. I felt it move slightly. 'Try that again!' I yelled down to Spoder.

The screen at the front of the cabinet started to close. It had real pressure behind it, the hydraulics irresistible. I scrambled backwards urgently, dreading what would happen if I too was caught in the mechanism. The screen closed.

I searched for the key, suddenly panicking that I might have dropped it irretrievably inside the cabinet. Then thankfully I found it, re-opened the screen.

Spoder's head was surprisingly now visible in the main part of the cabinet. It was all I could see of him. The rest of him was below ground level.

'Please help me out of here, sir!'

He managed to disentangle one of his arms and pushed it up. After a painful struggle he brought up the second one. In the confined space as I leaned into the cabinet it was almost impossible to get a lifting grip on him, but I pulled as I could while Spoder struggled below. He was much heavier than I had imagined, and his constant bellowing of frightened orders at me, and struggling with his elbows and arms, multiplied the problem of trying to hold and lift him.

Finally it was done somehow, and Spoder and I pushed back and away from the cabinet and sprawled together on the hard carpeted floor. One of his bare legs ended up beside me. I saw a smear of something old, brown and powdery, on his skin. When he saw me looking he sat up and brushed it away with a hand. He stood up, favouring his left leg. He rubbed his right ankle.

'So that's where they found Willer's body?' I said. Behind us the cabinet front screen was closing.

The screams from the Scrambler next door had ceased, but the music was still playing at maximum volume. After a few more seconds the grinding of machinery and metal wheels began again and so too did the delighted shrieking of the people.

'When Willer was shot he collapsed back into his cabinet, and his body remained out of sight in what the police called a basement.'

'So it's just a hole, a cavity,' I said.

'A hiding place designed for a vanishing illusion. But using it triggered the lock to the building, which is why the killer was trapped inside.'

Spoder took a few steps experimentally. He limped exaggeratedly at first, but it was clear he had not been seriously hurt.

'I dropped the file, sir,' Spoder said. 'I think it must be down there inside the cavity.'

'Are you going to go back for it?'

'Not ever! I can download the files again if I have to.'

'So leave it there. Let's get out of here.'

The lights were still on inside the museum, but the air conditioning had fallen silent. Spoder and I crossed to the exit. He was limping still.

I worked the door handle, a simple turn. It turned simply – but the door did not open. I pulled it hard. My hands were already wet with perspiration. Spoder elbowed me aside. The door was immovably closed.

'How the devil did that happen?'

'Ketty knows we're in here,' I said. 'She'll come soon.'

'What did you say?'

The endless music, the grinding of the engine and the screams of the riders drowned out our voices.

'Ketty!' I said loudly. 'She knows we're here. She'll be back soon.'

Spoder banged his fist on the thick door. 'Let us out!'

The Scrambler motor slowed, the rolling noise of the wheels quietened. People were laughing and calling to each other, not for now screaming with enjoyable terror. The music continued at full blast. We tried shouting again.

'In here! Ketty! We can't get out!'

'Help! The door's locked!'

The Scrambler started up again. The shrieks were renewed.

Spoder said loudly: 'Look, sir – that must be where the door was forced, after the murder.'

He was pointing at the area of the wall close to the handle and the heavy wooden frame. Although it had been expertly joined and repaired, and painted over, it was just possible to make out the irregularity, a sign of emergency renewal. Spoder was right. The door had been rammed open at some time in the past, forced violently through the frame. Long ago – maybe ten years ago?

'That's a weak area that we could work on . . .?'

I saw that Spoder's face and neck were wet with sweat. My shirt was sticking to me. It was getting harder to breathe. The temperature was rising.

We turned together back to the door, hammering our fists against the door, and the wall next to it.

'We're still in here! The door locked itself! Get us out of here! Help!'

The music played on, unstoppably, deafeningly. The screams went on and on.

'*Help!*'

18

The Alleged Safeguard

What with the various distractions that had been invading my life, since coming back from Dearth I had been lazy about opening physical mail. For many years any message of interest and importance has reached me, in the same way it reaches almost everyone else, through email or the internet. The arrival of envelopes has long been associated with energy bills, credit card offers, reminders about prescriptions, irresistible sales bargains for my household and garden, information about incontinence and impotence cures, and at certain times of year greeting cards.

The morning after I returned, late at night, from the silly incident in the holiday park on Sekonda, I woke up long after my normal time, feeling physically stiff and psychologically regretful. The experience there with Spoder meant that any career I might have been planning as an amateur sleuth was definitively at an end.

I put down some fresh food and water for Barmi. Knowing Jo would be back at some point, and that she would be here for only one day and a night, I tidied up and cleaned the house. After that I took the unexpectedly large heap of envelopes out to the patio, and started opening each one (a precaution against throwing away something I might actually want) before setting it aside for recycling. Somewhere in the pile I found, unexpectedly, a letter.

The envelope was addressed to Dr Todd Fremde. Inside was a letter, a real letter on paper, albeit one that had been clearly computer generated and personalized only by a scribbled pair of initials at the end. It was on the printed letterhead of the Dearth Plaza Hotel.

Dear Dr Todd Fremde,

After your recent stay here it was discovered that you did not surrender the mutability assurance key as issued to every guest, in your case identified to Room No. 627. Because this card contains confidential information, secured and encrypted, we would ask you to return it to us at the earliest possible moment. We are enclosing a prepaid and addressed envelope for your convenience.

If you no longer have the key, would you kindly use the same envelope to inform us of its whereabouts if known, or confirm that it has been lost or destroyed. If it is still in your possession, please do not hand it to anyone else. It must be returned to us. It would be an offence to try to sell it. Please note that it is inert because of password protection, and that none of the software is usable by non-staff members.

We look forward to welcoming you to your next visit.
Yours sincerely
T.I. (or T.J. or T.T. or I.T.)
For the Dearth Plaza Hotel, Dearth City

I searched, but I could not find the promised pre-paid return envelope. I checked the heap of paper destined ultimately for the recycling depot to see if I had thrown it aside by mistake, but it was not there. I put the letter on the recycle pile with everything else.

My priority that morning was to return to the publisher the page proofs I had completed reading. With the recycling of mail finished, I glanced through the proofs one more time, saw nothing else that needed attention, and put them with a short note into a padded envelope. I went immediately to the local mail office and sent them by priority service. They would be a day or two late arriving, but I always suspected that publishers, knowing well the forgetful ways of authors, announced a tighter deadline than was strictly necessary.

Afterwards I took out my notebook and made a few notes about what had happened when Spoder and I went to Sekonda. I was determined not to be any further involved in old murder mysteries, but I have long followed a policy of jotting down odd experiences. Ideas for stories are not always immediately obvious. Something I saw or noted or remembered from that day might be useful eventually.

In the afternoon I opened the computer document containing the first draft of my current novel, and read through it. It had been going well before my trip to Dearth, but with the extra days away from it all I could see now were examples of poor writing, weaknesses in the story and the characters.

I had been concentrating too closely on the creation of a feeling of threat, the background, and the working out of a plot. The characters looked unconvincing to me. I intended it to be a book about the psychological motive for murder, with four lead characters, all with complex and innocent lives, any one of who might turn out to be the killer. But with fewer than a hundred pages written it seemed to me that the outcome was already going to be obvious to the reader. I needed to close in on the book again, concentrate on it, rethink the structure of the plot, lay false clues, re-imagine the characters as well as the circumstances.

I knew I had been distracted not only by being away, but by too much puzzling over the Antterland murders. They were irrelevant to me, as Jo had reminded me.

After several hours of frowning unhappily at what I had done I took the decision to scrap everything and start again. I dreaded having to undertake the extra work, and I disliked the idea of an inevitable delay in delivering the completed book, but I knew it would pay off in the end. I had worked out what I thought would be a better way of tackling the book.

Within a couple of hours I knew I had made the right decision. I was soon working smoothly and, I hoped, well. Then, with about ten pages rewritten, I noticed a coincidence, a fragment of memory. I kept thinking about the short time I had spent on Dearth and the annoying enigma of mutability, the physical changes that were allegedly real at the time they occurred, but forgotten soon afterwards. The essential irrationality of that had always nagged at me.

Then it suddenly struck me that what I was doing to my novel draft was similar to what I knew of mutability.

The original text, the first draft, was forced into changes by my rewriting them. Once I had written them the new version seemed so natural, so organic to the book, that not only were they an improved version, I could no longer remember what my original draft had said. The outer perception of material reality, the inner perception of change without memory – as Frejah had tried to explain it to me.

The result was still only a first draft and would have to be revised before I sent it in as a finished manuscript, but I was confident that even with the extra work the overall delay would be slight. I worked on, encouraged by the thought. Hadn't Frejah said that Salay Raba was an island with incipient mutability? Well, then.

Re-interpreting the phenomenon of mutability in this way, as something I could understand, I began to muse about the possibilities of writing a story about it.

Jo arrived home while this was going on. To break off from work to be with her was something so constant in our relationship that it was ordinary, not an interruption at all. The next day she departed for the long trip to Muriseay, and I continued with the draft.

I worked for a week, enjoying being in the house alone, cooking for myself, looking after the cat, taking my daily swim from the beach across the road from the house, and communicating with Jo by internet every evening. It was the kind of stable, productive existence I most relished. I did not mind being alone – I liked company, I liked solitude. They were pleasures of different aspect.

Spoder telephoned me again. I had not expected to hear from him, and to be frank I was not particularly pleased to do so. He always distracted me. It was the first time we had been in contact since the day we had been finally released by Ketty from the locked magic museum, emerging hot, bothered and soaked in perspiration.

'Sir, did you ever wonder,' he said without preamble, 'what our man Willer did with the money he stole from his brother?'

A few seconds before the telephone rang I had been trying to write a long and probably over-complicated sentence. No problem – it happened all the time. I was realizing, halfway through, that it was too long and over-complicated, but to write it properly I had to finish it. After that I would go back and break it down into two or perhaps three shorter sentences. Then – Spoder.

It took me a few moments to focus on what he was talking about. A scattershot of events, motives and Willer/Waller, baseball bats and locked rooms. I had to pull back from what I was doing. I dredged around in memory for the names that were easier to identify. Lew? The other was called Dever? One killed the other, one of them was known as Willer, the other as Waller. I could not at first remember which. They had presented a fascinating puzzle at the time but they were not real people to me.

I had made notes. There they lay in my notebook, possibly of use one day.

A delaying tactic: 'How is your ankle, Spoder?'

'It turned out it was only a sprain. I took off the bandage yesterday, and the ankle feels sore but usable. But about the money—'

'Can this wait, Spoder? I'm working at the moment. Come over here tomorrow?'

'It was you who knew about the money.' Spoder had no sensitivity to the fact that because I sat around all day staring at a computer monitor I was actually working. He went on in the same rush: 'There was no mention of Lew Antterland's money in the police file, and then five years later Dever was killed. Once again nothing was said or recorded about the money.'

'Maybe money wasn't involved.'

'There must have been a huge sum.'

I reached across to the computer and saved the document I was working on.

'Couldn't it have been spent?' I said. I was at last starting to connect with him. 'Five years went by. Money doesn't last forever if you're determined to spend it.'

'There's been no sign of spending, though,' Spoder said. 'I've been doing some old-fashioned enquiries. Dever, the magician, was running that theatrical show for children, in a rundown amusement park. Not the sort of extravagant lifestyle some of those people in Ocean Domaisne enjoy. You've seen what his place was like. I made a routine search for his will, in case he had written one. In fact he had, and because all wills are published a copy of it can be viewed online, same as everyone else's. According to that he left most of his estate to the amusement place, Bonnzo's Holiday Park. It didn't amount to much.'

'Maybe he made the will before he stole the loot from his brother.'

'No – it was drawn up about a year before he, Dever, was killed. Like his brother, of course, Dever had been born into vassalage, but after he was moved to Salay Hames he was reduced to serfdom. Nothing was changed by becoming a self-employed magician. The Salay seigniory actually places magicians under the category of Mountebank. He lived in a trailer at the back of the park. He owned a car but it was in need of major repairs. He owned the usual stuff people buy for themselves, but nothing wildly extravagant and nothing close to that. He seems to have bought several pieces of magical apparatus. Those cabinets, for instance. I've discovered that large magical apparatus is usually built to order and is expensive, but I suppose the cabinets would be an affordable business investment to a working magician. Dever's biggest asset was the building, the museum. He left that as an entire bequest to the park. Apart from that he owned almost nothing.'

'So he must have done something with Lew's money. How much was it?'

'No way of knowing. Lew died fifteen years ago. The police know zilch about it.'

'So if we assume it was worth stealing, it must have amounted to a lot,' I said.

'Yes. That's what I'm thinking.'

'Could Dever have kept it as cash, and then lived on it?'

'He made enough from his magic shows to cover daily expenses. He didn't need to spend the money he stole. What I discovered is that his actual main source of income was a trust fund. It was paid to him every month by one of the clearing banks on behalf of a financial house in Raba City.'

'Is that where he stashed it?'

'I don't think so. It's a beneficial trust, the sort of thing you can't set up for yourself but has to be funded by someone else. I can tell you it is known as an Anonymous Mutable Beneficial Annuity, or an AMBA. I've tried to find out how he became involved in it, where the money originally came from, but that sort of fund is shrouded in deep secrecy. The payments are made through a protective network of holding companies, handling agencies, offshore fund managers and service regulators. Have you ever heard of an AMBA?'

'No,' I said. 'I know almost nothing about high finance. I'm a writer – I'm a low finance user.'

'Because of the secrecy I've been trying to investigate how they work,' Spoder said. 'How do you join an AMBA, for example? What do they invest their money in? Why are they never advertised? And so on. I called a few banks and was stonewalled. They know nothing, they say, even when I managed to get through to higher levels of management. There's no information about them online, except a few comments on random sites, mostly asking the same questions I was thinking of. The whole point of AMBA funds seems to be that they are surrounded by watertight secrecy and security. No one but the beneficiary knows where the money came from.'

'Any idea what they mean by a mutable annuity?' I said, having noticed yet again the re-surfacing of the word that had recently drifted into my life.

'I think it means something that changes.'

'I think you're right,' I said. 'So how does this affect the murder of Dever Antterland? And for that matter, of Lew?'

'The killer wanted the money, knew it was there. Presumably the killer was in on the secret – perhaps even he was also funded by an AMBA. Maybe even the same one? What's odd is that the money doesn't seem to exist. The cash you say that Dever stole from his brother doesn't show anywhere, and even today, ten years later, there's no sign either that Dever was robbed, or where his and Lew's money might be.'

'Presumably, when Dever was killed the capital invested in the fund went to whoever he left his estate to?'

'No, and that's the key to the problem. The money ceased to exist. The investment died with him.'

Throughout this conversation I was staring at the screen-saver on my computer. The fact that it had appeared was a clue to how long Spoder had been talking to me. I was being drawn into the Antterland murders again. I felt restless, felt my time available for my novel was slipping away. My document with the novel was saved – I shut down the computer.

'What sort of amount are we talking about, Spoder?' I said again. 'Thousands of thalers? Millions?'

'Yesterday I was talking to a former colleague who works in the Serious Fraud department. She said no one with an AMBA has less than millions.'

'This colleague – did she give any idea about how the fund works?'

'She had heard of them, but she said no one in the department had any actual experience of one. She's a cop. She wasn't stonewalling me.'

I was tiring of the conversation, becoming irrationally and perhaps unfairly irritated by Spoder's continued interest in a subject that, after all, I had started him on.

'So where does this leave us?' I said.

'I think that if we could trace whoever killed Dever, that would lead us—'

'Spoder, I think we should drop it.'

'Yes, sir. But if you don't object I'm going to follow it up a little longer. I think we are uncovering something really big.'

After Spoder hung up I stared at the dark computer monitor, then rebooted.

I worked hard on my novel for another five days, and by intensive redrafting I soon reached the same part of the story I had been writing before I went to Dearth. I had completed a roughly equal number of revised pages, but the content of the book was now so different that there was hardly any equivalence. Mutability of literature turned out to be an effective spur to rewriting. I was satisfied the four main characters were fleshed out. They all knew of each other but their lives remained separate. There was a looming sense of danger, but it was not focused individually on any one of the four.

Although I had already mentally picked out who my murderer was eventually to be, exposed climactically in the final pages of the novel, their tracks were carefully blurred with those of the other three.

One of those might or might not turn out to be the victim – I had yet to decide.

Unexpectedly, I felt myself easing off the novel again. Once I was through the intensive period of recovery and rewriting, my afternoons relaxing on the patio deck outside my study gradually grew longer. I watched more TV in the evenings. I still kept up a daily output of new pages but I knew I was cruising, not driving hard.

One afternoon, as I passed through the bedroom in search of a book, I noticed the key card I had inadvertently kept when I left the hotel in Dearth City. It was on the bedside table, partly covered by the base of my reading lamp. That's where I had put it earlier when emptying my pockets. I knew the hotel wanted it back. I kept meaning to look up the address and return it. I had seen the card every day, but had never got around to doing the necessary search. It felt low on my priorities.

I picked up the card, intending to do something with it at last, but as I held it and turned it over in my fingers I saw something I had not noticed before.

The top of the card, the laminated side, was familiar: it had a computer chip embedded in the centre, slightly towards one end. This presumably was what was read by the key mechanism in the hotel door. An arrow lightly engraved in the shiny white surface indicated the direction in which the card should be pressed into the slot.

But there was a second chip, or several more, buried on the underside of the card. These were less prominent, nano chips, visible as a tiny thin strip of serrated metal bonded into the plastic. The strip was less than a centimetre long.

I took the card to my study, where I discovered two new emails had recently arrived. I tossed the card on the desk while I read the messages. I replied to one of them, then picked up the card again.

My desktop computer, which I had purchased the previous year, had a card reader built into it. Never having found a need for it I had never investigated it. The longest slot was designed to take a card of five and a half centimetres, the standard width of debit and credit cards. Out of idle interest I took the hotel card and pressed it into the reader.

Nothing happened for a few seconds, but the signal light for the solid state disc drive indicated it was in use.

The screen changed to a pleasant pale blue, with the message: *Enter preferred language*. The first choice was *Archipelagian Demotic*. I clicked on it.

Next: *Enter your Social Level*.

I frowned, made a growling noise, rapped my fingers on the desk. I was tempted to pull the card out of the reader then and there. This was the enquiry I was habitually unwilling to answer. Who needs to know that, and why? What difference does it make to any damned software program? It was one of those intermittent reminders of the archaic and undemocratic social system which ruled our lives, and which most people ignored.

I pressed Return, to see if I could bypass the query. It returned.

There was a list of 'social level' options, the twelve familiar ones that allegedly defined the hierarchy of the Archipelagian society:

Serf, Citizen Serf, Villein, Squire, Vassal, Corvée Provider, Cartage Provider, Demesne Landed, Knight, Manorial Landed, Baron, Seignior.

In the anonymity of my office, and still grumbling, I was briefly tempted to pick one of the higher levels. I let the highlight bar hover over *Manorial Landed*, curious to find out what if any privileges would be given to those of such an elevated position. But then years of what I grudgingly admit must have been social conditioning kicked back in, and I clicked on *Citizen Serf*.

I knew my place. I never gave it a moment's thought, but I clearly knew what I was and where I was ranked. Forever a citizen serf! A writer, a humble scribe!

Another screen appeared. *Enter Password*.

This was the moment when, with hindsight, I should have ejected the card from the reader and rebooted the computer. Getting beyond a password was always an irritant, even though in practice most corporate passwords are banal and simple to guess. That evening it merely added to the aggravation and annoyance.

Staring at the screen I typed: *plaza*

The password was demanded a second time. I typed *plazahotel*

The password was demanded a third time. I typed *dearthplaza*

I was in.

Enter numerical location within 'dearthplaza'. After a moment's wondering, then some thinking, I typed my former room number: *627*

Now I was really in. The screen cleared to be replaced by the same pale blue, this time without message and without horizon. It was tempting to stare at it, imagine being drawn down into its limitless expanse.

A new message appeared. It said: *Installing temporary files. Do not remove the source*. My hard disc signal light began flickering at great speed.

Sense and computer experience finally returned to me in force. With a feeling of mild panic I jerked forward in my seat and jabbed anxiously at the eject button on the card reader. The card popped out.

The screen instantly said: *Replace source immediately. Registry files have been overwritten.*

I sat and stared at the monitor, indecision sweeping through me. What would happen now, if I switched off or rebooted? Alternatively, what would the software do if I let it continue?

I had been using computers for years and profoundly respected the rule that one should never run unknown or unverified software. This time I had blithely ignored that. The risk of viral infection was real. But then – I had state of the art antivirus software installed, and that worked reliably every day, neutralizing threats and calmly reporting its mysterious effectiveness of transferring malware into quarantine, or permanent oblivion.

I was curious about the software contained in the card – the hotel was a responsibly run business, part of a large chain of hotels, and two or three weeks after my one-night stay I was still wondering about what mistakes I had inadvertently made with this card. Wondering, but not obsessively so.

On the whole, I judged it safer to reboot.

Then the program message changed again. It was an identical warning about registry files, but now the words were displayed in a larger typeface, bright red, flashing urgently. *Replace source immediately.*

I pushed the card back into the slot. Installation of whatever it was resumed.

Half an hour went by. Messages appeared at intervals, informing or reassuring me that unexplained actions had been successfully completed, that old and obsolete files had been safely removed. It did not say which ones they were.

A narrow green bar at the bottom of the monitor screen was crawling with glacial sloth from left to right. It had a percentage sign above it. It slowly reached 50 per cent.

I went to the kitchen and put on a new pot of coffee. By the time the green bar showed 70 per cent I had finished drinking a second mug of coffee. I went to the toilet. I fretted with papers lying untidily on my desk. I walked around the garden. At 75 per cent it was seeming to slow. I went down to the beach and for a while watched the placid waves breaking against the shingle – the day was at last growing a little cooler. At intervals I returned to my study, hoping to find that it was over, but after the bar passed 85 per cent everything seemed to slow down even more. My hard disc continued to read or accept installation at high speed. Old files were still being deleted.

Finally, 100 per cent was achieved.

The monitor image returned to the pale blue screen, but my hard disc continued to run. I was tempted yet again to eject the card, reboot, hope for the best, but the instancy of the warning messages made me wary.

A new message appeared: *Enter your location.*

A pulldown menu was alongside, listing, as I quickly discovered, every island group in the Dream Archipelago. I scrolled down, fascinated to see this lexicon of the islands. I was astonished by the number of island groups whose names and therefore locations were unknown to me – I was surprised anyway by the sheer number of them. I press PgDn at least ten times, and I was still looking at island names that began with the letter 'A'. The list did not even include the many large islands, like Dearth, which stood alone in the sea. (Solus islands had a separate sub-menu, selectable at the top of the list.) The vastness of the Archipelago was something everyone was constantly aware of, but to see this listing of names was daunting and impressive.

I scrolled down to 'Salay Group' and clicked on it. The five inhabited Salayean islands were then listed. I clicked on 'Raba, the fourth'.

What is your specific area of interest on Salay Group: Raba, the fourth?

The choices presented below were, to say the least, numerous. There were several main headings, the first of which, unsurprisingly in view of the principal activity on Raba, was *Financial Services*. It was pre-checked with a boxed tick.

But there were many more: *Tourism, Retail Trade, Air Travel, Police, Arts, Social Services, Waste Disposal, Medicine, Building and Design, Topography, Hotels* – dozens more, each of which, after a single click, produced a new list of subsidiary 'specific areas of interest'.

As an experiment I clicked on *Arts*, then on *Literature and Books*, then on *Fiction*, then on *Novels*, then on *Commercial Novels*, then on *Writers*, then on *Detective Thrillers* . . . but suddenly some instinct made me pull back. This was going to be about me!

The software was obviously more than a mere database and I was unsure what it was intended to do. The sense of being selected as an individual target, in person, made me distinctly nervous. I was quite possibly the only writer of commercial detective thrillers on Salay Raba, the fourth. I had never heard of another, but I supposed it was possible there would be others. This would be one way of finding out?

But the last thing I wanted was to be personally identified.

I hit the *Return to Main Menu* option.

The fact was that I was uninterested in all the other options.

If you have spent most of your adult life reading and writing books, and using social media about books, and following book bloggers, and reading literary magazines, and finding emails from people who are interested in the same books as yourself, and if you write the occasional review of other writers' books, and if you have a circle of friends and colleagues also deeply involved with books in particular, and the arts in general, you end up with a fairly restricted but focused set of interests. It is not a position of superiority over others, but it does give you the point of view of the specialist.

Writers become interested in a hundred other unrelated subjects, but in an incidental, distant, practical way. They find out about things so they can put them in the next book, or at least hint that such knowledge is in the background of that book. Literature remains the centre of gravity.

Some non-writers might consider this to be an élitist attitude, but I think otherwise. It is the life I have always known and have become used to. I have been writing books for nearly twenty years, and for sixteen of those years I have lived contentedly with and worked alongside Jo Delson, herself a specialist of a similar kind.

I could not care less about Building and Design, Social Services, Retail Trade. Least of all about Financial Services, which as far as I was concerned might exist on another planet in another universe, and the people who prospered from it were alien to everything I knew or loved.

I was still mildly irritated by the software, by my running it, by what it seemed to imply.

I clicked on *Financial Services*.

The monitor showed the pale blue screen again, and the message: *Installing Financial Services Protocols for Salay Group: Raba, the fourth*. A new green bar began its slow transit across the bottom of the screen.

When it reached 5 per cent I left the study and went to the kitchen to prepare my evening meal. It was showing 32 per cent by the time I had finished eating. I watched the TV news, then a double episode of a crime series: 81 per cent. I used my cellphone to contact Jo, and we had a long conversation: 97 per cent.

At 100 per cent a new message appeared: *Mutability safeguards confirmed for Financial Services Salay Group: Raba, the fourth.*

Do you require regular updates? [y/n]

I clicked on No, ejected the card, rebooted the computer, read a backlog of emails and messages, dealt with those I thought should be dealt with, switched everything off, pushed the cat off my lap (but gently), and finally went to bed.

In the morning when I turned on the computer I discovered that a new software icon had appeared on my desktop: *Mutability Safeguard v.2.4.* The icon itself had been cleverly designed to suggest a mountain covered in snow that was trembling.

I selected it, deleted it. The icon disappeared.

When I went to the folder containing the documents of my new novel everything was untouched. The archive copies of my earlier novels were safe. Back copies of emails sent and received were the same as before. All the other work I had looked at recently, including my bank records and publishing contracts, seemed unaffected. I checked several different documents to be sure. I used the antivirus program to deep scan the computer. All was OK.

I went back to work.

19

The Journeying Boat

Towards the end of the week I needed to go into the local town to buy groceries and the other weekly requirements. The supermarket was not crowded and the shelves were as usual well stocked. With Jo away I had decided to try cooking some different dishes. At my last birthday she had given me a new cookbook, and I thought I would practise some of the recipes.

At the checkout I handed over a credit card, but the clerk could not make the electronic till interface read it. He asked if I had another card, so I passed him my bank debit card. This read normally. The clerk said they had been struggling all day with an intermittent hardware fault. Some customers had been obliged to withdraw cash from the ATM outside the building.

I was actually low on cash myself, so after I had put the groceries into my car I used the ATM. A message appeared on the monitor, saying that no cash was available.

I left the car in the parking lot and walked across the road to where there was a branch of a bank I sometimes used. It had a cash machine outside. It accepted my card, but would not read my ID number. I tried several times. I went inside the bank and withdrew cash from the teller behind the counter. She told me a number of customers had reported problems, but the cash machines were not operated by the bank. The company had been informed of the problem, and they had promised to fix it before the next day.

I stopped at a filling station to refuel the car. When I came to pay my credit card was accepted at the first attempt. I drove home.

While I was unpacking the groceries I turned on the small TV on the counter, and discovered a newsflash in progress. A troopship had run into difficulties in shallow waters close to the island of Fellenstel. The ship was aground and had developed a list, but so far there were no reports of casualties. The TV reporter said that there were believed to be more than two thousand young conscript soldiers aboard. Helicopter shots of the ship showed no one moving around on the visible parts of the vessel, and the lifeboats were still held high in station. There were several tugs and a salvage ship in the vicinity. The marine authorities were hoping to refloat the ship on the next high tide, although there were signs that the hull had been damaged. An amount of fuel oil had been spilled. The seigniory of Fellenstel was furiously demanding compensation from the Republic of Glaund, under whose flag the ship was sailing.

The TV channel returned to the programme it had been showing. I switched it off.

The passage of troopships through the shallow waters of the Archipelago was a constant cause of anger and concern among the islands. The mere presence of a military vessel was an outrage against the Covenant of Neutrality, the treaty which declared the whole of the Archipelago a neutral zone. Every inhabited island and island group supported and defended the Covenant.

The two warring countries on the vast northern continent, the Glaund Republic and Faiandland, were no respecters of

Archipelagian law. They transported their conscript armies to the south, where the war was being fought out on Sudmaieure, the unpopulated polar continent. Their war had been in progress for more than a century, in cruel and freezing conditions for the troops, with no apparent end in sight. Some of the troops were taken to war by air, but most of the unfortunate young people were crammed into the closed grey ships. The troopships were often too large for many of the channels between the islands.

Ordinary islanders, like me, felt unable to change or influence the situation in any way. For much of the time we lived our lives unaffected by it. Of course, there were protest movements, and I supported a relatively effective group on Raba. Once a year I would take part in a peaceful demonstration in the centre of Raba City. We never seemed to change anything, but it always felt better than doing nothing.

The only way we islanders could have a practical influence on the conduct of the war was in the matter of deserters. This was a subject of deep island pride.

A constant trickle of young people managed to get away from the icy theatres of war. They somehow eluded the military authorities and escaped by boat to the nearest islands in the southern Archipelago. They inevitably landed on one of about twenty islands adjacent to the war zone – the fighting was confined to a particular plateau on the northern coast of the continent, an immense and hellish plain of ice, frozen snow and broken rock.

These islands were in the sea facing the zone. They therefore received most of the deserters, who soon discovered three salient matters. Firstly, that they were not the only ones who had made the dangerous journey, and many others had attempted the escape before them. That the people who lived on all those islands were expert in sheltering and hiding the young conscripts who turned up from the chilly sea. And that well armed escouades of military police were also waiting, ready to capture them and return them to their units. The presence of the escouades on these islands was itself an outrageous breach of the Covenant.

The twenty islands of the south were considered heroic by the rest of the Dream Archipelago, and known informally as the Underground Islands.

The people of the Underground Islands had developed many ways of deceiving and eluding the military police. Most of the deserters were safely smuggled to other islands, further to the north and therefore more beyond the reach of authority. This was a process known as shelteration, a defiant and proud island tradition. Most islands had their own shelterate laws, differing in detail according to the nature of each island, but essentially the same.

Once free to travel, if at constant risk of discovery, some of the young deserters headed for their home countries. Islanders gave all the help possible, but expressed no opinion on this, nor offered advice, because they knew that even if they should reach home the young people would face arrest and imprisonment if and when caught.

The journey home was an unavoidably long and arduous one, crossing from one island to the next, necessarily passing through the unrelenting heat of the tropics. The majority of the deserters eventually lost the homeward urge. Most found an island where they felt particularly at home, settled into the community, began adopting their outlook and relishing the unaggressive ways of the islanders.

All islands had what were known as havenic laws and practices. These gave permanent refuge to the former deserters, with financial and practical help for those who wanted to stay, and who in time became islanders too.

Every troopship incident, and there were several every year, was a subject of immediate and intense local interest. Many outcomes were possible.

This latest accident was little different from most of the others, although the fact that the ship had been damaged and the conscripts were trapped below decks gave it an extra edge of nervy concern.

One general outcome that everyone dreaded was that should this Glaundian ship capsize or sink, or become permanently trapped in the Fellenstel shallows, she would be a major environmental hazard. Fellenstel was blessed with a coast and reefs renowned as nature and marine reserves. The disaster would also precipitate an urgent rescue attempt to save everyone on board. Releasing the young conscripts trapped below decks was a priority. It was why a hospital ship was hastening to Fellenstel, why swarms of Archipelagian rescue helicopters were in the air or on standby, why anti-pollution booms were already being laid around the area of the ship, why more salvage teams were on their way.

It was also why the ugly grey ship, if refloated, would present both a triumph and a failure: the former because lives would be saved, the latter because in everyone's mind was the need to get those young people off the ship.

I worked through the afternoon, but put on the early evening news programme, to catch up. The stranded troopship was the main story, but there had been no real change in the problem. Salvage crews were still trying to right her.

Later, the programme shifted to the local TV station, for Salayean news. Here the main news was the announcement of unexpectedly poor financial results from Raba's largest manufacturing and sales employer, a company trading online as RabaHome.com, a simple name that covered an immense network of factories, retail outlets and internet services. Although it was still for the moment trading normally, Raba Home Supplies had uncovered enormous and unexplained write-offs, creating a problem of insurmountable debt. The value of the shares had collapsed, and there were fears that the company might be taken over, or closed down entirely. Thousands of jobs were at risk.

I switched channels to a TV murder drama series I was following.

Spoder called me on the landline.

'Sir, there's a guy called Jackson or Jackerson who is trying to locate you.'

'Never heard of him. What did you say his name was?'

'He only said it once and I didn't really catch it. I think it was Jackson.'

'Would it be Jeksid?' I said.

'That sounds right.'

'Is he a cop?'

'He didn't say. I haven't met him – all this was on the phone. He didn't talk like a cop.'

'Do you know what he was after?'

'He wants your address,' Spoder said. 'Or failing that your landline number, or failing that your cellphone number. Your email would do.'

'No it would not. You haven't given him any of those?'

'Of course not.'

'Thanks, Spoder. Is he in contact with you now?'

'He said he would call again tomorrow.'

★

I had no idea what Serjeant Enver Jeksid would want with me, nor why he had chosen to get to me through Spoder. I was once again preoccupied by the news about the troopship stranded in the shallows off Fellenstel.

The vessel remained in peril. Although the emergency crews had managed to refloat and right her, the ship was being prevented from sailing away. The damage to the hull was being assessed by teams of divers. They reported that some repairs had already been carried out by internal patching, presumably by the crew. No more fuel oil was escaping into the sea. There was no information about the young conscripts still confined below decks.

The local news was also gripping, if for different reasons. The shortfall in the finances of RabaHome.com was now reckoned to be in the millions of thalers, the result of fraud. This had led to the consequent failure of their largest creditor, a major bank based in the financial sector of Raba City but with connections and influence all over the world. It happened to be the holding company of the small branch I had visited the day before, where I obtained cash.

Later in the afternoon, out of curiosity, I drove across to the area. There was a huge crowd of people outside the building, which was now closed and shuttered. Security guards were holding back the anxious throng. Although I often used that local bank for small transactions, my own main account was elsewhere.

In the distance, I could glimpse the silvery towers of the Raba financial district, rising above the trees, bathed in the sun, standing as if untouched by events, unexcited, unruffled.

As soon as I was back at my desk I checked online. My bank was unaffected by the collapse of RabaHome.com, and had issued a statement to the effect that it had adequate reserves to meet all its liabilities. To me, always a sceptic about utterances from large organizations, this sounded concerning. I noticed that the price of their shares had taken a slide, but to no greater extent than any of the other banks that day.

The next day came the news that the largest loan provider on Raba, which was mortgagee for more than two million homes on the island, had called in the administrators following a drastic reduction in their remaining loan capital.

Jo and I had managed to pay off our own mortgage two years earlier, so once again I was not directly affected by this disturbing news. However, house prices all over the island, as well as on the two Salayean islands closest to Raba, were predicted to fall sharply.

There was a distinctly silver lining to this cloud of gloom. I followed the news with a deep if guilty pleasure.

Properties in Ocean Domaisne, where most of the bankers, brokers and hedge fund managers lived, were said to have halved in value overnight. These expensive properties within the coastal gated community had famously been developed as a commercial enterprise. They were outside the rules and traditions of the feudal system, so were bought and sold freely and profitably on what was described as the open market. However, they also lacked the benign protection of manorial fiefdom, and so were utterly vulnerable to the whims of capitalism. There was no safety net from the seigniory, or from anyone else. They prospered alone, now they impoverished themselves alone.

The financial situation was looking bad in general. I listened closely to the news several times a day.

For now I felt relatively unaffected by the financial collapse. Jo and I discussed it nervously online every evening. We were cautious savers and investors. We had never actually owned much of value, so we habitually invested whatever spare money we had in fringe banks and small savings accounts. Most of these were linked to environmental schemes or projects. They did not pay much in interest or dividends so they were unattractive to people with real money. We had always assumed that in the event of some financial crash, if any of these savings were swept away our losses would not be great. And some of the places would probably benefit from their obscurity and manage to survive.

When the capitalists suffer, everyone else is affected to some extent. In my part of the island it soon became impossible to use plastic money. Cash was demanded everywhere. But even that meant driving around to find a bank that was still open and trading. There was always a long wait. Now there was a charge for withdrawing cash. Prices in shops were rising.

A spokesperson for the group that represented banking executives went on TV one evening. She claimed that the banks' IT systems had been hacked. Not only was data missing, vast sums of money, in transit between transactions, had disappeared. Their IT experts were working urgently on the problem, and it was expected everything would be corrected. Normality would return soon.

This supposedly reassuring message, or others just like it, was repeated every day. The financial chaos continued, worsening all the time.

I was working on my new novel.

'He called me again,' Spoder said, when he called me again.

'Jeksid? What did he say this time?'

'He wants to meet you, and get some answers.'

'Answers? From me?'

'That's what he said.'

'I've been wondering,' I said. 'If he's trying to make contact with me, why is he calling you?'

'I can explain that. He contacted Police HQ in Ewwel, the first. They know of my links with you, and so they passed him on to one of the station houses here on Raba.'

'You've never even been to Ewwel,' I said. 'Not as far as I know.'

'I was there briefly as a young man, sir.'

'I hardly know it. I've only ever passed through when changing planes. So how would they know about our so-called links?'

'Maybe someone there has read your books? You always print an acknowledgement. Anyway, I still have contacts. As you know.'

As I knew, perhaps, but not fully. Spoder covered his remaining lines of contact to the serving police with lack of detail. I assumed it was deliberate. I had worked with him on and off for several years and still felt I hardly knew him. I wasn't even sure where he lived, although he had once said it was in an apartment in an unfashionable part of Raba City.

He seemed able to access files and other intelligence remarkably quickly, almost as if he was there in the office and could download them, or walk across to a filing cabinet and pull out old papers. It made me wonder, often, how fully retired he really was. It was a reminder of Frejah Harsent's ambiguous working relationship with her force. Did all cops semi-retire?

As for Spoder, surely the police would have internal procedures to guard against the kind of enquiries that from time to time interested me? Because Spoder usually came up with the material I wanted I took advantage, and never asked questions. He was useful to me.

Writers lead quiet, unobjectionable lives, but on some subjects we are ruthless.

Spoder did not seem to behave like a cop – but then, how did cops normally behave? I had never been in the police, nor ever had any job like it. Being a police officer is just a job, but what does an ordinary copper think or believe when not at work? My guess is as good as anyone's. Writers make things up, we are professional deceivers. What we do not know, or can plausibly invent, we try to find out. Mostly we look in other books, we go to libraries, we browse the internet, and when we still can't find what we are looking for we ask someone like Spoder. We guess at the rest.

Anyway, novels are a form of entertainment. They are not documentaries.

'So this Jeksid,' I said. 'How was it left? Did he give you a contact number, or an address? Is he going to try again?'

'I could offer to meet him myself. He suggested that.'

'No – don't do that!' I said at once. The thought of Spoder acting as some kind of spokesman for me was alarming. Who knows what he might say, or inadvertently reveal?

'Then, if you did agree to meet him I could arrange to be there at the same time. Keep an eye on him, if you like. I thought he sounded a bit menacing.'

'You didn't tell me that before.'

'It was a sort of feeling I had. He said things that made me think he might be another cop after all, but he denied that.'

'He is a cop,' I said. 'A Dearth cop. Did he deny anything else?'

'He said he didn't want to hurt you.'

Three days after Spoder's call I heard on the news that the money missing from the accounts of RabaHome.com had been discovered. Officials from Raba Home Supplies, embarrassed and apologetic, blamed the omission on an accountancy error.

There was no explanation for this, but it was important news that the company was no longer in danger, and that the jobs of more than four thousand five hundred employees were safe. The head of the accounts department had been fired, and an enquiry was being set up.

The financial gurus were now certain that the unified computer system used in the Raba financial district had been targeted by a hacker, or by hackers. The hacker was believed to be based somewhere on Raba, or on another near island, but even the top software experts, who had flown in from all parts of the Archipelago, could not yet be sure.

That was unlikely to be the end of it, because the catastrophic collapse in the company's share price led to quick profits of millions of thalers for market speculators, who had taken out put options. Had these unknown, silent operators, gambling on a sudden price collapse, been given advance warning of what was about to happen?

Nor was it the end of the matter in other ways. The bank that went bankrupt remained bankrupt. Two more major financial houses had fallen deeply into the red – one that day, one the day before. Jobs were being lost, small companies as well as large ones were sliding into insolvency.

Meanwhile, credit was unavailable to citizen serfs like me. We paid in cash, but inflationary pressures were making cash worth less and less. The banks where cash could be withdrawn were harder to find every day.

I was for the time being relaxed about the state of the financial woes suddenly paralysing my island. Over the years I have discovered, by experience, that writers like me are relatively untroubled by the ups and downs of the wider economy. Of course we are victims of inflation. Sometimes, as now, we have to pay cash when cash is hard to come by. We suffer if interest rates are set too high or they sink too low. We see our pension savings devalued. Mortgage rates are too steep, and when they are not a mortgage is harder to obtain. In all of these we suffer the same as anyone else.

Equally, we do not necessarily benefit when things are going well. Twice during my writing career I have suffered serious downturns in my literary fortunes. These were brought about by titles going out of print, by sales of translated editions not materializing, overall by poor sales figures. Some of my books were markedly less successful than others. Both periods brought me hardship. I had to borrow money, Jo and I tightened our belts, we abandoned various plans for trips or holidays, we put off carrying out repairs to the house.

This is an illustration, not a hard luck story. Both of these personal downturns occurred at times when the general economy was said by seigniory market analysts to be booming. Inflation was under control, unemployment was low, house prices were rising, expensive holidays were being enjoyed by almost everyone else.

The difference is that in economic terms books are slow moving. This acts as an informal buffer against money-market madness.

For example: I started the novel I am writing now about three months ago, and it will take a few more weeks or months to finish. There will be a delay while the publisher decides whether or not to bring it out, but assuming all goes well the publisher will pay the usual small advance and eventually set a date. That is likely to be over a year and a half later. In short, the manuscript I'm working on now will not be published and on sale in bookstores until about two years after I began it. Any royalty income arising from the book will not reach me until about a year after it is published. The book trade rewards its authors slowly.

It is not of course my only book. The novel whose proofs I have recently read and returned was mostly written last year. It will be published early next year. Income from that will follow several months later.

I have a novel out at the moment, on sale in bookshops. Assuming the shops stay in business and ordinary people spend their meagre cash allocation on some copies (not a likelihood at the moment, I have to admit), I will eventually receive an income from it. That book was completed more than two years ago.

The slow production methods, and the sometimes unpredictable sales, mysteriously accounted for, therefore have a spreading effect. The novel of mine currently on sale in the shops is likely to suffer, but the next one might be launched into a more expansionary economy. The one after that – who knows? Things could be better, they might be worse. They have been both for me in the past. This does not mean I can be complacent.

The publisher, like the bookseller, might be forced out of business by the financial crash. That would be unquestionably tough on me, and on a lot of other writers too. But nothing like as tough as for those four and a half thousand RabaHome.com employees, or the tellers and ordinary staff who worked for the banks now bankrupt, who face the possibility of finding themselves suddenly and entirely without an income.

I was thinking about money, something I usually tried to avoid doing. But it reminded me that the University of Dearth Historical and Literary Society still had not refunded my expenses on that trip. Nor had they paid my fee.

I sent an email reminder to Professor Wendow, with copies to his assistant in the Revisionist History department, and the controller of the finance department.

That's something else writers have to do: beg for the money that someone else has neglected to send.

Meanwhile, the news from Fellenstel was good and bad.

The stricken ship had been patched up, then examined by marine experts. She was cleared to continue her voyage as far as the destination port named on the manifest: a military base on the coast of Sudmaieure. The ship had to be fully repaired and re-examined before she would be allowed to re-enter Archipelagian waters. Details of how this stipulation might be forced on a country fighting a war were not spelled out.

The darker news was that the young conscripts had been held below decks throughout the crisis, and were still confined in the crowded quarters as the ship sailed away. There was no information about their physical or mental condition after the ordeal. I could barely think about what they must be suffering.

The small armada of rescue tugs and salvage ships dispersed. Two of the larger tugs shadowed the troopship at a distance.

More than a week went by and I still had no response from Professor Wendow. I sent a second email pointing out that he had promised a prompt refund of my expenses. I added that to break a promise was unprofessional and would likely lead to stronger action from me. I attached copies of all my receipts, also his letter in which he had made the promise and offered the honorarium.

This is the second level of escalating reminders sent to re-calcitrant payers. Here the unpaid writer has thrown aside the begging bowl – now there are dark hints of connections with footpads and muggers. We all know that threats are a waste of time: what could I do in reality to coerce him? The money would only be sent as and when it suited the university finance department, but for the time being a bit of bullying had its own quiet satisfaction.

I received an automated reply within about fifteen seconds, one I probably deserved: Professor Wendow was on a twelve-month sabbatical and regretted he was not able to reply to emails in person. All enquiries should be sent to his assistant.

I had already sent copies to her or him: I knew only a surname and an initial.

Spoder telephoned me again.

'Sir, I wondered if you would put me in touch with an editor at your publisher?'

'My *publisher*?'

'Well, not necessarily yours. One of the others, if you prefer. You must know most of them – could you suggest some names?'

'Why on earth do you need to contact a publisher?'

Spoder was briefly silent.

'I've been doing a bit of writing,' he said in a moment. 'Nothing like yours, but I thought I might try to get it published. I've seen how you do it, how you take some of the things I tell you and turn them into a book. It looks so straightforward. I thought I could try that. Just an idea. Then I could find out if what I've written is any good or not. Maybe you could give me some advice?'

'What kind of thing is it? Are you writing a novel?'

'It's a sort of memoir. About my life before I joined the force.'

Images of unwonted autobiographical literary activity briefly danced through my mind. Hitherto unsuspected. What else was I likely to learn about Spoder?

'Can you tell me anything more about this?' I said.

'Next time we meet, sir.'

'I don't want to put you off. But you know, it takes many years to establish yourself as a writer. A lot of hard graft is necessary.'

'That's all right.' Spoder's voice was suddenly less assertive than normal, almost timid. He was backing away, sounding as if he wished he had not called. 'I have to go now.'

I realized I had been insensitive. I should have been more supportive.

'Let me read some of it soon?' I said.

'Yes, sir. If it's not too much trouble. Thank you.'

Before he could hang up I said: 'Did you ever hear again from the person you told me about? The man called Jeksid?'

'No, I didn't.'

I felt sorry and guilty after the call. Spoder was a good man and I believe he was hurt by my reaction. I regretted what I had said, and what I had not.

20

Engine of Destruction

I heard the car before I saw it. I would never have seen it anyway because the road runs at a lower level than our garden and was screened off behind the foliage of the trees. The sound of its powerful engine was distinctive, full of reminders. The smell of engine fumes started drifting towards me on the sea breeze almost at once.

I tried to ignore it. Was it Frejah Harsent? But she was half a world away. If it was her, how did she get her car across from Dearth? She could only have come by ship. Cars like hers were not a common sight on Raba outside the Ocean Domaisne, but because of the beach and the relative proximity of the wealthy quarter we did sometimes see over-powered roadsters similar to hers in our part of the island.

I was sitting on the patio outside my office, skimming slowly through a new book which I had received from an online bookseller that morning. It was an illustrated dictionary of the pathological terms applied to forensic procedures carried out on a body when the cause of death had to be scientifically established. It made for gruesome but fascinating reading. The publishers clearly intended the book for a general readership as well as a specialist one. Coloured photographs were included of many procedures in progress: close ups of bullet and knife wounds, arteries torn apart, crushed and broken bones.

To respect sensibilities, each set of illustrations was screened off by a covering page, which carried a warning as well as captions describing each picture concealed behind. This page had to be turned before the photographs became visible, which made seeing the illustrations optional, but at the same time introduced an unmistakable feeling of curiosity. Early on I succumbed to temptation, but after that I opted to leave curiosity unsatisfied. The captions alone were enough to make the stomach churn.

I would never have use for this degree of detail, now or in any future novel, but I saw it as interesting background intelligence. When writing about technical details I always wanted to be in possession of more information than I actually needed.

The car's engine continued to rumble in the sea road at the end of my garden. The familiarity of the sound made me want to retreat into the house, stay out of sight. A certainty was growing in me that it was not a casual visitor, someone who happened to have pulled up and was still waiting on the side of the road. I was sure it was Frejah. I had not been able to take in a single word of the new book from the moment I became aware of the car. I kept waiting for the driver to switch off the engine or drive away, or at least do something other than sit there with the engine running. The constant note was more distracting than a series of louder noises – it was like an unfinished sentence, music without a climactic tonic chord.

I put down the book. I had quickly become tense, curious, nervy. I crossed the garden, the comfort of our private space, then walked along the rough path Jo and I had made to the short flight of steps that led down to the road.

As soon as I reached the top of the steps I could see the car. It was either Frejah Harsent's roadster or one exactly like it.

The black bodywork glittered in the sunlight, shards of reflection shimmering as the engine turned over. The car I had once seen as beautiful and desirable now looked menacing, intrusive, frightening. I did not go down to meet her.

Since our brief meeting on Dearth Island I had often thought about Frejah Harsent, what she had said, the story she told me. I knew she had lied to me, but I still did not know why. Lying is something you inflict on people you know, the ones already around you, or people you intend to cheat or deceive. Why pick out a stranger then feed him a series of untruths?

There were still unexplained details I had not yet untangled. Why, for instance, had she given the name of the murdered man as Waller Alman? The Waller part of the name I understood, perhaps. But Alman? I was now certain the dead man was called Lew Waller Antterland.

That murder had led to another. She had not mentioned the death of Dever Willer Antterland, so presumably she had not been involved with it as a police officer. Or as anything else? But how could she not know about it? He was almost certainly the killer of Lew, the thief who removed Lew's money. So did she deliberately omit it from the story she told me? If so, why?

Over the past couple of weeks I had spent most of my time concentrating on the novel I was writing, and observing with a sense of combined fascination and dread the falling apart of the financial substructure of my home island. Yet the small mysteries Frejah Harsent created for me had never really gone away.

Because of the elevation of my garden I was above the low-slung car. From where I was standing at the top of the steps I could see down to Frejah, or more exactly her grey-haired head, glimpsed through the upper window of the gull-wing door. She was leaning forward, adjusting something on the dash. Did she know I was there? She gave no sign of it. Was I expected to walk down to the car, expressing my surprise that she had come to my house?

She moved her hands back to the steering wheel. The engine continued to rumble.

Stupidly, I felt immobilized by indecision, but it was not my own indecision. She had arrived unannounced at my house. It would not be a social call. She wanted something of me, something related to those old murders. I could turn around, step back into the covering shade of the trees, return across my lawn, pretend I was unaware of the car and had not seen her. Or I could walk casually down the stone steps, greet her in some way, speak to her, perhaps invite her in.

It was still less than two months since I had seen her last. I remembered the arrival at the airport in the freezing air of Tristcontenta Hub, chilled by a gusting wind and insistent rain, hastily retrieving my overnight bags and computer case from the trunk of the car. Horribly aware of the large, snub-nosed automatic weapon mounted in the trunk. Then a quick but conventional farewell: a slight and formal kiss on the cheek, a shake of hands.

She could have been any old acquaintance, dropping me off at an airport. In a supercharged roadster bristling with police instruments. With an automatic weapon close at hand.

In the end she made up my mind for me. While I was standing there wondering what to do I realized that Frejah had become aware of my presence. There was a movement of her hand on the steering column, then the gull-wing door on her side of the car smoothly raised itself. I went down the steps and stood beside her.

I said: 'Hello again, Commissioner.' A casual greeting, an attempt to try and counteract the negative feelings that her arrival had suddenly induced in me.

Looking up at me she waved a hand towards me. I saw that she was swivelling her body around, the manoeuvre I had had to master to get in and out of the car. Her legs were already outside the car, but she was having difficulty raising the rest of her body. She was pressing down awkwardly with her elbows, attempting to slide forward. She was holding her head at an odd angle. It made her look stiff, much older. When I had been with her on Dearth, just that short time ago, she had entered and left the car with smooth, almost agile movements.

I held out a hand to help her lift herself away from the low seat, but she waved it away impatiently, not looking at me. She levered herself into an upright sitting position, then managed to stand. She was unsteady, holding on to the car door for a few seconds. Once she was on her feet she stepped back a couple of paces. She looked hunched, reduced. There was no hint of familiarity between us.

'Fremde, you've been looking into matters that don't concern you,' she said. She was avoiding my eyes, looking somewhere behind me, not at me. Her voice was not strong – she spoke indistinctly, partly muffled by the constant loud rumbling of the car's engine.

'What do you mean?'

'You've been checking up on my story.'

'I wouldn't have done that if what you said was true. That's what made me interested in the murder – the fact that you lied.'

'What happened was more than fifteen years ago,' she said. 'It was one of the first cases I was involved with. I have forgotten some details. I wasn't lying. We were talking about your books, your writing. I thought you'd be interested in a real case, a real story. And you said you didn't understand mutability. When I went to Salay Hames for that case it was the first time I had ever experienced an extreme form of it. You and I were just talking in a car. It was a long journey.'

'No – I recorded it when we stopped in a restaurant. That was your idea. You wanted me to hear it, wanted me to react. I checked the names with you afterwards. It was more than just a casual conversation.'

'I should have said less. But you involved yourself.'

'Not directly.'

'Your associate – the retired detective, Spoder. He found the files. Then you went with him to Salay Sekonda.'

'Because the two killings were linked. The victims were brothers. Did you know that?'

'That's none of your business, Fremde.'

'You made it my business.'

We were both glaring at each other. She was certainly looking angrily at me, and without of course being able to see myself I felt I was facing her down.

I had prepared for none of this: five minutes before, I was peacefully contemplating punctured lungs and bullet exit wounds – a quiet pleasure, if inexplicable to many. I still did not know why she had come to my house, but the sight of her, the memory of that two-day drive across the grim landscape of Dearth, invoked by seeing the car again, brought rising to the surface thoughts of all the intrigue she had created afterwards. Until I saw her I had not appreciated how far under my defences she had penetrated.

I wished Jo were with me. She would at least have calmed me.

I turned away from Frejah in an effort to stop the argument from escalating into a full-on row. We were standing in the direct heat of the sun, while the fumes from the car's engine spread around us. I wanted to move to the side, circling her car, into the shade of the nearest trees, but it would mean stepping more directly away from her, around the obstacle of the halted car. I did not want to look or feel as if I was retreating from her, but she had parked at a sharp angle, making it impossible to step back into the shade without appearing to be doing exactly that. Everything had been disrupted by her arrival at the house.

'Frejah, what have you come here for?' I said.

'I'm here to warn you. Someone is looking for you, and if he finds you he's intending to kill you.'

'Are you serious? Someone hunting *me*?'

'That's what I said.'

'What the hell! You sound like someone from one of my novels.'

(I did not enlarge on this, but in reality she was sounding like someone from abandoned drafts of some of my early novels. That was a period of my writing signified by sudden declarations, sardonic laughs, threats uttered, features grimacing. Not now, not any more. Even back then there was not much of it. I was never good at writing violence, and verbal violence always felt false to me.)

'He is out for revenge against you.'

'*Revenge*? Who is he, and what does he think I have done to him?'

'My old partner on the Dearth force, Enver Jeksid.'

'Oh, not him again. He said much the same to my colleague Spoder. What interest could he possibly have in me?'

'He's dangerous. He has already killed at least once.'

'He's a cop. That's what cops do.'

'Enver is no longer with the force. He's disgraced, he has been put down to citizen serfdom. I haven't seen him in years. He was dishonourably discharged, which lost him his vassalage. He lives on Salay Tielet.'

'The third,' I said, by habit adding the suffix. Tielet was a long way from Raba, on the opposite side of the central lagoon of the Salay Group, a mountainous island dominated by a long-extinct volcano. It was the wine-growing island. Large herds of cattle were reared on the coastal plains. Salay Tielet was famous for its liberal havenic laws, making itself a destination for many fugitives. I had never had reason to go there. 'So what does Jeksid claim I've done to him?'

'He'll almost certainly tell you when he finds you.'

'If you know, tell me now.'

I felt I was teetering on the edge of a dangerous world I did not understand, a place of murder, revenge and threats. But was it real? I was outside my home, standing on the side of the road I crossed almost every day when I walked down to the beach. Traffic was driving past at normal speeds, although having to slow slightly to go around Frejah's roadster, angularly halted. Two young women in light clothes rode past on bicycles. They wobbled as they went around the car. Beyond us: the silver-blue sea looked glassy and still, as if becalmed by the hot sunshine. The familiar distant prospect of small islets. Yachts with multi-coloured sails tacked in the light breeze. People were walking their dogs along the green sward that separated the beach from the road. On the beach, many were lazing in the sun, others were walking or staring at the sea, or running down to plunge in. All this I knew and understood.

'He believes it was you who hacked the computer systems in Raba City,' Frejah said.

'And that affects him how?'

'He lost all his money as a result.'

'So has everyone else with savings on this island. Why should he blame me?'

'You took the mutability software from the hotel. He still has a police tracking device, and it identified you, your hotel room in Dearth. He's currently trying to find out where you live through your associate, Spoder.'

'This is ridiculous!' I said. 'I haven't the least idea how to hack software. I have trouble enough with my own desktop.'

'He knows you had the means and he believes you did it. He's serious about killing. He murdered my husband, he's going to kill you, and he's going to try to kill me too.'

'Kill you?' I said. The conversation had become surreal. I couldn't bring myself to believe a word of it.

'He will if he gets the chance. I'm planning to get to him first.'

'And that's why you carry a weapon in the trunk of this car?'

'One of the reasons.'

'You know where he is, then?'

'I know he's on this island now but I don't know where. He has a taste for cheap hotels, but there are many of those on the other side of town.'

I said again: 'Frejah – is this serious? Are you being serious?'

'Never more so.'

The engine of the roadster continued to throb noisily. It was a constant distraction and annoyance to me, worsened by the smell of particulate-heavy fumes. Raba has strict antipollution laws, and Frejah's ludicrously powerful car was in direct conflict with them.

'Can't you turn off the engine?' I said.

'I never turn it off – in case I need to make a quick exit.'

That made me smile: I imagined her slowly and painfully re-inserting herself into the sculpted low-angle driving seat, elbows and neck and legs stiff. She saw the smile.

'You really don't understand, do you?' she said.

'Why don't you just tell me straight what it is you know? Is that impossible? When we were driving to the airport we were speaking frankly—'

'That was then.' She held up a hand, and for the first time I noticed two of her fingers had splints, with bandaging around them. 'Things have changed.'

'Has someone beaten you up?'

'People don't get beaten up on Dearth. There's no crime on Dearth – remember? This was a transgression, one night just before I left to come here to Raba. We call it a bodily impairment intrusion.'

'Was it Jeksid?'

'Not Enver himself. Three of them. They were masked. I assumed he had sent them.'

'Were you hurt badly?'

'These two fingers were broken. I lost a tooth. Bruising all over my back and chest. My neck was wrenched. One eye was blackened. I suppose it could have been worse. I'll survive.'

Neither of us had moved away, but I felt that something had changed. A mutual connection we both rejected, but which bound us. Or that was what Frejah seemed to want me to feel, a mutuality with her. Standing there in the heat and sunlight, I still felt the tendrils of commonsense denial, the impossibility of it all. This plotting, these moves against each other.

'You said he murdered your husband. Are you certain of that?'

'It was a few years ago. Hari, my husband, was a police officer too, working undercover on Salay Ewwel, the first. We were separated, but still married. It was impossible to live a normal married life because of the work he was doing. My work sometimes was in the way too, but we were still fond of each other. We'd had a lot of good years together. He was a lifetime professional officer, committed to what he was doing, and I respected that. He was infiltrating a gang of drug smugglers, based on Ewwel but trafficking drugs to Dearth. He had a front, a drinks joint he ran in Ewwel Town. I was out of contact with him and had no idea where he was, but Jeksid traced him. He went to Ewwel and killed Hari. I'm sure of that, but Jeksid covered his tracks. He had no apparent motive, left no clues, no witnesses, no evidence, nothing that could link him to the murder. He had a clear alibi. He was still a cop at the time, and he got away with it. A perfect crime.'

'You said he was dishonourably discharged.'

'The police couldn't pin it on him – Jeksid was clever. He had done a brilliant job of covering it up. But I knew beyond doubt that no one else would have done it. Then some of the other commissioners started having their doubts. I said nothing to discourage them. About a year after Hari was killed they found a way to get rid of Enver. He was furious: he lost his vassal status, his pension, his good service record, everything. He blamed me – he knew I had worked out what he had done. I was the only one who could. He swore then he would get me. That's why I pack a weapon, yes. But mostly I've stayed out of his way. When he moved to Tielet, the third, I eased up a little.'

A perfect murder? I remembered Spoder's claim that the murder of Dever Antterland had taken place inside a locked room. Spoder had been right, in a way. Now this – the dream of every thriller writer, to think up a crime that was perfect, unsolvable, but at the same time possible, or at least made to seem realistic within the bounds of a novel.

But not so perfect if it led to Jeksid being given a dishonourable discharge?

'I'm going to leave now,' Frejah said. 'I don't like being in one place too long. Jeksid is somewhere near – he might still be using the tracker. He can pick out this car whenever it's running.'

'So why not turn off the engine?'

She waved at me with irritation. 'I told you.'

'If Jeksid doesn't know where I am, how did you find me?'

'I have a tracker too.' She indicated the car's bunch of antennae. 'Mine's better than his. Command and control, remember? But best not to take risks.'

She went around to the open door on the driver's side, then began the awkward and obviously painful procedure of easing herself stiffly back into the seat. I stepped forward to offer help, but she jerked her arm away from me. She half rolled into position. As soon as she was seated she touched the control on the steering column and the gull wing door began descending smoothly. She revved up the engine, which gave out a terrible roar and a cloud of dark smoke.

I said: 'But if you can locate me, why can't you—?'

Over the noise she said: 'You know too much, my friend. I will try to get to him first, but after that—'

The door thudded down gently into place.

A sudden, showy and unnecessary getaway followed: she accelerated hard, the drive wheels throwing up a cloud of grit and dust as they tried to find purchase on the road surface. I turned away defensively, rounding my shoulders, protecting my head. Gravel flew around me. There was a stink of burning tyre rubber. The sheer speed and acceleration of the roadster clearly took other drivers by surprise – it was being driven so hard that it snaked from side to side, at the outer edge of control. I saw one oncoming car swerve across the road to avoid a collision, lurching off the paved highway and on to the sloping sward that led down to the beach. The car braked on the grass, came to a sliding halt. People who had been strolling on the sward backed away, but no one seemed to have been hurt. Frejah's car roared on. Within only a few seconds the roadster had turned a corner and disappeared from sight, but I could hear the disagreeable and impatient thrusting and thundering of the engine for some time afterwards.

Normality returned. I heard birds, the sea breeze moving through the trees, the relaxed sounds from the beach. The driver of the car on the sward restarted the engine and drove carefully back to the roadway.

Inevitably, thoughts on being threatened with sudden death followed.

Although *just* a crime novelist I believe I share thoughts and ambitions no different from other novelists, and work in much the same way. A novelist creates a work of the imagination. Many novels are written in the realist mode, reflecting the world in which both writer and reader live. Even so, no matter how normal or familiar the setting of a novel might seem to a reader – with recognizable place names, for example, or remembered dates, historical events, perhaps even famous public figures – it is none the less a fantasy, a creation of the mind. Everything is made up.

It is made up because a novelist works in a state of mental and imaginative openness, of inventiveness, replacing the world of known facts with fabricated details, many of which might look as if they are the same, or almost the same, as those which are known. An historical personage in a novel – for instance a film star, or an important politician – is not the real figure known to history, but an imagined construct put to use by the writer. A fictional reconstruction of a war, a setting in a great or historical building, a famous love affair, a string of murders, remain fictitious for all their seeming accuracy to what is known.

The absolute familiarity of the world is for many writers too rigid, too well populated with knowledge, and in many cases is uninteresting because mundane.

There are degrees of this, as in all things. No generalization includes every novel. Some authors do treat reality as a literal matter, relying on it as an authentication of their world view. Others take flight on wings of fancy, dreaming of the fantastic, the magical.

For a writer of crime novels, or thrillers, the curse of reality is present in much of the genre, but most awkwardly in the fact of law enforcement.

The classic crime novel reveals the template that is the problem.

Suppose the body of a devious, adulterous and wealthy man is found in the conservatory of his large house. His son, alienated from his father because of an ill-chosen marriage and mounting gambling debts, finds the body. Three of his siblings have been at war with each other for years. A will has been lost or disputed. An ex-wife appears, not the mother of the gambling son. A secretary has just been fired, but still holds keys to certain mysterious rooms. The servants are divided between loyalty and self interest. Why does the son not call the police?

Because he knows, or at least because his author knows, that a scene of crime officer would soon arrive. The SOCO and a horde of uniformed cops would take control. The house would be declared a crime scene, and zoned off. Nothing could be moved or even touched. Photographers would record in minute detail the place where the body was found, and everywhere else of potential interest. A doctor or a pathologist would have to attend. Witnesses and dependents would be separated from each other for individual questioning.

Many readers will have a sceptical view of the efficiency of the police, especially in times of budget cutbacks, but in fact a modern force has a huge range of technical and scientific means of investigation. In recent years the work of identifying a murderer has been transformed by forensic science.

None of this is any good to a crime novelist. The crime must not be solved by experts, working out of sight in some laboratory. He does not want a helicopter with night-vision cameras to search the grounds. Instead, the bereaved family and their servants must gather, partly to reflect on the evil ways of the deceased, partly to accuse each other of complicity. They will each declare their own innocence, settle old scores, establish alibis, reveal the existence of hitherto secret promises or documents. There will be talk of sinister strangers moving silently through the shadows in the grounds.

Meanwhile, the sleuth, amateur or professional, will lurk quietly in the background, taking notes, interrogating suspects, studying railway timetables and the like.

The existence of a police investigation would ruin this.

Although modern writers have mostly dispensed with the template, elaborating and sophisticating it, the essence remains: a professional investigation does not make a compelling plot. The emphasis can shift to the police officer in charge: his or her weaknesses or strengths allowed to dominate the story. Details of police work can themselves make fascinating fiction of a different kind. Or the possibility of police intervention is removed altogether: a remote location for the scene of murder, landslides or snowdrifts preventing access, some social emergency tying up police resources, and so on.

The classic crime story was always a kind of artifice, and no reader or writer thought otherwise. But all thrillers, made as fiction, require special conditions for the story to work. Crime writers create self-contained worlds, or at least they carefully contrive a special area of the world that only seems realistic, where what we know about the reality of murder and its detection is set aside, forgotten. When we write crime we think little of real crime.

Frejah Harsent had tested my own understanding of reality. She brought what she claimed was a genuine threat of someone out to kill me. For some reason, she also accused me of knowing too much. That for me was unrealistic, unbelievable. It was she who knew nothing of me. She was a stranger who had power-driven jarringly into my life, created a web of lies, threats, old murders, false names. I still did not know why, and was beginning to realize that perhaps I never would.

In spite of what she said about my being in danger, how could I take any of it seriously?

I went inside the house, made myself some tea. I sipped it while I stood at the window looking out across the garden. I realized only then that for some reason I had closed the garden doors behind me. An instinct to lock myself inside against a possible intruder? I opened them again. Familiar sounds reached me from outside. The thought of some vengeful assassin, out to get me, prowling my island with a tracking device – it was ridiculous even to consider it as a possible threat.

This must be the saving grace of the real world, I thought. In crime novels and movies a murderous threat is taken seriously, at face value. It has an immediate and disruptive impact on the story. The intended victim flees to a place of safety, or rustles up some protection, or sets out on whatever it was that Frejah called pre-emptive self defence – attack being claimed by storytellers everywhere to be the best form of defence.

But fiction is made up. I was not. A feeling of everyday normality spread around me. I lived in a world I had found, not one I had constructed.

If you research the subject of murder and murderers you soon discover that fiction and the real world are entirely at odds. Far from there being some sort of criminal mastermind planning and preparing, fiendishly plotting killing schemes, most murders are impulsive, messy, sordid, and not at all mysterious. They occur as a result of fights and arguments, or most likely of all within a dysfunctional relationship.

Discounting acts of terrorism, more than half of all women murdered are killed by their spouse, their partner, their ex-partner or a work colleague. Roughly a quarter of all murdered men are killed by a friend or an acquaintance or at least by someone they recognize or already know superficially. When children are murdered it is most often, tragically, by a parent, a step-parent or a live-in partner.

In any police investigation of a murder, the starting point of enquiry is invariably within the immediate family, then to the circle of closest friends.

Only a minority of victims are murdered by strangers. Should you take comfort from the thought that if you are murdered the killer is likely to be someone you know?

Today I had received an indirect threat of murder, delivered by someone I barely knew, on behalf of someone I did not know at all. It seemed absurd.

The world you live in goes on around you in the same old way. Why should it not?

The threat only gains weight if you start believing in it, or if the people around you believe it. What, for instance, would Jo have to say about it? We could laugh it off together, as we often did about other things, small or large. Jo was my sanity resource. On the other hand, she sometimes took matters more seriously than I did. I take nothing for granted with Jo.

Would I still think it absurd if one day I noticed a disagreeable looking stranger with a gun or a knife or a club, clambering up the flight of steps from the road, striding through the trees and across the garden towards me, his manner single-minded and deadly? Would that be how this revenge was going to be taken? Somehow it still did not seem likely.

Or maybe a surprise attack? Someone who broke into my house earlier and was hiding as I came home late at night. A gunshot in the dark, a sudden clubbing with a baseball bat, a knife in the back?

I realized then that I was adumbrating the scene as if it was part of something I might write. The fallback position of every writer: events are useful, experience can fill in a plot, waste not, want not.

I would in fact write it differently. For me, a properly imagined murder would be prepared by deliberate imprecision. The victim would be in a strange place, feeling extra vulnerable. There would be the unknowable social conventions, possibly the language, the weather, the look of the people and the appearance of the buildings. The victim would already be disoriented by the sense of foreignness, isolation. Then by blurring, darkening or making the surroundings mysterious, by not describing motives, by having the threats less clearly uttered, all to misdirect the reader. False alarms, or real warnings? Techniques of delay or surprise or error to heighten the tension, in this imagined world, the one I would make up.

Instead, Frejah's scenario was this. A warm, sunny afternoon, with a light breeze from the sea. A ludicrously over-powerful car pulls up outside my home. It stands idling on the narrow coastal road, partly obstructing other traffic, two wheels up on the grassy verge that Jo and I from time to time have to cut back and make tidy. The engine, over-tuned, belches heavy gasoline or oil fumes, blatantly and uncaringly above the emissions limit for my island. Cars and bicyclists go past. Children play on the beach. An elderly woman, a senior cop past the age of retirement, known to me as unreliable at least, recently beaten up by masked men, utters mysterious threats, speaking of an enemy I do not know I have.

It was quirky, it was complicated, it lacked conviction. It did not have the atmosphere or the illusory feeling of reality that fiction should create. It was believable, but only because that was what had happened. It would never work in a novel.

Once again I felt irritated with Frejah. She was determined to drag me into her intrigues, her old police cases, the past murders she might or might not have investigated. For none of these I felt any responsibility.

I made supper, and afterwards had a long online chat with Jo. I said nothing to her of Frejah's visit. I watched the news on television, then downloaded a movie and viewed it with Barmi curled up on my lap. I went to bed late. (I did make sure all the windows and doors were locked.)

21

A Parity of Arms

Spoder came to see me. I invited him because I wanted at last to catch up with what he was doing. Because he lived in Raba City itself, I was also interested in finding out from him how the financial debacle looked from his perspective. He was eager to visit. He said he had news, things had developed. He roared up to the house on his motorbike within an hour of my call.

I was still following the daily news reports about the financial crash, which was growing worse and better in roughly equal proportions.

More banks and financial institutions had either had to close their doors, or were being administered by liquidation accountants appointed by the seignioral commissariat in Salay Ewwel, the first. On the plus side, a large number of new ATM cash machines had suddenly appeared in shopping malls, supermarkets, commercial centres and so on. People of course flocked to these, which fulfilled a real need, but their operation as actively reliable automats was strictly limited. Most of them became erratically unusable within about a day and a half of their appearance. Some were taken away and replaced. Naturally, there was always a huge rush to use a new ATM whenever it appeared.

A temporary compensation scheme had been hastily arranged by a group of the less badly affected banks. Although seeming huge by individual standards the fund was hopelessly inadequate as a way of bailing out the banks and other companies, but it was a much needed resource for many citizen serfs. Thousands had found their lives and homes seriously in jeopardy because of the crash. Emergency survival payments acted as a lifeline for most of these people.

Some of the more articulate victims of the crash went on television to say that the whole thing was illusory. There was no evidence of financial weakness, they claimed, and added that the so-called crisis had been devised as a way of amalgamating certain of the banks and other finance houses to strengthen their position. The cost of this was being borne by the citizen serfs whose savings were at stake.

It suddenly struck me that there was a similarity with the landslides and avalanches that killed people on Dearth but were in fact illusory, a psychological delusion of some kind. How long before we found out that the financial crash had never really happened?

Meanwhile, the authorities continued to insist they were closing their net on the mysterious group of hackers responsible for everything.

Every day I went online to check my own bank account. Every day I read the reassuring notes that the bank was riding out the storm of uncertainty sinking all others around. I doubted that was true, but there was nothing I could do about it. I was able to pay bills from the account, draw small amounts of cash from a handful of nominated sites, and I could of course pay into the account as much as I wished.

That gave me a thought. I hurriedly exchanged emails with the accounts department of the literary agents who paid me my royalties and other income. They were off-island and therefore likely to be unaffected by the crash. I instructed them not to send me any more payments for the time being.

Far away on the metropolitan island of Muriseay, north of the equator, not far from the forbidden and to me unimaginable countries of the northern continent, Jo made the same simple precautionary arrangement. We were both freelance workers. We could request the credit transfers to be resumed when the financial situation had stabilized.

Spoder arrived full of news and gossip about what he had seen around the town, as well as in the suburb where he had his apartment. It was all interesting, but nothing I had not heard about, or had not assumed was happening. I was happy to let it flow around me. He and I drank coffee together on the decking outside my office, relishing the shade and the steady draught from the electric fan, while an entirely normal and unthreatening summer's afternoon unfolded around us. I took him down to the roadside and showed him the tyre scorch marks, still visible, left by the roadster as Frejah Harsent accelerated away.

'Who is this woman?' he said. 'Is she the ex-cop from Dearth?'

'Frejah Harsent, a commissioner of police on Dearth. She claims to be still operative, and carries a warrant card or at least something that looks just like one.'

'Harsent – that rings a bell.' Then he shook his head, as if trying to erase the remark.

'Do you know her?'

'Let me think.' He leaned over to the coffee pot and poured himself a second mug. 'I think I heard the name recently.'

A silence followed. Spoder was not good at silences, because he made facial expressions and sometimes emitted grunting noises, but I knew to wait. After I had stared at him for a few seconds he began to look evasive.

'Tell me what you heard?' I said. 'It's not a Salay name, I know. Frejah Harsent said she was born on Hames, the fifth, but when she was six years old her parents moved to Dearth. She grew up there, and married a man called Harsent.'

'It was a man I heard about.'

'What was his first name? Was it Hari?'

'It was a case I was briefly involved in. I don't remember his name. It might have been Hari.'

'Was it a murder case? Where did it happen?'

'It was on Salay Ewwel, the first. Not so long ago – more recently than the murder of Dever Antterland, at least. I never had to investigate it directly, but these big cases generate a lot of paperwork. Some of the records came to the station house in Raba, and I was working on those for a while. There was something about the ballistic identity of the murder weapon. I remember scouring the files of registered guns, but we found nothing. The victim had his own similar weapon, but that wasn't the one used on him.'

'The man who was murdered was called Harsent?'

'I think so, yes. The thing is, it turned out to be another un-solved crime – in the end the file was closed. We heard from Dearth that they knew or suspected who the killer was, but he had an ironclad alibi and there was no evidence against him. They made the Ewwel force go through everything all over again, but they still found nothing. This information apparently came from one of the senior officers on Dearth, who said she was certain she knew who it was. But it was only a hunch, or perhaps hearsay. You can't arrest anyone on that basis alone.'

'And this informant – was it the dead man's wife?'

'Now you mention it, I think it was.'

'Then that would be Frejah, Frejah Harsent. She was a cop then, she's a cop now.'

'I think so,' said Spoder, again.

'Did she name the person she thought was the killer?'

'It's all coming back to me now, sir. I'm sorry – I should have made the connection myself.'

'It was Enver Jeksid, wasn't it? A serjeant on the Dearth force.'

'The man who is looking for you. Yes.'

'You spoke to him twice,' I said.

'Three times, sir. He made contact with me again this week. Yesterday, in fact.'

'When you spoke to him, did either of you say anything about this old case?'

'No – and he wouldn't. If it's the same man, he couldn't risk his whereabouts being known. He'd keep quiet about his past. Of course, I might have remembered his name, but in fact I didn't and he would have had no idea that I was connected with what he did. To most people his name wouldn't mean anything. That's why I'm sorry – I slipped up. But he's in an ambiguous situation anyway.'

'Why is that?' I said.

'In the first place, he was kicked out of the police in disgrace. I don't know the reasons, but it was a few months after Harsent was killed in Ewwel Town. Jeksid stayed on in Dearth for a while after he was fired, but eventually he moved to Salay Tielet, the third. Officially he is still a suspect, and when he left Dearth he became technically a fugitive. If the Dearth force knew where he was, they could try to arrest him. But there would be difficulties with that, too.'

'No extradition treaty?'

'None at all. The whole of Tielet is a refuge for deserters and other fugitives.'

Of course I did know that. Within the Salay Group, and probably elsewhere in the archipelago, Tielet was an island greatly admired for its liberal havenic policy.

'You were going to tell me about these calls with Jeksid,' I said. 'I need to know exactly what he said.'

'It's not easy, sir,' Spoder said.

'Can't you just tell me? You don't have to dress it up.'

'Oh, I do, I do.' He took a deep breath.

'Is this going to take time, Spoder?'

'There's a lot to tell, because Jeksid had a reason for contacting me.' His voice was low. 'He has found out more about me than I should like him to know. The fact is that I have never been completely honest with you about the life I lead. What I am doing now and the life I led in the past. I am not what you think, sir.'

'Is he blackmailing you?'

'He's using his knowledge to put pressure on me.'

'Are you now telling me that you were never a detective in the police?'

'No, sir. That is a matter of complete truth.'

'Or that you are no longer connected in any way with the police on this island?'

'Everything I have told you about my work with the police is true. I have never deliberately lied to you. I have simply omitted to tell you certain facts about myself.'

'We have an entirely professional relationship, Spoder,' I said. 'I accept you for who you are. You work well with me, and I'm not bothered by what you might have got up to in the past.'

'Well – it affects the present, too. When you know the whole truth about me, you might never be able to trust me again.'

'We'll see.'

'It's serious.'

I had never seen him looking so defensive, so troubled. I realized he had manoeuvred himself into a mental position where he saw no alternative but to tell me his story, and that I should therefore have to listen. He was almost wringing his hands in his earnest wish to own up, or confess, or whatever it was he thought he had to do. I was not anxious to hear it: what I said to him about our work together was true. For me it had been fruitful. I intended it to continue.

I wondered if our experience in the magic museum had unexpectedly opened the doors to this new frankness. I had not seen him since that day.

I collected up our coffee things and said I would brew a fresh pot. I left Spoder on the patio and retreated into the house. It was the work of only a few moments to prepare the coffee machine and rinse out the mugs. I stood for a few moments in the kitchen while the coffee maker popped and hissed, wondering how much in fact I wanted or even needed to hear Spoder's story.

Although I felt sceptical about Frejah Harsent's warning of a killer seeking me, there appeared none the less to be a link between me, Spoder, Frejah, Jeksid and Frejah's dead husband. I could not ignore that – I should listen to what he said.

As the coffee machine went into its familiar sounds of hoarsely gasping finale, I ducked away from the kitchen and went quickly to my study. Spoder was sitting outside with his back to me. I turned on my desktop, then as soon as I could I glanced at the emails that had come in during the interim. There were four: three were routine messages, one was from

Jo, confirming she would be in contact as usual that evening.

Before powering down, I clicked on my bank's icon and did the final check of the day on my account. I had already been in and out of the website about five times. Although I maintained an aura of indifference to the financial crash, I had become a compulsive checker of the health or otherwise of my own account.

I immediately wished I had not looked at all: large capital letters informed me that the bank had encountered what it called insurmountable problems. Official administrators had been called in, and all personal and business accounts were frozen. They assured savers and investors that their accounts were *safe and guaranteed*. There was nothing about current accounts.

I knew I was broke. Like hundreds of thousands of other citizen serfs on Raba I no longer had access to any of my money, apart from the increasingly worthless cash in my pocket. It was not a surprise after all the warning signs from elsewhere, but it was a substantial shock.

I went back to Spoder, put down the tray of coffee things. I wondered briefly about whichever bank it was where Spoder kept his own money, if he too had been affected. I did not ask. It was now late afternoon, but the sun, lowering towards the horizon, still gave out a powerful heat. The insects in the trees had not yet started their evening stridulation.

For a long time Spoder said nothing at all. I waited in the silence, thinking, inevitably, about money. Or the lack of it.

Then: 'The problem is, sir, that I don't know how to start. And I don't know how to say what I have to. I can only speak plainly: I am a lawbreaker and a fugitive from justice.'

22

The Story of DI Spoder (ret'd)

(I have tried to reproduce exactly what Spoder told me.)

Spoder said he was not an islander, that everything he had ever said about being born on one of Salay's islands was untrue. He said he was ashamed of this, that the lie had always been a background blight in his life, but when he was applying to join the Salay Raba police force he had mistakenly believed that advancement or promotion to senior rank, or transfer to the plainclothes detective section, would only be open to him if he was Raba born. Spoder said he wanted to graduate to detective work as soon as possible. He therefore presented himself in the best possible light, as he saw it at the time. He told me he had used identity papers that were copied and modified, and produced two false credentials from minor officials in Raba City. Later, he realized none of this was necessary, but he felt saddled with the lie and had never owned up about it. Over the years it had begun to seem true. Only now, with Jeksid trying to force his hand, was he able to confront it.

His beginnings were humble.

He came from Faiandland, the largest and most prosperous of the northern countries, and grew up in a suburb of Jethra, the capital city. He was born Yumi Spoder, a popular given name in the remote country area where his mother was raised, but he grew up hating it. The other children pronounced it 'yummy', a constant tease and affliction, as he saw it. As soon as he left school he used it as little as possible, a habit that persisted to this day. His father was a line engineer for an electrical supply company, while his mother was a junior school teacher. Yumi Spoder was therefore brought up by respectable and hard-working but not wealthy people. He had no brothers or sisters. In spite of the constant bullying, young Yumi was good at school and he intended to go to college when he left – but along with a great many young people in the same position he was to be denied that chance.

Faiandland was a country at war. Although it was a self-proclaimed liberal democracy, with an assembly of elected deputies, an independent judiciary and press, and a tradition of artistic diversity, Faiandland was embroiled in an unrelenting, shameless war with its neighbouring country, the Glaund Republic.

Glaund was the ideological opposite of Faiandland, a socialistic republic, a command economy, run by a military junta and using extensive techniques of repression and censorship to manipulate the populace. It too had an assembly of elected deputies and a tradition of the performing arts. Socially, Glaund was many years behind Faiandland. It too was fighting a dirty war.

Theoretically, the quarrel between the two countries was political, but in reality there were numerous areas of dispute over mineral deposits, oil fields, water resources and boundaries. Ancient grudges existed. Reasonableness did not. It was a war, and commonsense was the second casualty of war.

After years of destructive hostilities against each other the two countries drew up a treaty of disengagement. It was agreed that the fighting would be transferred to where military action could be unfettered without further damage to the infrastructure of either country. The southern continent of Sudmaieure therefore became the battlefield of choice, the war quickly evolving into a military confrontation for which there was no conceivable end.

Yumi Spoder was conscripted at the age of seventeen. After several weeks of basic training he was taken to the port where one of the many troopships was moored.

He said to me: 'All through training it was rammed home to us that life in the Faiandland army was hard but fair. We were trained to obey orders, no matter what, without hesitation or thought. We were trained to march, to dig temporary defences, to fire rifles and missiles and rockets and cannons and mortars, to engage in hand-to-hand combat. All these I saw, reluctantly, as the work of a modern army. I was too young to have shaped my own ideas, except in the most general way. I was not a pacifist, nor was I enthusiastic about having to kill the enemy. I learned during training that the way to survive the army was to turn off all private feelings of identity or individualism. My escouade was my only group of friends, the escouade serjeant was my only god. Time would pass. We were assured that military service would last no longer than two and a half years, at the end of which we would be returned home. All this I accepted. But nothing had prepared me for the conditions aboard the troopship.'

The first sight of the ship was alarming to Spoder and the hundreds of other conscripts. It was painted matt grey, but over the years many huge streaks and blotches of rust had spread across the hull and around the rivets. One long part of the hull, extending down below the waterline, had been replaced without being painted, so you could still see the streaky brown-red of anti-rust paint. The vessel lay low in the water.

The escouade serjeant marched the young soldiers to the quayside, then read them their orders: he would not be boarding the ship with them. He added that he was instructed to tell them what they would find once they boarded the ship. He said that it was fully modernized and air conditioned inside, that there were shared cabins with four comfortable bunks apiece, space for relaxation, shower rooms, and so on. There were adequate facilities for recreation: a large gym and exercise hall, a cinema, a library, even a small swimming pool. The food was good and nutritious, better than anything they had been given during training. Each escouade could appoint a spokesperson, who would be able to pass on ideas, requests or complaints to the ship's crew.

The serjeant brought them to attention, then marched away. An hour later the squad was still waiting on the quay, with all the other escouades of conscripts. No officers or NCOs were there. It was wintry and cold on the bleak and exposed quay, and the young soldiers became restless to be on the ship. Eventually, they began to drift towards the nearest gangplank and went aboard.

Thus they discovered the first casualty of war: truth.

Spoder said that what they found on the ship were conditions so foul it seemed inevitable that disease would be rife. The interior had apparently never been cleaned: there was filth everywhere, and the air was rank and disgusting. There were no cabins, only narrow stretches of bare deck, and nowhere to sleep other than in some hard, cramped space on the deck, shared with others. The food was more or less uneatable. There were no facilities for exercise, there was no escape from the constant heat, noise, stench and crowding. Once the ship set sail it was impossible to move up or down to other decks. Everyone was grouching and complaining and selfishly argumentative – it was not long before the first fights broke out.

The hell of the boat continued for what Spoder estimated was at least four days. The lights were never dimmed, and there were no routines by which the passage of time could be measured. Spoder said he managed to grab some light sleep about ten times, always in short, disturbed sessions. He was soon hungry, exhausted, nauseated, frightened and angry. Then the ship ran at full speed on to some rocks.

There was an explosive, grinding roar and the entire vessel jerked violently upwards. Instantly, all the lights went out. Everyone standing was thrown to the deck. In the total darkness there was complete chaos. Spoder suffered a series of violent blows from men behind and around him. He returned them reflexively. Everyone was fighting for survival, scrambling and kicking against each other, forcing themselves upwards, trying to find air and light and freedom. Then the ship rolled to one side, with the tortured racket of the splitting hull against the rocks, amplified by the bare metal plates and bulkheads of the ship's construction. The screaming and shouting actually intensified. Spoder said he found himself cushioned by many bodies as he fell, so although he was smothered and trapped in the confusion of the heap of struggling men, he suffered no serious injuries.

Sea water was gushing in through unseen fractures in the hull. The flood quickly reached where Spoder was trapped, pouring with terrifying pressure around his head and over his face, surging around his chest. He struggled to be free of the bodies holding him down, but everyone around him was doing the same. They were trying to lunge upwards in the total darkness, fighting for air. An instinct made Spoder force his way in the opposite direction, down through the flailing limbs and the icy water. He slipped through a thicket of unseen kicking legs. He was swallowing the salty sea water, feeling as if he was inhaling it. Terrified, choking and spluttering, he was suddenly able to work himself free of the others. Still in absolute darkness he dragged himself and waded further away: the sounds of distress behind him were horrendous.

A glimmer of light ahead! Spoder pulled himself towards it. He was still floundering in freezing cold sea water up to his waist, sometimes deeper, clambering over the bodies of many others. The shouting was less now, as the water continued to flood in. After a long struggle Spoder saw the source of the light: one of the bulkhead hatches, firmly locked throughout the voyage, had burst open under the stress of the ship's crashing halt. When he finally staggered up to it he saw a metal staircase beside it, a ship's steep ladder, but because of the list it was now almost horizontal. He worked his way along it, emerging unexpectedly into brilliant sunlight. Because of the extreme list the outer deck was vertical, a wall, and when he let go of the final rung he slithered down, crashing against various pieces of deck equipment, and immediately plunged shockingly into the sea.

The wreck had already attracted a small fleet of rescuers, an ad hoc flotilla of small boats and yachts. After ten minutes trying to stay afloat, every breath feeling as if it was his last, Spoder was hauled from the water by the people in one of the boats. Within half an hour, he and four other young conscripts, also dragged in a wretched state from the sea, were taken ashore.

Spoder spent five days and nights being cared for by a couple who lived on a farm in the hills, away from the sea. The island against whose rocky shallows the troopship had crashed was called Nelquay, in the temperate zone north of the equator. For the time being the island would be safe from the escouades of military police sent to search for conscripts who had survived the wreck, but they would inevitably arrive in force in the near future. There were ways he could avoid being captured. The people caring for him said he would be given all the help and advice he needed.

On the evening of the sixth day he was taken to a meeting in Nelquay Port. Apart from fourteen young soldiers still being treated in hospital, all the known survivors were there. It was estimated that more than sixteen hundred young people had died in the disaster, but around one hundred and fifty were still alive. Spoder realized immediately that he had escaped with comparatively little harm to himself – most of the other survivors were in a bad way.

A spokesperson from the island seigniory addressed the meeting, pointing out that the survivors had three choices. She said they must urgently decide what they wished to do.

The choices: They could wait on Nelquay for the arrival of the feared 'black caps', the military police escouades, then surrender to them. This would probably be in the next day or two. Or they could go into hiding, or disperse.

If they surrendered they would be treated by the military police as army deserters – because of this they faced the death penalty. In practice, execution was not likely to be carried out, as capital punishment had been abolished for many years in Faiandland itself. However, they would probably be sentenced to death, immediately commuted to a long spell of imprisonment in a military prison camp, followed by a return to the unit they had joined. The spokesperson added that high speed military vessels had already been detected leaving the southern mainland, probably heading for Nelquay, and they were expected to arrive within the next forty-eight hours.

The second choice was to remain on Nelquay and attempt to hide from the black caps. The woman said that the islanders of Nelquay would help them hide, and do what they could to protect them from capture. She explained Nelquay's havenic and shelterate laws, which meant that among many other provisions no islander could be punished for hiding a deserter, or in this case a survivor from the shipwreck, but if any of the conscripts were discovered they would be immediately taken into custody. She added that staying in hiding was a viable option, because the people of Nelquay had substantial experience from past incidents. They were adept at concealing and smuggling escapees.

However, there was a final choice. This was to disperse and depart from Nelquay to any of the score or so of other islands in the close vicinity. From there they should quickly move on to the many other islands, in every direction, losing themselves in the hundreds of thousands of islands and island groups spread across the Midway Sea. They should travel alone or, at most, in pairs. The black caps routinely patrolled on many islands. Nowhere was completely free of them, but there was safety in small numbers and a willingness to keep travelling. Observing that all the survivors from the ship were young, the seigniory official pointed out that the logical overall direction of travel might seem to be homewards, to the north. She knew the urge to return home was strong, but she spelled out the risks of re-arrest should they make it back. She reminded them of the islands' liberal shelterate laws that gave powerful if not complete protection from the escouades.

Finally, she said that the seigniory would give a useful sum of travel money to anyone wishing to move from Nelquay, and would provide advice about local ferry services departing in the next couple of days. Extra ships could be put into service if needed.

Spoder said he took the third choice. He travelled alone, but about fifty others were with him on the first of the ferries. Soon after that the opportunities of the sheer number of other islands made sure that the concentration was quickly dispersed. He transferred from one island to another, almost at random, usually changing ferries as soon as he arrived in another port. Within ten days he had landed on the island of Quy, smaller than Nelquay and with a warmer climate. Here at last he rested. But only for a while.

Spoder told me that over the next five years he discovered how to survive as a fugitive. He changed islands constantly, never remaining in any one place for more than a few weeks, however safe or attractive it seemed. He found jobs in most of his ports of call, begged in the streets in some others. He matured, learnt skills, made brief friendships. He was constantly alert for the arrival or presence of the black caps, terrified of what would happen to him if he was apprehended. He soon realized that most of the ordinary islanders shared his hatred of the squads of military police, and it was the local people who would tip him off if they heard of black cap activity close by. He had one close encounter with an escouade on the island of Demmer, but he successfully eluded them and did not see any others. He never lost his fear of them.

On Manlayl, the only island on his long itinerary where the benign climate and the way of life tempted him to settle permanently, Spoder met and was befriended by a former fugitive, called Thuneton.

Thuneton was some forty years older than Spoder, a deserter from the Glaundian army. He said little about himself, but one day he told Spoder the story of how he and three others had managed the near impossible: an escape by boat from the mainland of Sudmaieure. They had been chased by an escouade of black caps in a power boat, but managed to elude them when a bank of fog drifted up from the frozen coast. After a chaotic and almost disastrous landing on the shores of an island called Luice, he too had wandered for many years from one island to the next, in constant fear of his life. Finally, here on Manlayl, he married. He was now naturalized as a citizen serf of the island. His wife had died, but he had three islander children, all now adults. He said that because of his approaching old age the threat to him from the black caps was minimal, and if he was found by them the havenic laws would protect him.

Thuneton explained to Spoder why he believed islands like Manlayl were mostly safe from the escouades. Almost all the deserters fleeing from the actual war tended to fan out in an ever widening northerly direction. Islands to the west and east of this huge area were relatively unvisited by fugitives, apart from people like himself who had been on the run for many years. Most of the Archipelago was of course outside the escape sector.

Manlayl was one of those islands, but not, according to Thuneton, sufficiently far away to be completely safe for a young man travelling alone. To the black caps he would be an obvious target.

A few weeks after this, Spoder decided to forgo the scenic beauty and pacific lifestyle of Manlayl, and put more distance between himself and risk of capture. He travelled south and west, heading down into the equatorial zones.

After two more years of travel Spoder came at last to the Salay Group. The ferry took him to the port in Salay Ewwel, the first, where he had discovered ahead of time that there were plenty of opportunities for work. After his many adventures across the islands Spoder had decided what he wanted to do: his travels had made him resourceful, self-sufficient and able to think for himself. He had worked in dozens of different jobs, most of them menial, but now he wanted to put his skills and abilities to use. He had had first-hand experience of policing work, most of it on his behalf, through his contact with the various shelterate laws on different islands. He had formed a strong wish to join the force with the aim of becoming a detective. He moved to Raba, where he made the mistake of lying about his background, but he was accepted and began the training scheme.

Spoder said he had served as a Raba detective for years, gradually promoted, committed to the work he was doing, enjoying the increasing responsibility. He said nothing about his present status with the force, and once again I did not enquire.

Then he said: 'I have to tell you what happened to the other young people who escaped from the ship at the same time. Most of them became cops, like me. It's not widely known, but there are former deserters and fugitives on almost every police force in the Archipelago. I began to find this out after I started regular work, and was part of the team. It makes sense, of course. Once you're in the police the black caps are no longer a problem, and the life you have been forced to live while on the run turns out to be the best basic training you could get. If you can survive several years of island hopping, having to look out for yourself, then you end up self disciplined, capable, knowing the difference between right and wrong, and you've found out about human nature from the ground up.'

'That makes you into a cop?' I said.

'It makes you suitable to become one.'

'Some people have a more sceptical view of the police,' I said, suddenly remembering the ex-cop Jeksid, for some reason hunting me down and allegedly wanting to kill me. When

I noticed Spoder's reaction to that, I added: 'As a matter of interest how many other fugitives are in the police? Here, on Raba?'

'When I first joined the Raba force there were sixteen ex-deserters on the roll. One of them was my immediate superior, and the station superintendent had been on the run thirty years before. At the moment there are about a dozen, all of them junior to me. There'll be a new intake of cadets later this year, and some of those will almost certainly be fugitives.'

A swift twilight had passed while Spoder was telling me his story, and now we were sitting in the humid darkness of the early evening. I turned on the patio lights, and the ones in my study behind us. Large insects soon swarmed towards the deck. We retreated inside, closing the windows and doors. I was hungry – a dilemma because Spoder was showing no signs of leaving, and I would either have to cook something for us both or send out for food.

Then I remembered that apart from about fifty thalers I had in my wallet, I was broke. For the first time in my life I felt a fleeting sense of panic about money. I was no longer so sanguine about the crashing economy.

I said to Spoder: 'Do you have any money on you? I've been wiped out today.'

'My bank foreclosed yesterday,' he said. 'I have about a hundred thalers in cash. Plus some savings in an account I can't get at.'

'I had savings until earlier today. Are you going to be all right?'

'I've no idea, sir. It's too depressing to think about.'

'I can cook omelettes and potatoes for us both. Is that OK with you?'

'I'd like that,' Spoder said.

'We could go to a restaurant, but I don't want to spend the cash I have, not until I know the exact situation.'

'The exact situation is that we're cleaned out.'

'Let's eat,' I said. 'After that I want to work.'

Twenty minutes later, sitting at the long table in the large kitchen/diner, while we finished what felt at the time was possibly the last meal ever, Spoder suddenly went to his jacket, slung on the seat of one of my chairs. He withdrew a thin sheaf of papers from an inner pocket. He had folded them down the middle, lengthways, to fit his pocket.

'Sir, I said I had a reason for wanting to tell you what happened to me when I was a teenager. And how as a result I came to be in the police a few years later. At the time I thought I was the only fugitive who moved over into the law, but as I've described it turned out to be a common route. It's not widely known to the public. Although throughout the islands there's a great deal of sympathy for the young people who escape the war, there is a belief at every level of policing that this is a subject that should not be made widely known. Hundreds of people like me are still being hunted, we are in breach of the laws of those distant countries. And we are the law enforcement in the islands.'

He placed the papers on the surface of the long table, and flattened them with his hands to smooth out the crease.

'This Enver Jeksid we have been talking about. The former police officer. Sir, he came to visit me yesterday. He turned up at my apartment without warning. At the time he came to my door I was trying to find out what had happened to my money, so I couldn't have been less ready for him. I had no idea who he was: when he said his name I didn't connect immediately. He did not look as I expected, because of the things he had said. The insinuations, the sense of a threat against you. He did not frighten or intimidate me. But he said that because the island where he came from, Dearth, was close to the southern continent, he had contacts with the Faiandland forces there. I took that to mean he was threatening to expose me.'

'Surely the escouades, if they found you, could not arrest you now?'

'You mean because of my age? That's right, of course. But they could make life difficult for me, and perhaps for my children.'

'So what did he want?'

'He's using me. He wants to meet you. He has promised there is no threat to you.'

'That's not what Frejah Harsent told me—'

'He swore he is no danger to you.'

'Was he carrying a gun when he came to your flat?' I said.

'Not that I was aware of. The only thing he had brought with him was this.' Spoder indicated the low pile of papers lying on the table in front of him. 'He wants you to read what he says. I read it last night – he described it as a confession but to me it seemed more of a boast.'

'A confession of what?' I said.

'He claims to have killed Hari Harsent, the husband of the woman cop you know. He said you should read it.'

I stared at the pages, lying on my long table. They were handwritten.

'Why are these people around you?' Spoder said. 'Who *are* they, and where have they come from? The Harsent woman and the man who claims he killed her husband. She says Jeksid intends to kill you too. He denies it. All three of them are police officers, or were. They were involved somehow in the murders of the twin brothers. You know, I'm much more concerned about the future of Terrik and Noella, my own children.

They're grown up and have their own lives and know nothing of this, but I'm suddenly bankrupt and every plan I had for them, to leave them something to provide for their future, all that has been suddenly undermined, taken away. That's much more important to me than the intrigues of these ex-cops.'

'I agree,' I said, knowing the words were inadequate, feeling great sympathy for him. He lived alone. At least I had Jo. I was feeling the separation from Jo intensely at that moment. She was due to leave Muriseay in a couple of days – I could barely wait to see her again. I felt certain that once she was home all this intrusive madness of fast cars, guns and ex-cops would somehow go away. Meanwhile, what I had was Spoder and his story, now Jeksid and what appeared to be his. I added: 'Frejah Harsent said that Jeksid claimed to have committed a perfect murder.'

'That's more or less what he says here. He's stricken with guilt, but a part of him is bragging about it. It doesn't make for pleasant reading.'

'I don't believe in a perfect crime,' I said. 'Crime is too crude, too rough, too negatively intended, for perfection.'

Whatever Jeksid had done it would not have been perfect. I remembered the many articles and books on the subject that I had read over the years, written by my fellow crime novelists. It was a subject of recurrent interest in the unusual, generically defined but popular business I was in. I was interested in it too.

The gist of the argument was essentially this: murder, one of the worst of all crimes, was only perfect if there were no witnesses, no known motives could be proved, no incriminating evidence was either left at the scene or found on the perpetrator, no connection at all existed between the killer and the victim. Preferably, ideally, there would be no corpse lying around after the event, so that a forensic examination by a doctor or a pathologist was not possible. If any of those conditions was broken, then it was not a perfect murder.

On the other hand, if all those conditions were exactly in place then, ironically, it became a murder not worth writing about in a thriller. Thus the essential contradiction that always frustrated crime writers.

In the real world some people were undoubtedly murdered from time to time in inexplicable circumstances. Killings in this sense would include murders, but were not in themselves mysteries. A body might be found on the side of the road, the victim of a hit-and-run incident, perhaps a deliberate one (murder) or an accident (careless or dangerous driving). The car would bear revealing damage, but if it took several days to be traced, then there was time for the damage to be repaired or the car disposed of. In another example, someone else might be stabbed to death in a fight outside a bar or a nightclub, after which all the witnesses and the perpetrator fled. Or there could be a totally innocent victim shot at random by an armed sociopath who had never killed before, went into hiding and who never killed again.

A murder was often unsolvable, but that did not make it perfect.

Nor did it make it thrilling or mysterious. Such murders were not the stuff of the kind of novels I and all the other crime writers liked to write. Who can solve the unsolvable? Who may be tempted by perfection? Novelists often were. But then novelists sometimes cheated.

Spoder said: 'Jeksid prepared it as a perfect murder, sir. And I believe it would be unsolved to this day if he had not written this account of it.'

'Hari Harsent's wife Frejah knew it must be him. She told me she had him drummed out of the force because of it. That alone removes any claim to perfection. And, as you say, the fact that he has written a confession has the same effect.'

'His wife Frejah, his widow, accused Jeksid only on suspicion. This is proof.'

'How long ago was it?' I said.

'Nine years. I'm not sure when these notes were written.'

'The other murders we've heard about were even older. They are all beyond the reach of justice now.'

'Not if Jeksid is still alive. He's somehow involved in them all.'

I was growing tired of the subject. It was past the time in the evening when Jo and I made internet contact. I also wanted some time to myself – I was desperate to look around on the internet and explore just how bad the financial crisis had become. It was no longer of purely academic interest to me, if it ever had been. I had much on my mind. And Spoder had been here at the house since late afternoon.

'Will you leave those pages with me?'

'These are photocopies – the originals are locked away at my apartment. Are you OK reading his handwriting?'

I glanced again at the top page. The handwriting was large, squarish, obviously put down slowly and carefully, a childish hand, intended to be legible. The writer in me winced at the spelling mistakes – I saw five in the first couple of paragraphs. It's a writer's curse to notice such errors, another kind of quest for perfection. As usual I felt guiltily supercilious for noticing.

'I can manage,' I said.

Spoder left the notes lying on the long table in my kitchen. I glanced at them again, put them aside.

I wanted Jo, and as soon as Spoder's motorbike roared away into the distance I put in the call. She was waiting. We spoke for an hour, mostly about the work she had been doing, and would be completing the next day. She showed me several photos of her set designs. I was pleased for her and impressed, and from what she told me it sounded as if the artistic director of the theatre was too.

Later we turned, inevitably, to the problem of money, but even in this she was optimistic. She told me that the next day, before she flew home, the theatre would be paying her the fee, and she had already arranged for it to be settled in cash, in thalers.

I said: 'Spoder stayed for dinner this evening. I thought he would never go.'

'Did you make him an omelette? He likes eggs.' She was invoking a private joke: Spoder invariably said he was not hungry, but ate anything that was given him. Jo always said we should keep eggs on hand, a quick fix, an easy dish to come up with for him at short notice.

'You left a lump of cheese in the fridge. And there were some eggs. I'll go out tomorrow and buy some more food. I've enough cash for that.'

We talked until late, and when we finally said goodnight I was feeling happier than I had for several days. I went around the house, following a recent habit: making sure every window, door and screen was locked. I was irritated with myself for doing so, but I did it anyway.

I glanced at the local news headlines on TV. The financial crisis in Raba City was still the headline news. This time it was about the suspected cause of the problem, a software glitch, an attack by one or more hackers, now definitely believed to be based in Raba City or close by.

It was after midnight, but I was still wide awake. I picked up the papers Spoder had left for me, and began reading.

23

The False Inspector Harsent

The account of Det. Sjt Enver Jeksid (ret'd)

The hotel was in a side street, close to the harbour. It had three storeys and faced directly on to a square. A street carrying traffic ran on the far side of the square. Behind were some empty outbuildings and a yard where rubbish was thrown. A rambling flowering plant grew out of control over the main facade, obscuring some of the windows. Inside, the building smelled of sweat, old piss, stale tobacco smoke.

The place was a dump but it was good enough for what I wanted. I paid in advance for two nights but the guy on the desk gave me no receipt. I had checked in under the false name I was using, so I didn't complain. He asked me to sign a register: the page he gave me was free of other signatures. I wrote in *Det. Sjt Waller Alman, Dearth Police*. I flashed the warrant card. The desk guy barely glanced at it: it was a fake, but a good one, good enough for his glance. Good enough also for a closer look. I had made sure of that.

I carried my bag up two flights of stairs. The lock on the room door was loose and inside only one light bulb worked. The bed smelled of other people.

I left the room and walked around the town. It was my first visit to Salay Ewwel. The night was warm but a mist drifted in from the sea and a light rain fell. The streets glistened. I stayed in the shadows of buildings, away from the streetlights. All lights were haloed by the misty fall. It was a town for sailors, drug dealers, the rootless young, the lost, the vengeful. A town to die in. I found a diner where I could eat standing. I kept my collar turned up.

I walked some more until I came to the bar that Hari Harsent ran, the one he used as a front. I clocked it from a distance, noted where the street doors were. I couldn't go in – if he was there Harsent would recognize me. I walked past several times, peering in through the small windows, mosaics with coloured glass. I rehearsed walking away from it, looking for routes through narrow streets. Afterwards I went to a movie house, but left before the end of the main feature. I'd slept through most of it.

The next afternoon I went to the police firing range. I had to sign for the piece, show my warrant card. Again I used the name Det. Sjt Waller Alman. The woman at the desk barely glanced at the card or the signature. She issued me with the standard semi-automatic, the same as the one used by most cops, the same as the one I kept at home. The serial number engraved on the barrel was recorded against Alman's name.

The rule was the same here as at other police ranges, and loosely applied. We were all cops. Alman was recognized as a serving officer. After training with the weapon I would be able to check it out for official use for a fixed period afterwards. I specified two days. No questions.

I paid the deposit. I bought three clips of the range ammo, then went with an instructor. We both put on eye guards. I wore white cotton gloves. The instructor fired a few rounds to check my piece, watched me take five shots, then she left me. She muttered that she could tell I was a good shot. My right shoulder is weaker now, but I had trained to the level of senior marksman. She wouldn't know that. She was right – I'm still good.

There were guys in the lanes on each side of mine. I guessed they were also cops. The shooter next to me was a rookie. His shots were missing because of the recoil. He hadn't yet learned how to brace. He had an instructor showing him and he was learning well. The cartridge casings from his gun flew away from him, some landing close to where I was standing. A sign on every lane said spent cases must not be touched. I saw staff who cleaned up every time a lane became empty, before the next shooter took over.

When I was finished the target was spindled back to me. I needed it to collect back the first half of my deposit. As the target arrived I turned towards it, bent down and scooped up a small handful of the rookie's casings. I held them in my gloved hand until I had the target in the other. Then I found a natural way of sliding the cases into my pocket. There were four. I might need all of them but one should be enough.

I went back to the desk, handed in the target, picked up my deposit and left. I was wearing the gun in the holster provided by the range. I dumped the cotton gloves in a trash can in the street. The bin smelled of rotting food and some kind of sickly perfume.

I went to a shopping complex and found a place that sold cheap clothes. I bought a shirt, trainer pants with deep pockets, slip-on shoes, more pairs of cotton gloves. I had everything bagged by the assistant at the check-out. I never touched any of them, except through the wrappings.

I walked back to the hotel. It was still daylight. The room felt airless, midges hovered in a thick cloud outside the window. The rain had finally ceased in the middle of the day and since then the temperature in the streets had risen. With the window open the room was filled with the sound of cars, motorbikes, music and voices. I lay on the bad-smelling bed for two hours, eyes open, staring at the ceiling. It was crazed with hairline cracks. Sunset came quickly and darkness fell. I was calm. Everything was ready.

I took a clip of ammo from my bag and slotted it into the handle of the gun. Ten rounds, standard issue. One shot would be enough. Maybe two would be necessary.

I practised raising the weapon, clasping it between both hands, taking aim, bracing against the recoil. I had been carrying a weapon most of the time I was on the force, but had never discharged it in anger. Dearth was free of violent crime, of all crime. Like the others I went twice every month to the local firing range. Like the others I kept my gun cleaned and oiled, ready for use. But I had never shot anyone before.

What else could go wrong? The gun was prepared. I was prepared with the gun.

There would be no witnesses. Hari's undercover deployment was temporarily in suspense, which was why I had chosen this time. I knew where he would be, what he would be doing, what time it would end.

The sound of gunfire at the moment of action? Police automatics are semi-silenced. The barrel has two baffles in an extra chamber. Official policy: weapons must not unduly alarm or disturb people near by. The discharge was loud, but not as loud as most people think a gun sounds. Hari's combined office and sleeping room was above a music bar. There was live rock music three nights a week – this was one of the nights. I had checked the band: they were loud and used pyrotechnics in their act. Pyrotechnics make a noise too.

Clothes: I would change at the last minute. (I glanced at my wristwatch.)

The rookie's cartridge cases I had picked up at the range: ready.

Alibi: no one knew I was on Salay Ewwel. I had travelled as Waller Alman and would fly back to Tristcontenta tomorrow under the same name. If the traffic copter was in use, I could blag a ride back to town in that. I was rostered for duty every day I was away from Dearth, but I had volunteered for the standby list, as everyone did from time to time. I had done this before. Patrols went out, transgressions were dealt with, the reserve was never called in. By law there had to be an extra officer on standby readiness, but the call never came.

That's where I was: on standby at home in Dearth City. Everyone on the station would confirm it.

Mutability? The curse of every investigation on Dearth. All detectives were on their guard, because evidence could change, or could be said to have changed. We had to become experts in reading it. Dearth Island was positioned on a geological fault above several gravitational anomalies. Mutability could kick in without warning, because of local effects. Things happened. A power spike usually, but often faulty IT on some nearby corporate system, an obsolescent memory card on someone's washing machine, a hotel door unlocked incorrectly, a personal computer loading bootleg software.

Nothing like that was a risk on Salay. There was only a single geological fault, and that was beneath the central lagoon. Gravity normal. Nothing would change. What had just happened would always lead to what would happen next. Reality could be trusted.

But I remained aware. The old Dearth habit.

I paced around the squalid hotel room. The moments dripped by like the runnels of sweat inside my shirt.

Jeksid discontinued.

★

I turned away from Jeksid's account, rubbed my eyes. It was late, and my mouth was dry. Jeksid was starting to tire me. I ran a glass of cold water, wondering if I should close down for the night and read the rest of what he had written tomorrow.

Spoder had summed it up.

'Who *are* these people?' he had said, in a rare for him display of feeling. This sudden vehemence had startled me more than the remark itself. I thought he took these old incidents more seriously than I did, but at that moment he had caught exactly the same feeling as mine. Frejah Harsent in her souped-up car and uttering her implausible warnings, now this ex-policeman proud of his gun skills, going about a law enforcement job in a place where there was allegedly no crime, where he carried a weapon everywhere but had never fired it, bragging about being a senior marksman. The Dearth habit of distrusting reality, because it was believed to change.

And it was all long in the past. The Antterland twins, one of them murdered fifteen years ago, the other five years later, now this about Hari Harsent, nine years ago. Who knew anything about these people when they were alive, who cared now about who had killed them? They all seemed cut off from the flow of life, from family and lovers, even people who merely cared about them. Only the fact that they were murdered, and that the murders appeared to be linked, made them more interesting in death than they had been in life. Their fates survived in closed police files and confessions that were suddenly produced. Who are these people, and who *were* they?

The novelist in me – I could not help seeing it this way, because that is what I do, what I am – simply could not respond to these people. Mystery and crime novels are often thought to be entirely about plot, but in reality like all novels they are driven by character. People are depicted as having real lives, with complexities, worries and satisfactions that have little to do with the main story.

I knew almost nothing about Lew Antterland, beyond the fact he was murdered. He owned a baseball bat, he had a lot of money, he had a twin brother. (But what was his job? Where had the money come from? Was he in a relationship with a partner? Why had he moved from Dearth? Why was he killed?) His brother Dever was slightly more interesting: a small-time magician, and the likely killer of Lew. What would drive a skilled magician into murdering his own identical twin? How did he first become interested in magic, and why? Dever too had money, but it was buried in a secret trust fund. (Who later killed him? Where had the money come from?)

Frejah Harsent had been intriguing for a while, but the more I knew her the less I thought of her. She depicted surfaces of herself, not the deeper reality. She was involved in every one of the murders. This Jeksid: I had learned nothing about him that made me visualize him, see him as a person. For now, in his account, especially in his account, he came over as a set of actions and intentions in ways I had read a score of times in second-rate thrillers. No imaginative spark. A good editor would send any description of him back, saying that the character needed fleshing out more.

I looked back at the last page I had read: Jeksid was describing his familiarity with the effects of mutability, but reflecting that they would not be a problem on Salay. The people I had met from Dearth all seemed obsessed with this subject – perhaps they had a right to be. So maybe we who lived on Salay should be more sensitive to it?

Reading about mutability again had raised in me the uncomfortable feeling that I knew more about mutability than I would admit, even to myself. The long-term stability of the financial sector on Raba, much as I loathed it, was an undeniable fact of life on this island. Yet the present devastating collapse of major parts of the sector had followed soon after I played around with the software I discovered on the hotel key card.

A mutability safeguard – what was the harm in that? What indeed?

The authorities had been saying for a long time that the banks' secure computer systems had been hacked into some-how. Was I indirectly responsible for that? Even directly?

Money and high finance were a system of belief. The price of shares rose or fell, not only because a corporation was doing well or badly, but because enough investors expected it to do well or badly. Or thought it would. Or were willing to gamble that it would. It was an activity that was purely abstract, psycho-logical. They speculated with opportunities and options. They never saw or handled money – they just lived for the idea of it.

I was a hands-on user of money: I earned it, spent it, lost it, saved some of it. In this I was a true citizen serf. I had no belief in money unless I could see it or count it, an entirely practical matter.

The onset of mutability was a kind of belief system similar to high finance. There were practical effects and consequences (the events were real), but afterwards only the results counted, so no one believed that the process had really happened (the events became abstract).

Did my hands-on spending of my earnings, and that of hun-dreds of thousands of citizen serfs like me, eventually build up to such a total that our spending gained a psychological dimension in the glass and steel towers of the financial district? That my weekly buying of groceries encouraged or discouraged those who would run a pension scheme, or an insurance policy, or who were moneylenders? So that money was both real (actual spending) and abstract (a belief system)?

Feeling stiff with fatigue I went to my study and booted my desktop. When everything had loaded I looked for the icon on my desktop called *Mutability Safeguard*. Then I remembered I had deleted it. Only the icon had disappeared – the program was still installed. I located it, opened it and waited for it to load. I entered the password. I went to the main menu.

At the top there was a message: *Salay Raba, Financial Services Protocols – Mutability Safeguards installed.* Beneath that it said: *Upgrade available. Install now? [y/n]*

I hastily clicked on No.

I noticed another pulldown menu headed *Settings*. Among its many options was: *Remove Salay Raba, Financial Services Protocols – Mutability Safeguards? [y/n]*

I clicked on Yes.

My hard disc was humming as it worked busily. I was holding the key card from the hotel in case I was ordered to re-engage the 'source', but it seemed the program could be uninstalled without it. There was no sign of the slow-moving green bar at the bottom of the monitor display, glacially reporting percentages. I was yawning, my eyes were tired.

At last the message came: *Salay Raba, Financial Services Protocols Uninstalled.*

In the morning I ate breakfast at the long table, Jeksid's handwritten notes lying across from me. I fed Barmi the cat. In my study I sent a brief email to Jo, letting her know I was up and about. I read other emails, and looked at my regular social media feeds. I did not look at any of the online news services. I did not open my bank's website.

I returned to the kitchen/diner, sat at the long table and

carried on reading Jeksid's account from the place where I had stopped, after his unappealing image of the runnels of sweat.

Jeksid, continued:

I was ready to go. I first removed my street clothes, then put on one of the pairs of cotton gloves. I removed each garment in turn from the store's plastic bag, cutting off identifying labels: size, manufacturer, country of origin, laundry instructions. When all the garments were ready I pulled them on over my own underclothes.

I made sure the safety catch was on, then slipped the gun into the deep pocket of the trainer pants. In the other pocket I put the four empty bullet cases I had taken from the firing range, then thrust in the rest of the cotton gloves on top. I removed my own shoes and put on the slip-ons. I glanced at my watch.

It could still go wrong.

Transgressions in Dearth City were often solved because matters ran out of the control of the perpetrator. The act of doing something wrong can break down your reserves, your sense of cool. In the heat of the moment you think nothing of impulsively punching someone in the face, but moments later, when you've done it and your victim is lying huddled on the floor, perhaps with blood oozing, and you know you've really done it because your hand is hurting where contact was made – your understanding of the violent act has changed.

Human responses, emotional and mental, cannot be controlled or predicted. Transgressors give themselves away. Their behaviour changes – some become defensive and guilty, other toughen up, act more brazenly.

But I was calm. I was a trained cop. I would be calm throughout. I had prepared for many weeks and travelled a long way to achieve this. I had researched, had timed every move and action, factored in alternatives, errors. If there were any slips I had backups ready.

Hari Harsent was the brains behind the original deal. Hari had made us rich, but I knew he was greedy now for more. I was probably next on his list. Greed put us all at risk, as Lew had discovered, fifteen years earlier. Hari had taken his share of that result, he had his pay as a cop, and the bar he ran in Ewwel Town was a business that brought in more. None of it was enough for him. For some, having more is never enough.

The physical layout of Hari's bar was this. On the ground floor was the small stage where the music acts performed, with a raised section, lights, power sockets, and so on. There was a cleared space for a crowd, or for dancing. Around the edge were seats and a few tables. The area behind the bar was where the staff area, kitchen, toilets, etc., were situated. On the floor above, Hari's personal space was directly over the bar. When not on police operations he relaxed there every evening a band was playing. He stayed out of the way, listening on large relay speakers. He played the music loud. He rarely, never, went down to the bar while the band was playing. He was alone, stayed alone, deep in a big chair, drinking hard from a table littered with bottles.

At the end of every gig, while the bar was still open, Hari would go downstairs, talk to the bar staff, see some of the regulars, chat to the band members, perhaps share a drink with them. All this I knew.

I checked my preparations one more time, then I slipped out of the hotel without being seen, into the humid night. Once I was on the main street, music blared from doorways and windows, and from small speakers attached above the stalls of street traders. Crowds surged by. Prostitutes were on every corner. The smell of spicy meat smoking on the charcoal braziers of the vendors was appetizing. I walked on. I was not noticed. Who in the crowd would see me or recognize me?

I followed my planned route. It was about half a kilometre from the hotel to Hari's bar. I was tempted to hurry but I was sticking to my plan. I maintained a steady pace because I did not want to get out of breath.

I came to the square where Hari had his bar, went to the building and pushed through the doors. A support band was playing, not well. The place was full but not yet crowded. Most of the people were much younger than me. I had not thought of that. I felt prominent for being older. I bought a glass of beer, but I held it without drinking more than a couple of sips. I made eye contact with no one. The support band were coming to the end of their set. They were running late, but I could wait.

They cleared away their kit – the roadies of the headline band moved in quickly to set up their sound and lights. I waited, watching how they worked, connecting the amplifiers, play-back, and so on. Soon, the band members themselves moved to the platform, and started a sound check. That was my cue.

I put down my beer and followed the signs to the toilets, beyond a double swing door. I walked past them and pushed open a door marked Private. Behind this was a staircase. I went up one step at a time. There was a thick carpet. The top three steps turned and opened straight into Hari's room. He was in his chair, alert, upright. He had heard me coming. For a moment I was uncertain: he had a mass of wild hair, and a bushy beard. His undercover image.

He recognized me at once. Of course he would know who I was.

'I expected you here one of these days, Enver. But you can go now – we agreed never to meet. Leave now!'

'Never to meet in public. That's what we said. There's no one here.'

Sounds from the bar were being relayed through the loudspeakers: shouted conversations over the background recorded music, glasses and bottles clinking, bangs and random amplified notes from the band's instruments as they were set up. The drummer kept pounding at his bass.

'You're here for a reason. What is it?'

'We had a deal, Hari. We agreed on it, said we would stick to it. It was fair to us all and it was going to set us up for life. But you killed Willer, you broke the deal!'

'It was already broken, when Lew Antterland broke it.'

'That was a long time ago. You didn't have to shoot Willer.' I noticed then that there was a baseball bat leaning against the side of his chair. I pointed to it. 'Is that Lew's?' I said. I could see the sports club badge still attached to the stock, close to the maker's stencil. 'I gave him that as a present when he left school.'

Hari reached down and took hold of the bat. He laid it on his lap, hands cradling it.

'I found it in his house. Want to have a close look at his suicide weapon? Real close?'

Anger coursed through me – Hari had also tensed.

'You know Lew didn't kill himself!' I said loudly, against the noise from below. 'How did you get hold of his bat? All the evidence was being held by the police on Hames.'

'They released it, let me have it. The inquest was over, the verdict made sense to them. They could close the file. I went to Lew's house one day, when things had quietened down.'

'You had no right to do that! I should have been told! It belonged to my son!'

'Yeah, well – you never were much of a father to him, were you, Enver? I thought having the bat might be useful in this place, and with the work I do. People like you come up those stairs more often than I like. I need to have something by my side, to settle arguments.'

'You can put it down, Hari.'

'No – you're here for an argument.' He had not moved from his chair, but his hold on the baseball bat was steady. 'Tell me what you want.'

'I want to know why you killed Willer.'

'You know exactly why. He murdered Lew, took the money. I was pissed with him.'

'Five years later?'

'I wanted to be sure. I thought for a while you might step in and do it yourself. Willer was also your son, your responsibility. But then my assignments were changed, and getting to Salay Sekonda became something I had to do while I could still travel. He knew too much, and I needed the money to buy this place. You were paid off too, so what's your complaint?'

I said: 'No complaint, Hari. But I didn't want or need the money enough to have my only remaining son killed.'

'Maybe now it's different. That's why you're here, isn't it? Cops aren't paid too well, as we both know.'

'I'm thinking ahead to retirement,' I said. 'The money counts, yes. Next year I'm going to want a bigger share of the deal.'

'You won't get it from me.'

Hari braced suddenly, and he stood up. I took an unguarded step back. I realized he was still strong, easy with his movements. I was younger than him, but his undercover work had clearly kept him fitter, more active. I had a stiff hip, a lower back I had strained too often. My right shoulder was weak. I could not raise myself out of a chair like that any more – I had to shift my weight, get my legs in the right position, lever myself up. The days when I ran in pursuit of wrongdoers were long over. I was an office cop now, working out the remaining years.

Hari was hefting the baseball bat in an aggressive way.

'Keep your distance, Hari,' I said, alarmed by the speed of his response.

At that moment there was a howling noise from the speakers, as someone downstairs grabbed the microphone. Holding it too close to his mouth, and speaking too loudly so that every breath was a harsh rasping noise, the man began some kind of heavily distorted announcement about the band who were about to play, which group would be coming to a later gig at the end of the week, a ticket-only event, something about where the tickets were available, then a list of the names who wanted songs dedicated to them tonight, mostly women's names, on and on . . .

Hari and I stared at each other across the room, I could not believe he was once the friend I had known, the ideal of a trusted cop, looked up to by everyone who worked under him. He was an inspector now, my superior officer in theory and reality, but his special duties had made him look like a dishevelled, dissolute wreck, a transgressor. As the voice downstairs broke off, Hari shrugged as if to indicate he heard something like that every night. Still neither of us moved. I was aware I was only a single step away from the top of the stairs, that if Hari made a rush at me I should fall or be knocked backwards. But to move forward would seem to be initiating something.

As the microphone downstairs rattled back into its stand, Hari said: 'Are you here because my wife sent you? Do you still work with her?'

'No – she doesn't know. No one knows. We're both on the force, but I never see her. We agreed not to meet when other people were around, remember?'

'And you can arrange that?'

'She's senior management. We stay clear of each other.'

From below, a thudding drum beat, a jangling electric guitar. The sound of the band exploded into the room. A vocalist started shouting *la-la-la* sounds in time with the music. The building resonated with bass notes.

I pulled the gun from the deep pocket of my trainer pants, releasing the safety in the same motion. I held it in my right hand, pointing at Hari. It was not how I had imagined it would be. Hari swung the baseball bat above his shoulders, stepped with shocking speed towards me. There was no doubt what he would do if he reached me. We were about three metres apart. I pulled the trigger.

Even drowned by the sound of the rock music, the gun's discharge sounded loud. The weapon jerked in my hand, wrenching my weak shoulder. I missed! Hari was almost on me!

I took the gun in both hands, fired again at close range, no time to aim. This time I hit him in the shoulder, pushing him violently backwards and away from me, spinning him around, making him fall. The baseball bat twisted in the air and landed on the floor.

Hari doubled up in pain, but he was trying to crawl, squirming across the floor towards the top of the stairs. He was yelling.

I moved back from him. Blood was already pumping from his arm, his shoulder. I was shocked by how the blood surged unstoppably out of him. I hadn't expected that. I wanted none of it on me. It was appalling! I had to finish him off. I fired a third shot! I was desperate, frightened, certain someone would come rushing up the stairs to investigate. I missed him again, but he was on the floor. It was difficult to hit a low, moving target. Now he had changed direction and was crawling towards me. I wanted him nowhere near me. I had to avoid getting his blood on me at all costs.

He was yelling something at me, but his voice was distorted by pain and on the speakers the vocalist was chanting the words of the song. I was shocked by the ferocity and anguish of Hari's expression. With his good arm he tried to grab my ankle, but I leapt out of the way just in time.

I saw the baseball bat – it was within reach. Hari saw me looking, saw me stretching my hand towards it, and with a tremendous twist of his body he rolled over to it. I grabbed it, then swung it at him like a club, catching him a glancing blow on the side of the head. He howled in pain, but managed to raise himself into a crouching position. I knew with an extra surge of terror that if he was able to take hold of me, if only with one hand, he would certainly go on to kill me. I swung the bat again at his head – it hit him hard but it did not slow him. Then a third blow. This time I brought the bat down from above on the front of his head, using all my strength.

I felt something breaking. I thought it was the bat splintering, but then I saw the thick, dark blood erupting horribly from the top of his head, just above his face. Hari fell back again, and was still. Then he rolled in an agonized spasm, turning on one side. I tossed aside the bat. which rolled across the floor.

I fired a fourth bullet into Hari's chest, aiming at his heart, but leapt back and away as if propelled by the recoil.

He did not react to the shot. He was unconscious or already dead.

Everything changed.

Horror and fear filled me. Now he was still. I was appalled by what had happened, what I had had to do, how difficult it was to kill a man. The blood was spreading in a thick pool around Hari's head and shoulders. I had no idea.

My instinct was to flee, throw aside the gun, rush down the stairs, push through the crowd in the bar, escape to the street.

The rock music thudded and screeched on. I was paralysed. I could not look at Hari. I was still terrified of him. In case he moved.

Fragments of my plan returned. I noticed that one of the bullet cases I had fired was on the floor, now being overtaken by Hari's spreading blood. I leaned over it, kicked it away from the blood with my foot, rolled it by pressing on the thin carpet, trying to wipe away some of the blood.

I had discharged four rounds. I looked around for the other three cartridge cases, dreading that they too had been covered by the flood, or that Hari's body had fallen on them, or that they had simply bounced and rolled somewhere I could not see or reach them. I was able to spot two of them straight away, but the fourth eluded me. I had to bend down, constantly terrified that someone downstairs had heard the noise of the violent struggle and would come up to investigate. Kneeling, I stretched out across the floor, feeling and groping for the small metal cylinder.

Then I saw it – it too had been overtaken by the spreading of Hari's blood. Once again I rolled the casing out with my foot, and made a rudimentary attempt to clean it by wiping it on the carpet. I had Hari's blood on my gloves, on my shoes.

I held in my right hand all the cases from the four bullets I had fired. With the other hand I reached down into the deep pocket of the trainer pants, located the cases I had picked up at the range, and scattered them on the floor around Hari's body. Two of them fell into the pool of blood. I then clicked the safety catch on and slipped the gun down into the same pocket, together with the cases I had used.

I took off the cotton gloves and stuffed them into the same pocket. From the other I pulled out a clean pair.

The band was coming to the end of the number with a series of crashing climactic chords. I hurried away, down the stairs, pushed through the connecting door and entered the bar through the swing doors. No one turned to look at me. I pressed through the crush and made it to the street. As the door closed behind me everyone was cheering and waving their arms towards the stage.

I was in shock from what I had done. It was the first time I had fired a gun with intent, the first time I had killed. And the club. I could not forget the feeling of violently swinging the club against Hari's head. I had done that. The memory would haunt me forever. Hari was someone I had known for many years, a colleague, a friend even, an important part of the plan we had devised, married to a senior colleague.

Superintendent Harsent, when the news reached her, would know immediately that I was the killer. It didn't matter what steps I took to eradicate the evidence – she would know. She and Hari had separated some time earlier when he began undercover work, but they never completed a divorce. She could destroy me. She was the main weakness in my plan, but I pinned my hopes on the fact that she was as guilty as me. If she used her insider knowledge to incriminate me she would lose as much as I would.

I could depend on that. I had to depend on that.

The small square outside Hari's bar was closed to traffic, and a crowd of young people were enjoying the hot night while the music spilled out. Many were standing, but others were sitting on the patch of grass in the centre of the square. I saw one of the vendors waiting beside his brazier, and in spite of the bloody crime I had just committed the smell of the spicy food was almost irresistible.

I hurried from the square and followed my planned route through side streets and alleys, heading towards my hotel and the harbour beyond. Away from the area of Hari's bar the streets were more crowded. Traffic drove by slowly, weaving between people sauntering in the roadways. The vehicles made a racket and left a stink of exhaust fumes.

I felt the weight of the gun and the empty bullet cases in my pants pocket, knocking against my thigh with every step, a steadily beating reminder of the horror of what I had done. I tried to control the fear that was in me. I was certain that by now someone would have found Hari's body. The police would be called and they would immediately start searching for whoever had killed him. I was listening for the sound of sirens as I went swiftly along, but there was too much loud music being played everywhere. I felt prominent because I was a stranger in the town, and because most of the people who were out in the streets that night looked decades younger than me.

I struggled to be calm. I told myself, saying the words under my breath, that all would be well when I had dealt with the gun.

But I had not expected so much blood. I knew without look-ing that my slip-on shoes had been in the spilled blood as I searched for the spent cases. My trainer pants too – I had been kneeling. I imagined a trail of incriminating bloody footprints following me. Had any of Hari's blood spurted on to my shirt? I did not dare to look back or down. And there was blood on the cotton gloves, which I was wearing when I picked up the bullet cases. These gloves were now stuffed into my pocket with the four casings. I imagined traces of blood seeping out through the cheap synthetic material of the trainer pants.

And although I was wearing a fresh pair of white gloves, had there been some of Hari's blood on my hands when I pulled them on? Were traces of that blood even now oozing through the glove material?

I did not look, could not risk looking. Worse, I could not risk discovering the truth.

Stay calm, stay calm. It became a mantra. I could not have regrets. I could not think myself wrong.

I reached the harbour area. The largest part was the main port for the inter-island ferries, as well as the longer haul passenger and cargo services. A tall ferry, blazing with deck and navigation lights, was slowly approaching the terminal. Another was already departing, heading out across the sea.

There was also a small harbour where the local fishing fleet was based, its outer wall facing the open sea. This quay was sparsely lit at night. It was a quiet period in the harbour as most of the fishing vessels went out at night. I could see the ice and auction shed on the shore – all lights were off.

I was soon on the long outer arm of the fishing harbour, the dark sea heaving below me to my left, the calm waters of the harbour on the other side. My hip was sore from walking, and my weak right shoulder was aching. I went on, from one dim pool of light to the next. There was a long gap between lights where the quay wall turned at an angle to contain the harbour.

In the middle of the gap between lights I scooped the four spent bullet cases from my pocket and tossed them into the sea. The soiled gloves followed, and after a moment's thought so too did my slip-on shoes. The sea would not destroy them, and one day soon they would turn up in the harbour or on one of the beaches as jetsam, but they would be bleached of all signs of Hari's blood. Also of any traces of my skin or perspiration that might otherwise be forensically traceable to me.

Finally, the gun. I looked around, suddenly concerned that someone might be watching. But I was alone, in darkness. I released the clip of unused bullets and fingered them free of the spring loader and down into the sea. Then I broke the weapon open, slid the firing pin from its mount — that too I dropped into the sea. I returned the gun to my pocket.

Now walking barefoot, I went slowly back along the harbour arm. It was painful to walk, but I felt safer than before. No bloodied shoes to worry about. Just before reaching the harbour road I saw a litter bin. It was crammed with used drink cans and food waste. I dropped into it my cotton gloves, pushing them down beneath the top level of waste.

When at last I came to my hotel I noticed the street vendor I had seen earlier. He was working hard for a group of customers, standing close by his brazier, making up portions of sliced broiled meat with a handful of salad, crammed into a pitta. I passed him, went to my hotel. I wanted to change my clothes, rest my feet — I had not walked barefoot in city streets before.

In my room, under the dim light of the single bulb, I stripped off the trainer pants and T-shirt, bundled them up. Next, I attended to the gun. The ammo clip was inside, but empty. I had brought a replacement firing pin with me, concealed in my luggage. I pushed it into place.

Now, apart from hand and fingerprints, the gun was unidentifiable. The gun itself was already registered by the firing range to 'W. Alman' — that thin disguise would not of course resist good police work, but I had the resources to deal with it. When I handled the baseball bat I was wearing gloves. The bullet cases I had scattered around Hari's body were from another gun, the one the rookie had been using at the range. The bullets they would find in Hari's apartment, and the one (or two) somewhere inside his body, were not from those cases. The firing pin was not the one that had detonated the charge in the bullets. The barrel, if examined, would reveal that the bullets had passed through, that it was the murder weapon, but there were no other traces to identify it further.

Wearing another pair of cotton gloves I wiped the gun clean. I laid it on the table beside the bed.

I filled the hand basin with cold water. I rinsed my hair, then washed my face, hands, chest, everything.

I lay on my bed for half an hour, listening to the sounds of the night through the open window.

Finally, I dressed in my own clothes and shoes, then went down to the street. I walked across to the vendor and bought some food. The cauldron beneath his cooking plate was glowing bright red in the breeze from the sea. He passed me the filled pitta, with a paper napkin and a wooden fork. He sold me a bottle of iced water too.

I said: 'When you're finished for the night, how do you deal with the hot coals?'

'It's charcoal,' he said, looking beyond me, hoping for another customer.

'So how do you deal with the charcoal?'

'What do you mean?'

'Do you just leave it here on the side of the road? Do you have to put out the fire?'

'Incinerator,' he said, nodding in the direction of the hotel.

I remembered the untidy yard beyond the building. It was an enclosed area, behind a high chain link fence and an unlocked gate. 'You dump it over there?'

'Incinerator. The town truck clears it out at daybreak.'

The pitta sandwich was delicious but I didn't want to take it to my room. I strolled around, eating and remembering — remembering most of all. Memories filled me. I couldn't finish the sandwich.

Back in the room I stayed obstinately awake. I kept trying to justify what I had done, make excuses, but then would turn defiantly against myself. Hari was dead! It was done at last! The sounds from the street gradually quietened. It was long past midnight. When the stillness had lasted for more than an hour I left the bed, and picked up the small bundle of clothes.

The main door to the hotel was closed but not locked. No one was on the desk, or in the tiny office behind. I went out into the silent streets.

I doubled back, walking along the narrow street that ran beside the building, to the yard. The gate was wide open. The whole area was a mess, with rotting rubbish spilled on the ground. Several immense hoppers lined one side, waiting to be emptied or carted away. At the back of the yard was a walled area, which the pitta vendor had identified as an incinerator. It was in fact just an area where hot cinders from braziers could be dumped at night. It was obvious that the contents of more than one brazier had been emptied here. There was a wide and multi-peaked mound of cinders and ash, emitting heat while not actually releasing flames or smoke. Patches glowed bright red where the breeze caught them. Sparks briefly flew.

I tossed my incriminating clothes as far towards the back as possible, then watched for as long as it took for smoke to rise.

No sleep followed, that night.

In daylight, when the town was awake, I walked to the police shooting range. I arrived a few minutes after it had opened for business. The woman civilian worker I had previously seen on the desk was not there. A young guy had taken her place. I was wearing the last of my cotton gloves. I flashed my Alman warrant card at him, then handed over the gun in its holster.

He took the weapon from me, opened it expertly, removed

the firing pin, examined it, then put it back. He noted down the number engraved on the barrel.

'Have you brought back unused rounds, Serjeant Alman?' he said.

'No.'

'OK.' He typed something on his keyboard, then handed me the refund of the deposit. I signed for it as W. Alman.

The next day I flew back to Dearth, using the Alman identity for the last time. I had to wait a while at Tristcontenta for the traffic helicopter to arrive, but I was home before midnight. The day after I put on my usual work clothes, pulled on the ID lanyard, and reported to the station. As usual I was rostered for desk work.

The news of the death of Detective Inspector Harsent broke towards the end of that day. He was a well known and popular figure on the station, at least among the more senior officers. He had been working undercover for so long that recently appointed officers knew of him only by reputation. The station went immediately into mourning, a formal roll was called as a tribute, an investigation was announced to work alongside the homicide squad of the Salay Ewwel police. Many officers volunteered to take part, but I did not. I saw Superintendent Frejah Harsent during that day, but she either did not realize I was attending the roll call, or did not notice me. For all of the next day the mystery of Hari Harsent's killing was covered by television, press and internet news media.

I continued to work my shifts at the station, but was fearful of being challenged. I fretted endlessly about the effectiveness of how I had concealed the evidence. There were two weak areas I was painfully aware of: the knowledge that Superintendent Harsent would deeply suspect me of the crime, and the fact that I had strong personal links with the victim.

My working belief about Frejah Harsent appeared to be correct. She was herself too deeply involved to reveal her knowledge, or to make accusations against me. I rarely saw her again, except on the most formal of occasions – if she came to the station when I was working there I never had any contact with her. She knew what I knew, and vice versa. There was a silent pact between us, and it held.

More concerning were my links to Hari Harsent, and this was because effective investigation by the homicide team could discover them. There was a direct causal link between the murders of my two sons, and the death of Hari Harsent. However, both the police cases of Lew and Dever had been closed, Lew's because his death had been declared a suicide, and Dever's because no suspect had ever been identified or arrested. As the weeks went by, none of those links to me were discovered. I knew of course who had killed Dever, and so did Frejah Harsent. For different, or in fact similar, reasons we maintained our silence.

The strongest link, in theory one that could be revealed by good police work, was the nature of the financial investment that Hari and I had shared. An opening of that matter would incriminate me beyond any reasonable doubt, because it would establish not only the connection between us, but the motivation for the killing. I was helpless before that.

But the money was in an anonymous fund, it was spread between document banks and unnamed investment houses, it was long-established and had been set up years in the past – even the bank officials who drew up the agreement would not only not remember any details, most of them by now would be retired or even deceased.

The worst moment during the investigation came about seven days after I returned. I was working at my desk when two uniformed officers from another force approached me (I later learned they were from Salay Ewwel), ordered me to stand up, then demanded I hand over my firearm. Of course I did, fearing the finger of suspicion had finally landed upon me. Only later that day did I discover that every semi-automatic weapon issued in our station had been taken away for forensic and ballistic examination. Mine was returned to me ten days later. So was everyone else's.

24

The Concatenated Man

I went to my office. I took the photocopies of Jeksid's story with me. I laid them out next to my desktop computer, and spread them so that the right-hand edges of most of the pages were visible. I lifted one page after another, scanning quickly over what I had read, deliberately skimming the description of the brawl that led to Harsent's death. I never enjoy reading about violence, even in fiction. If Jeksid's story was true, or even partly true, then it was so much the more unpleasant.

I had other things on my mind. These included enquiring into the state of financial health of my bank, to me an urgent matter. I still had only a few thalers in my pocket until Jo came home. The bank's website had not been refreshed since I last looked. I turned to the local news: nothing had developed there either, from what I could tell. No new financial corporations had declared imminent bankruptcy overnight, but the general sense of malaise amongst the people who lived in Ocean Domaisne remained high and all-consuming. It depressed me simply to listen to those interviews, even with people whose obsession with wealth was alien to me.

I tried to contact Jo, but she was not online.

I felt the day starting to slip past me, with nothing achieved. I took a break and walked across to the beach, stood by the shallows and stared out to sea. This was not Salay's central sea lagoon, but the Midway Sea itself. Our view of the open ocean created a constant temptation to travel, to follow the apparently close allure of the horizon, to discover and explore the subtropical islands to the north of us, and east and west. Jo had suggested a holiday at the end of the summer – perhaps it was time I took her up on that. By then my new novel should be finished and delivered, and I would have no more literary commitments for a while.

Back at the house I tried again to contact Jo, but she had left a message for me saying she had to be offline for a few hours. I knew it was her last full day at the theatre. Her plan was to pack up her stuff in the evening and catch the red-eye flight from Muriseay to Ewwel, the first, which took off after midnight. I would drive to Raba airport and meet her from the inter-island shuttle during the morning.

In the afternoon I settled down to a series of detailed searches of the social records of both Dearth and Salay Hames, the fifth. It had not occurred to me that the murdered twins were relatives of the other people. The revelation that Lew and Dever were the sons of Enver Jeksid had come as a significant surprise, something which seemed both to explain and obscure a great deal.

The registry data available about births and deaths, and so on, became more inconsistent and unreliable the further back I looked. The file storage formats and general organization of the records created puzzles I had to keep working at.

I could turn up no birth records for the twin boys, either in the Dearth social archives, or in Salay Hames. Frejah had said they were Dearth citizens: I searched the serf, villein and vassal categories from both islands.

In the Dearth Vassal Court of Marital Union and Dissolution

I came across a summary (only) of a suit of dissolution, in other words a divorce, made by the plaintiff, one Enver Woller Jeksid. He was suing for dissolution on the grounds of desertion by his wife, Jessa Jeksid. He lodged an appeal against a previous court decision, which had granted custody to Jessa of their twin sons, then aged two years, but the appeal was turned down. Jessa was granted leave to travel away from Dearth, with the condition that her ex-husband be allowed full access to the boys on request.

I soon found Jessa's birth record: she had been born into the Dearth vassalage as Jessa Alman. She was approximately the same age as Enver Jeksid. They had married young and the marriage did not last long: between three and four years. I could not discover why custody of the boys had been granted to the mother, although I knew in most divorce cases involving children that was what happened. There was one unsubstantiated allegation of neglect against Enver Jeksid, but he emphatically denied that and it was not raised again.

In the archived gazetteer of the Dearth police I discovered that Jeksid had joined the force two years after his marriage broke up. He was then twenty-five years old. After three years he was moved to the Transgression Investigation Department as a plainclothes detective. He was promoted to detective serjeant two years later, having displayed, according to the gazette, 'commitment and determination' in his work.

From this information I worked out that Jeksid, the man Frejah alleged was hunting for me with deadly intent, was now sixty-two years old.

While searching through the gazette archive I looked to see what I could find out about Hari Harsent. Harsent was five years older than Jeksid and at the time Jeksid was recruited Hari was a detective serjeant in the TID. According to the file,

Harsent was promoted to detective inspector a year later. In the same year he married another young officer, Detective Serjeant Frejah Garten. There was no further information about Hari Harsent's career after that, presumably because for several years he was working undercover. The final entry reported his death at the age of fifty-eight, nearly a decade ago.

I frequently remembered Spoder's querulous demand: 'Who *are* all these people?'

I was beginning to find out at last, and even had some idea of what they looked like. I had already seen the photos of Lew and Dever Antterland, for instance, and the police archive carried a blurred photo of Hari Harsent in the years before he was assigned to undercover work. Of course I had met Frejah several times, but Jeksid remained an enigma. He was the one I knew least and, unexpectedly, through his written confession, the most about.

Spoder was on my mind. Then Spoder called me on the landline.

'Sir, I have some important information for you!' he said, while I was still lifting the receiver to my ear. 'I have had good news, and I have made some interesting discoveries about these cops from Dearth.'

'Tell me the good news,' I said.

'Well, it is only good for myself, but as you showed some sympathy, which I greatly appreciate, I must tell you. I was in contact with my bank this morning, and the website claims that their cash machines are all operative again. I went straight down to the nearest one, and it was true. My account will be back up and running again tomorrow.'

'Spoder, I'm genuinely pleased for you. I was worried.'

'And the savings account, where I have set aside something

for Terrik and Noella, that is going to be restored before the end of the week.' There was a slight pause, then: 'Is your own bank functioning again, sir?'

'Not yet, not as far as I know. But I'm OK for now – Jo will be home tomorrow, and she is bringing some money to tide us over. It's not a problem, or not yet. What is the information you said you had found?'

'It's about the Dearth cops. Are you still involved with the mystery?'

'Of course I am,' I said. I had resigned myself to following the path to its conclusion. 'I want to see the thing through. What have you discovered?'

As often before, it turned out that Spoder's research covered much of the same ground as mine. I listened carefully to him without commenting, noting down a few extra details I had missed or skimmed over. Spoder was a thorough researcher.

He told me about Jeksid's early marriage and divorce, the loss of his small children in a custody dispute.

'I have to say I felt some sympathy for him there, sir,' Spoder said. 'I can't imagine anything more hurtful than to lose contact with one's pre-school children. But it seems to have been an angry divorce, and Jeksid deliberately kept away from his wife and children after they left. He made only two contact visits after the divorce. His wife, Jessa, moved to Salay Hames, the fifth, with the man she had met. As you know, travel between Dearth and Salay involves a substantial journey.'

'When were these visits, do you know?'

'The first was a year or two after they split up. The second was some years later, when the boys reached the age of sixteen – it was probably a birthday visit.'

'This was when he gave the baseball bat to Lew?'

'I think that's right. He would almost certainly have given the other boy a present too, but I've no idea what it might have been.'

A memory of an inscription in squarish handwriting flashed like a shard of sunlight glimpsed through trees.

'I think it was a book,' I said. 'An instruction manual of magical techniques.'

'Yes – I suppose that's possible,' Spoder said, apparently not too interested.

'Tell me about the man Jessa moved to Hames with,' I said.

Spoder re-engaged with his information.

'You won't be surprised to learn that his name was Antterland,' he said. Amongst the relative flood of new information I had been absorbing, it had not yet in fact occurred to me that I still did not know why the twin brothers had that name, but I said nothing. If Spoder had not telephoned when he did I would have guessed anyway, but he was a long way ahead of me here.

He went on: 'Antterland was not from Dearth – it's not clear where exactly he came from. Somewhere else in the Archipelago, obviously. He travelled around a great deal, maintained an air of intrigue about his doings, was secretive about his meetings and sometimes used false names. His real name was Raffe Antterland, and he was a businessman of sorts, a self-styled entrepreneur, constantly setting up schemes and companies, then selling them or using the equity to raise more capital.

'He was about ten years older than Jessa. They met while he was negotiating a string of business deals in Dearth. He seems to have dazzled her. It must have been love at first sight, because within a few weeks of meeting him Jessa packed up her life and moved with him to Salay. After her divorce finally came through she and Antterland married. They set up a home on Salay Hames. As far as I can tell this was the same house in which Lew was later killed.'

I tried to imagine what Enver Jeksid must have gone through during this period. He and Jessa were so young, still in their early twenties. It was a sad story: a recent marriage, sudden abandonment and desertion, removal of the children to a distant island. Presumably the relationship turned toxic. She had met and married another man, a business operative with plenty of money. She changed her name. Perhaps Raffe Antterland seemed glamorous, a bit of a cad but attractive with it, high on his success, a deal-maker who used other people's money.

'When were the boys given Antterland's name?' I said.

'I haven't been able to date that exactly,' Spoder said. 'It appears to have been soon after she remarried.'

'And was Jeksid a Dearth cop at this time?'

'No – that came a year or so later. He had another job – I don't know what it was. He gave that up and applied for a police cadetship. When he was recruited as a full constable he appears to have thrown himself wholeheartedly into the job. A way of keeping his mind away from other things? He did well. A lot of new police officers are like that. They often see joining the police as a new start, a chance to put things behind them. I know the feeling, sir. That was me too. For the first two years I was the keenest young cop on the force.'

Like Spoder, I felt some sympathy for the young Enver Jeksid. He was still more or less unknown to me, but I was glimpsing the details of his life as they took on a comprehensible shape.

I said: 'Spoder, have you written all this down?'

'No – but I've sent you links to the internet sites where you can find everything.'

'Thank you.'

Yes, but that meant of course I would have to spend more

time looking through these old records. Many of the links Spoder would have sent me were likely to be duplicates of sites I had already found, or mirror sites with the same data. I didn't want to discourage him. Then the others, the ones I hadn't yet seen: it would be a case of working through them to confirm what Spoder had just told me.

'Couldn't you print out the relevant ones, and let me have them next time I see you?'

'I've already emailed them to you. It's always best if you have the original data. You told me that once.'

'I know.' Spoder was only doing exactly what I asked of him. I went on: 'So where were Jessa and her husband when Lew was murdered?'

'That is something I haven't been able to find out. All I know is that Lew was living alone.'

I took a break from the phone call, and told Spoder I would look at what he had sent me, and call him back. I tried contacting Jo again – she was still not answering, but I knew she was likely to be busy. I made some coffee, then strolled around the garden in the warm sunshine. Barmi was sunning himself outside the garden windows.

I returned to my desktop computer and started to search the links Spoder had sent. The story had finally taken hold of me. All these people, all these old killings. They were gaining in depth and solidity for me at last, becoming human. Everything would make sense in the end.

As I suspected, Spoder had sent me links to a number of sites I had already visited, which I skipped. I bookmarked several others, experimentally following a few more links from some of them. He had, for instance, sent me a website of newspaper cuttings about Frejah Harsent: news of a medal she was awarded for long police service, an announced promotion to superintendent, her involvement in a long search for a particular transgressor, her appointment as commissioner, the first woman on Dearth to reach that level of policing. There was a photograph of her as a young woman, another one that was more recent.

I believed she was the key to all the killings, this entanglement of police officers and the murders they were involved with, long ago.

I called Spoder back. It felt like an old-fashioned novelty to keep speaking on the landline.

'Thanks for what you sent me,' I said. 'It's a sad story.'

'If anything it gets worse. I've been looking in the Hames newspaper archives. When the two sons were adults, aged twenty-four, Jessa died. She was in hospital for a minor operation, but sepsis set in and they couldn't save her. There were other medical complications. The story appeared briefly in the newspaper, but there were few more details. I'll send you a link to the archive entry. Lew was still living with his mother in Hames City, and to a certain extent also with his stepfather, Raffe Antterland. It was around this time that Dever went to live and work on Sekonda. According to a newspaper in Corlynne, the town where the carnival is, a young magician had been hired to entertain visitors at the park. They say little about him, but he was already using Willer as a stage name. Raffe was increasingly absent on his travels and Lew was often alone. After Jessa died, Dever did return to Hames to be with his brother, but he never stayed long and his absences grew longer.'

'So what happened to Raffe Antterland?' I said.

'It's impossible to tell. There's no more mention of him – he was at Jessa's funeral, but after that he seems to disappear. The Hames census return, which was taken the following year, shows Lew still living at the house on his own. Dever was by then permanently on Sekonda – I think we both realize he was probably opening his magic theatre at Bonnzo's Park, or at least getting it ready. But there was nothing about Raffe Antterland. I've tried all sorts of census searches on his name – it's not a common one but there are Antterland families on several islands in the Archipelago. None of them is the right one. No Raffe, or anyone with even a remotely similar name.'

Spoder sometimes amazed me with his thoroughness. 'How long did it take you to search for all that?'

'Not long.'

'Do you suppose Raffe died too?' I said.

'Not likely, is it?' Spoder said. 'Not in the way Jessa died. She was ill. He might have died around the same time, or later, but there's no record of that anywhere. He could still be alive today. Probably is. I came to the conclusion he just took off after she died, and left the two young men to fend for themselves. He doesn't seem cut out for family life.'

We agreed to leave it at that. I told him Jo was returning the next day, so I would not be thinking about 'all these Dearth cops and their murders' for a few days at least. Spoder sounded amused: I think we shared a feeling that we had found out everything about them that it was possible to know.

Afterwards, I checked my bank's website. Nothing had changed for the better.

I went to my usual social media feeds, browsed around. Some of the people I knew who also lived on Raba were talking about the chaos the financial crash had brought to their lives – their worries, the desperate attempts to buy food, and so on. For them the crisis continued. I added nothing to the debate, with the uncomfortable feeling of almost certain responsibility looming around me.

But it was not a crisis for all: several people said that they had found cash machines that were working again, and, like Spoder, that their bank had promised everything would return to normal in the near future. A lot of messages went to and fro, about whether one should move to a different bank, how to do it, and so on. Again, I added nothing to the comments.

After this, I carried out a more detailed search for information about my own bank, but again received negative answers. Negative in the sense that nothing appeared to have changed for the better.

Thinking about that shadow of responsibility, I remembered the way I had used the software on the hotel key card to invoke a mutability safeguard, so-called. I thought I had uninstalled the program, or at least that part of it. I wondered if there was some residual effect still present. Should I check the program?

Nervously, I thought not. It was a beast. I went to the kitchen and made myself more coffee.

While I was there I found a long forgotten can of soup in the cupboard and warmed it up, trying to avoid thoughts about the mutability of old food. The can must have been sitting there at the back of the shelf, unused for at least a couple of years. The soup smelled all right so I consumed it anyway, but immediately afterwards I drove to the local grocery and purchased a few basics: milk, bread, eggs (thoughts of Spoder), cooked meats, salad vegetables, some cans of beer. I was astonished by the prices: most of my remaining cash was used up.

In the calm of the afternoon, with no phone calls from Spoder, with no more links to follow, with no rumbling exhaust of an over-powered roadster, I thought that if I proceeded carefully through the mutability software I might be able to discover what in fact it had done. I remembered how long it had taken for the program to load – afterwards I had discovered a note of the huge amount of internet data that had been sent to and fro. I also found allegedly temporary files on my hard drive in obscurely named folders.

I located the program and ran it, went carefully past the questions about language, social level, password, location, software update (I clicked on No). I saw the menu I had used before, and pulled it down. The option for *Financial Services* under *Salay, Raba* was still pre-ticked. I moved the cursor to the box, and unticked it, just in case.

I then tried looking in more detail at the various front menus, searching for some idea of what the program was capable of doing. The *Help* page, written in coders' geek, contained a note of recent upgrades to the software. While I was looking at the *Help* option I searched for warnings about the possible side-effects of the program. There were no warnings: all the documentation under *Help* was cursory and opaque.

I selected *Exit*.

Immediately, a message flashed into sight:

You Have Concurrently Safeguarded a Background Option:

Salay Group: Raba, the fourth – Arts / Literature and Books / Fiction / Novels / Commercial Novels / Writers / Detective Thrillers

Do you wish to Deconcatenate this Option? [y/n]

I stared at the screen.

What did that mean? A 'background option'? I did not remember doing more than going through those menus – was that enough to initiate the program? And did I wish to 'deconcatenate'? Deconcatenate *what from what*? If I clicked No, would that mean the option would be concatenated? *With what*?

Had the people who wrote the program used the word 'concatenate' in the usual sense of linking one thing to another? Or was it computer jargon, perhaps specific only to this program?

Only to this moment of software choice, a single use, in this particular program?

I remembered the evening when I had gone through the menus, looking for some subject in the options that might mean something to me, might be relevant to the life I knew, playing around experimentally with what I entered.

I also remembered shrinking back from going any further: unless there was some other writer of commercial detective thrillers living on Salay Raba (and I had never heard of one) then the program was going to zero in on me. Here – this house, perhaps even this room. Me, protected from mutability. Concatenated.

My cellphone made the beep that meant a text message had arrived. I picked it up. The text was from Jo: AT MURISEAY AIRPORT. WHAT ARE TIMES FOR RABA SHUTTLE FLIGHTS? HOME AT LAST!!! SEE YOU TOMORROW! JO XXX

The inter-island shuttles took off every forty-five minutes throughout the day – some flew direct to Raba, others stopped at intermediate islands. This meant that the scheduled times for arrival were erratic. I hurried away to the next room, where we kept the most recent shuttle timetable. I knew roughly what time her overnight flight from Muriseay would land at Salay Ewwel, so I picked out the three most likely connecting flights. I quickly composed a reply, listing the departure and arrival times of all three, but added that she should text or call me once she was about to board the plane. I would then still have time to drive to Raba Airport to meet her.

She replied at once: THANX!

I walked outside, holding the cellphone in case she contacted me again. It was the delicious hour of the evening, when the sun was going down, the air was still warm, and the cicadas had not yet started their nightly celebration of insect rapture.

I believed that with the running out of interest in all those Dearth cops I had everything to look forward to. I was thinking actively about the next scene in my novel draft, glad to be getting back to it after so many interruptions. Jo was likely to be at home for an extended period. We could plan that vacation.

I finally returned to my office, where the computer monitor was still showing the attractive pale blue background. While I had wandered around outside in the balmy air I had made the decision simply to click on No, and then be done with it. However, there had been a development while I was away.

The screen said: *Mutability Safeguard Timed Out. Option Auto-Concatenated.*

When I touched the keyboard, the program closed.

25

Todd's Last Case

We are close to the end. How is it going to turn out?

First I must prepare the ground for what is likely to happen.

There are two major problems with any mystery novel or detective thriller. The first is the almost invariable subject: the presence of death – the problem of the way death is handled in crime fiction. The second is the unavoidable anticlimax always present, lurking blandly at the end of the book.

Neither of these appears to affect the popularity of the genre with readers, nor do writers pay much attention to them from the evidence of the books they write, nor even when they get together socially or at crime fiction festivals.

Death and anticlimax are surely a contradiction in terms?

Death is unspeakable, partly because of the dread we all feel about it, but also because of the inherent unanswerable question facing any novelist: what can be said about it now, or indeed at any time, that would be original, profound or helpful?

Even so, in all the arts, literature in particular, death and the prospect of death, and the process of dying, are subjects which are recurrent themes. Just like describing the birth of a child, the movement of the seasons, the passage of time, the falling in and out of love, a spiritual awakening or renewal, the approach or fear of death provides a theme of classical unity and grandeur.

But outside the arts death is a personal tragedy. The death of someone close to us is always a shock, even after a long illness has been endured, or the deceased passed away after reaching a great age. It is a cause of inconsolable upset and a feeling of helpless loss. For the person who dies it is an entry into the fathomless oblivion from which there is no return, no reporting. Death is a mystery solved by everyone, but only once and always too late – the experience cannot be described, so we cannot therefore learn about it from others. Some deaths are harder than others for the survivors to bear: the death of a child, of a new lover, of a close parent, of a brother or sister.

Sometimes, when we hear of the death of a stranger, occurring in peculiar or unusual circumstances or as a result of violent action or an avoidable accident, we are moved to the same sense of dismay and loss, even though all we are told about it is the terrible context. We know nothing of the person. The human condition ensures that we identify not only with the one who has died but with the people he or she was closest to.

All this is because we know our own deaths are inevitable and final. We do not know when death will strike. We live our lives in expectation.

Descending to the practical: a writer of thrillers deals with death on an almost daily basis. Most crime novels include at least one death, and in many cases that will occur close to the beginning of the narrative. The rest of the writer's work is therefore with the consequences. How was the murder actually carried out? Who did it? Why? Was it really a murder or only an accident?

Some novels include several killings.

In the classic mystery a body is discovered: in the library, in the garden, in the drawing room, in the cellar, in bed, in some improbable place in inexplicable circumstances. For the writer and reader this is the start of the mystery, and is essentially a mere plot device. The story becomes concerned with what is not clear about the death: the motive, opportunity, money, property, relationships, grievances, jealousy, secret dealings, legacies, and with the investigation, the police procedure, the role of the detective, the identity of the killer. We find out about these as the story develops.

The tragedy of the death is taken for granted, or ignored. The emotional impact on the people closest to the victim is only sketched in, or glossed over – after all, from the point of view of the plot the relatives are probably among the chief suspects.

In the more sophisticated thrillers of the modern age, the emphasis shifts and the background is ramped up. We learn of political shenanigans, of foreign powers, of secret police and secret societies, of traffickers, of rings of predatory sex perverts, of drug barons, of global corporations, of high and low life.

The psychological state of the criminal has become crucial: we become interested in the psychopathy of the serial killer, the weird obsessive life of the loner, the deadly methods of the professional assassin.

Where once the protagonist was a sleuth – a private eye, an amateur detective, a police officer working alone – now we are more likely to follow the enquiries of professionals who are to one side of the main action. The central character becomes a leading criminal lawyer, or a forensic pathologist, an academic criminologist, a journalist, a social worker.

But the existence of the dead victim, although often skilfully polished up and made subtle and unusual by the writer's description, remains none the less a plot token. The killing provides the stimulus for the story, and the main story duly follows.

The unique tragedy and dread of a sudden death is passed over quickly.

It is not the role of a thriller writer to lecture the reader on the awfulness of death. The reader anyway is not interested in that. Thrillers are written to divert, inform, create a sense of mystery or entertaining tension. People read books for pleasure, thrillers and crime novels no less.

Then there is the matter of the anticlimax.

Many thrillers or mysteries take the form of a puzzle. The inexplicable situation is the body that has been found, while the puzzle lies mainly in working out who was responsible for the killing. Suspects and motives abound. The sleuth slowly unpicks the facts. The solution is almost never obvious – the reader is snared by the idea of a puzzle, reads on, waiting for the moment of revelation.

Mystery writers are ingenious. Like the murderers they dream up, they weave a web of deception and misdirection, and also like the killers they drop occasional clues for the alert reader to seize upon – though rarely obvious enough for the reader to out-guess the author. It becomes something of a game, the writer and reader vying to come to the solution.

But isn't the solution to a puzzle inherently unsatisfactory? A let-down, an anticlimax? The sleuth produces the astonishing truth, and we react to the cleverness or otherwise of the sleuth. We do not congratulate the murderer on his/her ingenuity, we do not pause to mourn the dead victim. We see the solution to a puzzle. We close the book.

This is of course an oversimplification. My ingenious colleagues frequently think of many ways to outpace the puzzle, to give it relevance beyond the story, to suggest a universality of mystery. Many thrillers do not provide a solution – my own books often avoid the scene of final revelation where the plot is explicated. The displacement of the protagonist to a less involved character, the forensic pathologist and so on, has the same effect of distancing the writer and the reader from the superficial mystery. It opens other possibilities about the characters and the crime they have been caught up in, or a deeper interpretation of the world the characters live in, as well as other facts and the relevance of the clues.

Many readers say they enjoy the puzzle, though. There are clearly no answers to this.

I have prepared the ground because I knew we were moving towards some kind of final confrontation.

I had slept well overnight and I was up and alert. I was waiting for Jo to call me from Salay Ewwel to tell me she was boarding one of the inter-island shuttle flights. But earlier in the morning Spoder used the landline to tell me that Enver Jeksid had discovered my address, and that he wanted Spoder to come with him to the house straight away. I told Spoder that I would not be there, that I was meeting Jo at the airport. But it seemed inevitable that sooner or later the story of the Dearth police and their string of old murders was going to come to a head.

I braced myself for an anticlimax, but not eagerly.

Jo was one of the first passengers to appear through the arrivals gate. She was laden down. She was tugging a large wheeled case I had not seen before, as well as her usual travelling bags. I rushed to help her, and we stood hugging for a long time.

In the car she talked excitedly of what she had done and achieved, the people she met, the project she was working on, the future plans.

'Does this mean you will have to take more trips to Muriseay?' I said.

'Only occasionally. No more long visits, anyway. I'll be sub-
mitting my designs online. It's all worked out. We've shared
software, and they've set up a protected internet page where
we can discuss ideas. I'll probably have to go back to the theatre
for dress and technical rehearsals, and the opening, but mostly
I'll be working from home. When I go next time, you could
come with me?'

Maybe I should. Long ago, Jo and I had agreed we would
not routinely accompany each other on work trips away from
home. There were a few exceptions, but most of our visits
to festivals, artshow openings, conferences, gallery parties, conventions, etc., were taken alone. The trouble and intrusion of
unnecessary work-related travel was most of what we wanted
to avoid – my recent trip to Dearth was a case in point. It
would have been a complete waste of time for Jo. But in recent
months, now she was branching out, Jo had started taking on
some adventurous and interesting commissions. She clearly
wanted to share them with me. I was more than willing. It
would be fun travelling with Jo when she was doing so well.

She showed me some coloured sketches she had made of the
set designs she was working on. Because I was driving I could
only glance at them while she held them up. I said I would look
properly later.

We skirted around Raba City on the freeway, the glass towers
of the financial district glittering in the sun.

I said: 'I should warn you. When we get home we're likely
to be receiving some visitors.'

'Not Spoder?'

'Spoder, yes . . . and one other.'

'Not today, Todd. Please put him off! I've been on planes for
ages. I haven't eaten a proper meal for hours, I want to shower,
wash my hair, change my clothes—'

'This is going to a be a short visit, I promise you. You don't have to talk to him, even see him.'

'No, Todd. I'm too tired and hungry to have Spoder around the house. I just want a quiet day at home. That bloody motorcycle.'

'We can stop somewhere on the way and find something to eat. Then when we arrive home, you don't have to see Spoder. I'll take him out to the patio. I'll get rid of him as soon as I can.'

'Why not tell him to come back another day?'

'It's not possible this time.'

After a short silence, Jo said: 'Is this something to do with those old murder cases you said you've been researching?'

'Yes – but this is the end. I need just a few minutes, and he and the other person will be gone.'

'Who is this other person?'

'He's called Enver Jeksid. Maybe I haven't mentioned him to you before. He's one of the police who was involved.' I could not remember at that moment how much I had kept Jo abreast of the story. 'I have to meet him – he's come to Raba specially to see me. I'll get rid of them both quickly.'

We stopped at a roadside restaurant we both knew well. Nothing more was said about the imminent visit. Sitting opposite her I could see she was elated by her successful trip, but that she was exhausted after the long flight. I knew and understood how Jo felt about my involvement with all those Dearth cops. I had said to her I would be concentrating on my novel again. I felt guilty, slightly deceitful. I did not want to ruin the pleasure of her return. It was an unfortunate clash of private life and work life, but not really even that. The Dearth murders, as I now thought of them, had become a kind of displacement activity away from my writing, my real work life.

A little under an hour later we continued. It was not far to the house. As I turned the car into the access road that runs behind our house I saw a Raba City taxicab driving out. I paused to let it pass. When we reached our house we could see two men were standing outside, looking expectant, as if they had just hammered on the door.

One was of course Spoder – the other? If I had had a mental image of Enver Jeksid before then, it was replaced forever by the reality. Jeksid was a short man, slight of build. He had his back towards me when I first saw him, and when he turned he did so with physical awkwardness, as if he had a damaged hip or knee or foot. He was leaning on a metal cane. He had a small sand-coloured moustache, and his grey hair had thinned to a few patches across his narrow head.

Jo said: 'Oh, please! I wish you hadn't arranged this today, Todd.'

'I'm sorry, but I didn't set it up. Spoder called this morning, just as I was about to drive to the airport to collect you.'

'I'm going to take a shower, and keep out of the way. I'll see you later. Don't offer them food, OK?'

She let herself out of the car, walked quickly past the two men, giving a brief smile of recognition to Spoder and a polite nod to Jeksid, then let herself in with her key. I followed her.

I led the two men through the house, then outside to the decked patio. I was mildly annoyed to discover that I had left the house without closing the large window door that led from my study to the patio. It was hanging wide open. When I pushed it closed, it swung open again on its hinges. For some reason it stubbed against the frame. I was trying not to regard Jeksid too closely, but I felt that nothing about his physical appearance could have been guessed from the account he wrote of Hari Harsent's killing. But then why should it have done? He was describing what he did, not what he saw in the mirror. All the assumptions were mine.

He walked slowly, favouring his left side over the right. I wondered if he had suffered a stroke, or was just developing the physical weaknesses that often hit in later years. The other day I had estimated his present age at . . . what? Sixty-two, I thought, which was not by modern standards the depths of old age. He looked older than that, more frail.

I keep only the two folding chairs on the patio, as well as a low table, but remembering the promise of a short visit I had made to Jo I did not offer them seats. Jeksid stood close to the edge of the deck, leaning on his cane.

'You're Enver Jeksid,' I said. 'Former detective serjeant with the Dearth police.'

'Yes.' His voice was louder and clearer than I had expected.

'Well, I am Todd Fremde and I understand you have been trying to find me. I must ask you to make this quick, as I have plans to spend the afternoon with my partner.'

Spoder spoke across me. 'Sir, I should warn you that I believe Jeksid is carrying a weapon.'

Jeksid raised his arms, so that his jacket parted at the front. There was no belt holster around his waist. He lowered his arms quickly, placing his weight on his cane again.

'No, I am not,' he said. 'He has no reason to suspect me of that. I am here because I want some information.'

'He is wearing a shoulder holster under his jacket,' Spoder said.

'That's not true,' Jeksid said, but made no effort to disprove it.

'Go ahead,' I said. 'Just tell me what it is you want.'

'My life has been ruined,' he said. 'I consider you to be partly to blame. Both my sons were murdered. Their mother left me for another man, someone much richer than me, and now she is dead too. I worked hard for the police for more than thirty years, but they cashiered me out of the force because they suspected me of what they called a serious transgression. I was believed to have killed another police officer, who was working undercover. They had absolutely no evidence I was involved, no proof. I was completely innocent. I was sacked without an honourable discharge. They even cancelled my pension. I moved away from my home island, Dearth, and since then I have lived peacefully on Salay Tielet, the third. I blame you for none of these events. But my only source of income is a private trust fund, and that has lost all its value. It is now worthless. I know you are responsible for that because you stole a software card from a hotel in Dearth City and have been using it to hack into the banks that support me.'

He was not telling the whole truth. I had read his confession – as Spoder had told me at the outset, it was not only an account of what he had done, but also a boastful claim about skilful concealment of evidence. If he was prevaricating about that now, what else was a distortion?

Spoder, standing to one side by the table, said: 'There is some evidence that the high economy is recovering. Most banks are about to restore people's accounts. I heard it on television this morning.'

'No, that's not true,' Jeksid said. He turned back towards me. 'And it's irrelevant to what you have done to me. I'm bankrupt, and I need you to do something about it.'

'I think it's just a matter of time,' Spoder said. 'One of the biggest investment banks in Raba has discovered software errors that were probably responsible. Or partly responsible. This bank is the central lender for many of the trust funds and annuity holders.'

'That's too late for me. My money's gone. I want payback.'

At that moment I heard the sound which I had recently come to associate with a woman I hoped never to see again: there was the loud growl of a highly tuned car engine, close to the house. I listened, hoping it was the souped-up sports car of one of the rich kids who from time to time drove at insane speeds along our streets, but this time the engine cut out.

I said: 'Wait here!'

I hurried towards my study. The door was still open – I invariably kept it closed. As I went through and by habit pulled it behind me I heard the door banging against the frame. As soon as I was through the doorway my foot caught against a raised floorboard, standing proud from the rest of the floor by a couple of centimetres. I tripped and sprawled forward. I managed to catch hold of myself on the edge of my desk, so I did not crash to the floor. But who had moved my desk? It was normally never as close to the patio door as this. My desktop computer was where it should be, but the power lead was stretched tight from the socket on the wall to the back of the case. It usually lay untidily across my floor – I stepped over it a dozen times a day. It was a hazard now, stretched so tightly, so I tugged the cable out of the wall socket and laid it on the floor.

I hurried through the rest of the house. Who had opened the corridor windows? There was a mirror in the hallway, cracked from side to side: a jagged line across the pane, but the glass itself had not fallen out of the frame.

I rushed outside. Frejah's black sportster had squeezed past my own car and was now stationary on the gravel hardstanding. The engine was not running, but the gull wing door on the driver's side was fully raised. Frejah was inside, straining to clamber out. I went to stand beside her.

I said: 'Would you like me to help you out of the car?'

'This time, yes.'

'Why are you here?'

'You will find out. I've come for Jeksid. He's carrying a huge grudge against you, as well as against me. You mustn't listen to him.'

I gave her both my hands, and she used them to pull herself upright from the moulded car seat. I noticed that her damaged hand was still bandaged – she positioned it so that I gripped her wrist as I helped her up.

Once she was up she straightened her back and legs, but the imperious posture I had noticed when I first met her was gone. She hunched her shoulders, she held her head at a slight angle. She flashed a serious look at me, then went back towards the car. She leaned forward, reached inside. When she turned towards me again she was brandishing the gun I had seen stored in the car's trunk.

She was not pointing it at me, but the sight of it was frightening. I moved back from her.

'Put that away, Frejah,' I said. 'You don't need that.'

'I need it,' she said. 'Jeksid is here, isn't he?'

'Yes.'

'He killed my husband, and he carries a gun everywhere. I'm not going near him without this.'

'He's already denied that he's carrying a gun.'

'So am I. You're imagining it. OK?'

She pushed brusquely away from me, past me, and went up the steps into my house. I followed her closely. At the far end, along the central corridor to the left, I could hear the sound of Jo playing music on the radio. The shower was running, but the door was still open. Frejah appeared to be about to set off in that direction.

I said, quickly, pointing towards my study: 'If you want Jeksid, he's this way.'

She walked ahead of me. I noticed she was limping. Jeksid limped too. I had a random thought: had Frejah sent two of her own goons to beat him up?

It was absurd. It was terrifying, but still absurd.

Two people old enough to know better, both becoming physically frail, both carrying loaded guns, heading for a confrontation in my house, on my patio, the place where I normally sat around in pursuit of doing nothing, and where Barmi liked to crawl on to my lap and fall warmly asleep. My house, my property – these people had no business here. My partner was in the house, unaware of what was going on.

I should take control of the situation, demand that they put down their weapons, tell them to get the hell out . . . but I felt ineffectual. I knew no more how to handle this real situation than I was able to write similar scenes convincingly in my fiction. People sometimes commended me for the cerebral nature of my plots, the internalizing, the insights into motives and feelings. What they did not know was that I shied away from the violent clichés that appeared in so many crime novels because I was hopeless at writing them. When details of criminal activities were needed I took some ideas from Spoder, wrote down what he told me, let him check the passage before I finalized the book.

'Go through the door on your left,' I said, like a realtor showing a client around a house. Frejah pushed it open with her free hand, the one that was bandaged.

I wanted these people out of my house. I glanced at my wristwatch. The hands were settled on midnight, or midday. The sweep second hand was not moving. I shook my wrist, trying uselessly to restart the watch.

We crossed my office. Had the desk moved even further towards the patio door? The room seemed disproportionate, wider, shorter, the ceiling was lower. The whole room looked and felt as if it were expanding. No, it was shrinking. Another mystery!

Ahead of me, Frejah stopped suddenly. She looked around the room, then turned back to where I was behind her.

'This is familiar,' she said. 'What has been happening here?'

'I really don't know.' Through the open door to the patio I could see both Spoder and Jeksid. Spoder looked wary and alert, but Jeksid was leaning back against one of the supporting pillars. He looked disagreeable.

'There's something mutating here,' Frejah said. 'In this room. You told me there was no mutability on Salay.'

I had no idea how to answer that, my feeling of ineffectuality deepening with every moment. Then she obviously noticed Jeksid standing on the patio. She strode forward purposefully, but halted in the doorway, deliberately allowing the gun to hang from her lowered hand.

Jeksid reacted immediately: with a slow movement he slipped his right hand under the front of his jacket, and extracted his gun. He held it between thumb and forefinger, showing it was there but that he was not about to use it. He allowed it to dangle.

Spoder moved bravely to place himself between them.

Three ex-cops, two loaded weapons, and me. And suddenly my cat too: Barmi, always unselectively social, had jumped up from the garden to the decking and was now rubbing himself affectionately against Jeksid's legs. Jeksid seemed barely to notice. Cats are invisible to some people – I have never known why. His gun was pointing straight down at Barmi, the barrel only millimetres away from his trusting head.

I shoved past Frejah, idiotically raising both hands in the air, then bent down and grabbed the cat. I took him to the edge of the patio, lowered him to the grass. I tried to make him run away, but he sat down stubbornly and began washing.

Spoder said: 'I want you both to put down your weapons.'

Frejah shook her head. Jeksid said: 'Like hell.'

Spoder turned to me and said: 'Sir, what should we do with these two?'

Somehow, without real preparation, almost accidentally, I had found myself in the role of the sleuth. I couldn't avoid it. I had spent too long trying to work out what they had been up to. It had to be completed somehow.

Still feeling unequal to the task, I said: 'I want to be sure I know the extent to which these were involved in the murders, then they can go off somewhere else. They can shoot each other there if they have to. Not here, not in my house.'

The angry silence persisted.

'You say you want to be sure,' Spoder said to me. 'We know what they've done. Jeksid gave me his confession to read, and Frejah Harsent was obviously complicit in the murder of the first of the two brothers.'

'I had nothing to do with that!' she said, turning towards him. 'I was sent as an investigating officer.'

'We know what your version of that is,' I said. 'What you told me was full of lies. We know the two of you went to Lew's house after he was murdered.'

'I might have forgotten some of the details. It was a long time ago.'

Then arrived the final moment of revelation and accusation, the sort of interrogation scene, sleuth against suspects, that I never wanted to write, in fact never knew how best to write. Only the sleuth and the reader are seeking information at this late stage. Why should the suspects answer incriminating questions? Why do they feel the need to explain?

'I'm not too concerned with that,' I said. 'What I want to know is where the money came from, the money you used to set up your scheme.'

'We came into it,' Jeksid said.

'As cops? How do cops come into money? Does that mean you stole it? Or it was given to you as a bribe?'

'It was given to my sons. Raffe Antterland was a philanderer, a dishonest businessman and disgustingly rich. Once my ex-wife died, he obviously decided he didn't see himself in the role of stepfather, so he ran off somewhere. We've never been able to trace him. Before he left he gave Lew a large leather shoulder bag, and he said: "This is for you and your brother, also for your father, and for anyone else who can use it." Note that he said: "also for your father, and for anyone else who can use it." Inside were stuffed hundreds, thousands, of high-denomination thaler notes.

'Those few words caused endless trouble between us. Lew told me what Raffe had said the next day. Dever was there, he heard them too. They both confirmed it. But later, the boys decided that Raffe had meant something else, that he intended the money only for them.'

'They were acting like serfs,' Frejah said contemptuously.

I pressed on. 'Do you know why he gave away all that money?'

'It was guilt,' Jeksid said. 'I met Raffe a couple of times. He was a feudal snob – he had bought and bribed his way to the level of cartage provider, as if that mattered, but he knew that when my wife Jessa left me for him, the boys would automatically be reduced to serfdom. That's what happened – it's the law. I think he intended they should have enough money to buy their way back, at least to vassalage.'

'They were serfs,' Frejah said. 'They deserved to stay that way.'

Jeksid glared at her. His gun hand twitched.

'So you went across to Salay Hames and helped yourself to it?' I said.

'No!' Frejah interceded. 'That was not the idea at all. We wanted to help. It was a family crisis for Enver. He wanted to go and see his sons, and because I was his police partner he asked me if I would go with him.'

'That's right,' Jeksid said. 'But we needed time off work and had to get the permission of a senior officer.'

'My husband Hari was the obvious one to ask. He decided to come with us. All three of us travelled to Hames together.'

'Was this before Lew was murdered?' Spoder said.

'About two years before,' Jeksid said. 'We had the best interests of everyone at heart. Lew and Dever were obviously arguing about what to do: they both wanted the money for themselves. At first we suggested a three-way split, but I kept being reminded of what Raffe was supposed to have said. It was Hari who came up with a solution.'

'He suggested setting up a tontine,' I said.

'A what?'

Both Jeksid and Frejah looked blank, and Spoder shook his head.

'You created a tontine. That's an investment shared equally between a number of different people, each of whom has to sign a binding agreement confirming the deal.'

'We bought into an AMBA,' Frejah said. 'Not – whatever you said it was called.'

'It's known legally as a tontine. The AMBA is just the kind of capital growth fund in which you invested the tontine – I assume Hari had some information about that?'

'He said he knew a professional outfit on Raba who would set it up for us. It was all above board, nothing illegal.'

'I never said it was illegal.'

'So how does it work?' Spoder said.

I said: 'Everyone has to agree absolutely to the terms.' I said to Frejah and Jeksid: 'Is that what happened?'

'Eventually, yes. Lew and Dever agreed to it because we pointed out that they were the youngest of the five of us.'

'That's my understanding,' I said. 'Tontines are sometimes set up to benefit children. Once the agreement has been made, everyone has an equal share in the money. They all receive the same regular annuity as income. It's at a much higher rate than would be produced by a normal investment. If one of the signatories dies, that particular share is then redistributed to the others. The survivors' annuities increase, but also their share of the capital. In your case, you all owned one-fifth of the equity at the start, but as soon as anyone died that share would increase to one quarter each. After the next one dies, it would increase to a third each. Your plan, I think, was that in the end Lew and Dever would survive the three of you and receive a half each of the investment, which because of the amount of time that had passed would be much larger. The last one alive receives everything.'

'But what happens when he or she dies?' Spoder asked.

'The investment bank keeps everything that's left. But by then there will be none of the tontine members left to care. They lived well on the annuities, but they no longer have any interest in the capital sum.'

'Used to live well on,' Jeksid said sourly. 'Because of your intervention, the fund has collapsed. Not a cent more is likely from it.'

'Don't be hasty,' Spoder said. 'I heard this morning—'

'I know what you said. I'm sick to death of promises from people like you.'

'I'm a retired cop too.'

'Yes, but you're on a pension.'

'Mine collapsed last week,' Spoder said.

Jeksid glanced away with irritation.

'What seems to me went wrong was Lew cashing in his part of the fund,' I said. 'Is that right?'

'Absolutely,' Frejah said. 'He acted like the common serf he had become. He and Dever had never been close, and after Raffe Antterland disappeared their relationship went from bad to awful. Lew was jealous of Dever because both of them had once planned to be magicians, perhaps even working together. But Dever went on with it, practised his tricks every day, started performing, started making a living from it. All Lew had was the house, which was beginning to need major and expensive repairs, and the monthly annuities. They were no better than anyone else's. Lew let it be known that he had had enough of the annuities, and was going to take out as much of his capital share as he could. He saw it I think as a way of getting at his brother. Dever went round to argue with him about it, a major row developed, and – you know what happened next.'

'Lew committed suicide,' Jeksid said. 'That's what the court said.'

'Let's speak plainly,' I said, ignoring him. 'Dever murdered Lew, and disappeared with the cash. But what did Dever do to get himself shot five years later?'

'He kept Lew's cash,' Frejah said, while Jeksid looked increasingly restless. 'He lied and lied. First he said he didn't have it, then he said he'd paid it back into the fund. If he did, we would never know, except that our annuities had gone down and they never went up again. Or not to an amount that would tell us the fund had been restored. Dever was difficult to pin down to the facts – you know what he did for a living. He was slippery, tricky. He would disappear for several weeks, then afterwards pretend he had been in his little magic theatre all the time. This went on for about two years, but then Hari lost patience with him. He had just been transferred to Salay for his work, and—'

'He killed my son,' Jeksid said with a growling sound. 'I lost both my boys!'

'Afterwards, Hari located the cash. It was still in the leather bag that Lew had used, stuffed under the bed in the mobile home where he slept. Hari paid it back into the fund.'

'So why was Hari killed?'

'He murdered my son!' Jeksid said again. I noticed that his grip on the gun had changed: his hand was wrapped meaning- fully around the bullet chamber. I did not like the mood he had dropped suddenly into. Frejah had not appeared to notice. I tried to signal my fear to Spoder, but at that moment he had his back turned towards me. He was moving around one of the patio chairs, closer to me.

I said: 'Jeksid, put your gun down.'

He looked at me, his face contorted with anger. I thought I saw him raising the weapon, but in fact he was massaging his right shoulder, flexing it. Then the gun did move in his hand.

Jo suddenly appeared at the door from the office. I turned to- wards her. She was wearing one of her thick bath robes.

'Todd, the water heater's gone wrong! The water ran cold for ages, then suddenly started blowing steam—'

Spoder shouted: 'Look out, sir!'

I looked back at Jeksid. He was levelling his gun at me, brac- ing his shoulder with his free hand. I saw a flash. I heard a loud bang.

In that same moment something powerful slammed into my chest, throwing me helplessly backwards. The agony was instant. As I fell I bashed my head against a hard object behind me.

I heard the shot! *I heard the shot!*

My last living thought. I sank quickly into deathful oblivion.

There were attempts at resuscitation.

I heard sounds, felt movement. People were shouting instructions to each other. I was in a vehicle. I had things strapped to my hands, my face, my chest. Nothing hurt. If this was death it was not what I expected. I drifted away again.

I woke up in a hospital bed, at first seeing with unfocused eyes, my mind wandering. Jo was beside me. It was two days later, she said. Gradually I retuned my senses, focused on Jo and the room I was in. Now I was aching. My head and neck were constrained in some kind of harness. Jo was holding my hand, pressing her face close to mine. I felt her breath on my cheek.

At first it was enough to be alive. There was nothing to say about that. Later Jo told me what had happened.

'Spoder is a hero,' she said. 'He saw Jeksid's gun, and as the shot was fired he pushed you away. He just swung his arm around and punched you massively in the chest. You stumbled back through the doorway, and hit your head hard on the edge of your desk. It was right behind you. There's bullet damage in the bookcase against the far wall of your study. I haven't checked yet which ones they were, but a couple of paperback thrillers were shot. On the shelf of books where you stack the books you never read.

'When the paramedics arrived and saw what had happened to you they assumed your neck was broken when you fell backwards. It was not, although it's going to be stiff for a long time

309

to come. The impact was a severe one, though, and you've had concussion. And there's a big bruise on your breastbone. That's where Spoder punched you.'

'Spoder didn't get hurt, did he?'

'No, he's all right. He says his hand is sore, but when I asked him about it he said it was already feeling better. I think he didn't want to admit he'd hurt himself.'

Time passed pleasantly, or as pleasantly as is possible when connected up to drip feeds and monitoring equipment in a hospital bed. I was so happy to be alive! So happy to be with Jo. I never let go of her hand. We talked quietly of this and that: memories, plans, hopes. Nothing that would be important to anyone else.

Finally, I said: 'Jo, what followed? I mean afterwards. Did Jeksid shoot anyone else? What did Frejah do?'

'Things happened really quickly. Everyone was so shocked by the gun going off that it completely broke the tension. Jeksid threw his gun on the floor, and was complaining about a painful shoulder. Spoder grabbed the gun and disarmed it, in case. Then he went across to the woman – that was Frejah Harsent, I later found out.'

'Yes.'

'He took her gun away too. She was meekly compliant. For a long time they both obviously thought that Jeksid had killed you.' She reached into the shoulder bag she had brought in with her, and produced two pieces of tempered metal with shaped points. 'Spoder wants you to have these as souvenirs.'

'What are they?'

'He said they were the firing pins from their guns. He removed them. Both weapons are useless without them.'

'But what happened then?'

'Nothing at all. Someone called an ambulance. I think that was Spoder. Whatever was going on was over. Frejah Harsent and Jeksid stood around, not saying anything, looking embarrassed. Then they shook hands! Even before the ambulance arrived they went out to her car together, that ostentatious black thing with all the antennae, and she drove away with Jeksid in the passenger seat. That's how quick they were to leave. After the paramedics had assessed you and injected you with painkillers, they told me I should follow them to the hospital in about an hour's time. We knew by then you were not about to die.'

I gulped. How does one respond to that sort of information? Jo added: 'I was still in my robe, so I rushed around and managed to dress properly before I drove to the hospital.'

'And Spoder – was he shaken up by the shooting?' I said.

'He still wouldn't talk about his hand, but I know he hurt himself. I've never seen anyone punch so hard! He kept saying how sorry he was he had hurt you. That was more important to him than the fact he had saved your life. I think he was more shocked than anyone else by what had happened, but he repeatedly said he was going to be OK. I made him some coffee, and then he said he was hungry. By this time I was feeling so fond of him I said I'd fix him something. I found some eggs in the fridge.'

'So you made him an omelette.'

'Yes, of course. Then I called a taxi for him.'

I held her as tight as I could, while we both giggled about our dear friend.

Our revels now had ended. The story was told, the puzzle explained. The antagonists were reconciled, and melted away into the warm air of a Raba summer. The involuntary sleuth was thought dead, but was miraculously alive. No one else had to die, but two unread paperback thrillers remain forever unread. The weapons were disarmed, the cat was safe and well. The author's saviour and hero was tucking into an omelette and a cup of coffee.

A perfect conclusion, one anticlimax leading into another. It would never make a book.

Two days later I was discharged from the hospital, as fit as possible if not entirely recovered. I had a hell of a stiff neck, and I was convinced Spoder had accidentally cracked a couple of my ribs. It hurt to breathe deeply but one of the doctors advised me to try breathing shallowly.

My desktop computer, although looking in some indefinable way *different*, appeared to be working normally. I went into the mutability program, and deconcatenated the one remaining project. Then I uninstalled the whole program, rebooted to be on the safe side, and dropped the hotel's key card into an envelope, ready to be returned whence it came.

An hour later my watch was showing the correct time. My bank re-opened for business.

The next day I was sprawling on a recliner on the patio, with Barmi sleeping warmly on my lap. The door to my office had swung closed. I was once again looking at my manuscript in progress, working on the next chapter. Jo brought me an envelope that had just arrived in the mail. It was addressed to Dr Todd Fremde. Inside was a cheque from Professor Wendow's Revisionist History Department, for the refund of my expenses and my honorarium.